MY ONE NIGHT

An On My Own Novel

CARRIE ANN RYAN

MY ONE NIGHT

An On My Own Novel
Includes the prequel MY FIRST GLANCE

My One Night
Includes the prequel, MY FIRST GLANCE
An On My Own Novel
By: Carrie Ann Ryan
© 2020 Carrie Ann Ryan
ISBN: 978-1-950443-12-3

Cover Art by Sweet N Spicy Designs
Photo by Wander Aguair

Praise for Carrie Ann Ryan

"Count on Carrie Ann Ryan for emotional, sexy, character driven stories that capture your heart!" – Carly Phillips, NY Times bestselling author

"Carrie Ann Ryan's romances are my newest addiction! The emotion in her books captures me from the very beginning. The hope and healing hold me close until the end. These love stories will simply sweep you away." ~ NYT Bestselling Author Deveny Perry

"Carrie Ann Ryan writes the perfect balance of sweet and heat ensuring every story feeds the soul." - Audrey Carlan, #1 New York Times Bestselling Author

"Carrie Ann Ryan never fails to draw readers in with passion, raw sensuality, and characters that pop off the page. Any book by Carrie Ann is an absolute treat." – New York Times Bestselling Author J. Kenner

"Carrie Ann Ryan knows how to pull your heartstrings and make your pulse pound! Her wonderful Redwood Pack series will draw you in and keep you reading long into the night. I can't wait to see what comes next with the new generation, the Talons. Keep them coming, Carrie Ann!" – Lara Adrian, New York Times bestselling author of CRAVE THE NIGHT

"With snarky humor, sizzling love scenes, and brilliant, imaginative worldbuilding, The Dante's Circle series reads as if Carrie Ann Ryan peeked at my personal wish list!" – NYT Bestselling Author, Larissa Ione

"Carrie Ann Ryan writes sexy shifters in a world full of

passionate happily-ever-afters." – *New York Times* Bestselling Author Vivian Arend

"Carrie Ann's books are sexy with characters you can't help but love from page one. They are heat and heart blended to perfection." *New York Times* Bestselling Author Jayne Rylon

Carrie Ann Ryan's books are wickedly funny and deliciously hot, with plenty of twists to keep you guessing. They'll keep you up all night!" USA Today Bestselling Author Cari Quinn

"Once again, Carrie Ann Ryan knocks the Dante's Circle series out of the park. The queen of hot, sexy, enthralling paranormal romance, Carrie Ann is an author not to miss!" *New York Times* bestselling Author Marie Harte

MY FIRST GLANCE

AN ON MY OWN PREQUEL

By
Carrie Ann Ryan

MY FIRST GLANCE

See what happens before the night that changes everything in this prequel novella to My One Night by NYT Bestselling Author Carrie Ann Ryan.

After mistakes and false starts, 1 thought I'd finally worked my life out. It took eighteen years before I found my brothers, the ones pushing me into this direction. Now I'm faced with another decision, a new school, and a set of roommates I didn't know I needed.

Only after one glance at her, I know everything might change yet again.

Chapter 1

Dillon

"ALL I'M SAYING IS, IF YOU'RE ANXIOUS ABOUT WHAT SHE'S thinking, you should just ask her," I said, leaning against the bar. "She'll tell you, you know. She's not the type of person to make you guess what she's thinking. But you *do* need to ask her, or she'll feel like she's bothering you."

My brother, Cameron, raised a brow. He was good at it, just like his twin, Aiden. They could always raise that single brow and make it look as if they knew exactly what you were thinking, even if *you* weren't sure where your thoughts were headed.

"Really? You believe that if I just simply ask her, she will tell me exactly what she's thinking? And there'll be no weirdness."

I shrugged. "I don't know, why not? It just makes sense to me."

Cameron snorted. "You know, for someone so young, you sure do think you know all about love and relationships."

I scowled. "I'm twenty. I'm not young. I've been through shit." That was an understatement, and when Cameron just gave me a look, I shrugged. "What? It's the truth."

"You're right. You have been through shit. But have you been in love?"

I shook my head. "No, but I listen to the girls, and they all say communication is vital. Therefore, I should try explaining it to you once again. Talk to your wife."

"He's right, you know," Violet said as she walked into the bar, her smile cunning yet full of love.

I loved my sister-in-law. She was brilliant, beautiful, and loved me. I had been eighteen when I met her and fell head over heels for her, just like Cameron had. The fact that I had just moved to Denver after nearly stirring up my life meant I hadn't been in the best headspace to make friends.

But, somehow, I had gotten close with my brothers, the ones I hadn't grown up with thanks to my mom and the choices she made. I'd also made friends with the women my brothers had fallen for.

They all tended to coddle me, even though I was twenty years old. But they needed something to focus on. That way, they didn't have to deal with other things in their lives. At least, that's what I told myself when they got over-bearing in comforting ways.

They mothered me, and I usually let them. I loved them. Not that I got too emotional about it when I was in front of them. At least, mostly.

"You are supposed to be at work," Cameron said as he

slid off the stool and prowled towards his wife. There was no other word for it. Cameron *prowled*. He was like a cat on the hunt, and his prize was right in front of him. His wife leaned her head back and grinned, then practically moaned right there in the middle of the bar as her husband laid one on her.

I rolled my eyes and took a sip of my Sprite. It sucked that I worked in the bar my family owned and I wasn't even allowed to taste the wares.

"Get a room," Brendon said as he walked in, sliding on his jacket. He had worked at the bar that morning, but I knew he had meetings with potential clients later. He was smooth, wore a three-piece suit better than anyone I had ever seen on TV, and had a wicked grin for his wife—and another for everyone else.

"I'll get a room. Maybe the office upstairs," Cameron said, leering at his wife.

Violet blushed, even as she rolled her eyes. "You need to behave."

"And when has that ever happened?" Brendon asked, snorting.

My smile widened. "It is true. He is the least behaved out of all of us."

"Ouch," Cameron said, his eyes going wide in mock-affront. "I can't believe you said that when Aiden's in the kitchen in the back, and we all know he's the worst of us."

"I can hear you," Aiden said as he slid two plates across the open window pass-through.

The Connolly Brewery was family-owned and operated, even though I hadn't known about it until I was forced to move back to Colorado. It was a long story that I tried not to think about in detail too often. But all in all, it meant that

I now lived with my brother, Cameron; his wife, Violet; and occasionally slept in the spare bedrooms of my other two brothers and their wives. I needed to move out, and though I had tried the dorms at my university in downtown Denver, it hadn't worked out.

I hadn't been a normal eighteen-year-old—or nineteen-year-old, for that matter. While everyone had wanted to party and have fun and enjoy life, I'd been forced to focus on other things. I had wanted to join in but living at home and saving money while still working had been the best for me.

And all of that brought me back to why I was sitting in a bar. I had a few things to ask my siblings, and I was petrified that they wouldn't agree. I blinked myself out of my thoughts as someone moved closer to me.

"You look like you have a lot on your mind," Violet said as she tapped my nose with a finger. She smiled softly, and I lowered my shoulders, tension releasing from my body. My sisters-in-law could do that. They saw right through to your soul. It was a little nerve-wracking sometimes. But at other times? It was perfect.

"Talk to me," she whispered.

I would…just not right then. I needed time. Or maybe I just needed the spine to do it. Instead, I smiled. "I thought that was Cameron's line," I said, not wanting to get into that conversation yet. I needed to do a few things first. I had to formulate my thoughts, and frankly, I wasn't sure I could.

An email burned a hole in my pocket where my phone rested, and I was terrified that I might continue hiding from what it said.

Violet gave me a look that said she'd talk to me soon about what was bothering me. "You know, the kid is right,"

Violet said as she turned on her husband. "You should talk to me."

Something in her tone made my brows rise, and I looked over at Brendon. He shook his head. He didn't know what she was talking about either.

"Okay, would you like to tell me what's going on in that mind of yours? You're starting to scare me." Cameron straightened as he spoke, and I was grateful that even though we were in the bar, only our family and Beckham, the bartender that should practically be family, were there. It was right after the lunch rush, and I knew the next rush would be there in a minute, and I'd have to work at waiting tables. For now, though, we had a moment of peace.

Violet just shook her head. "Well, let me see. What exactly are you saying is wrong with me? Am I being weird?"

I winced and slowly moved away from Violet, just in case she took a swing. A gentle one because it was Violet, and she would never hurt us, but Cameron did tend to have that effect on people.

"That's not what I said," Cameron grumbled. "Well, just that you've looked tired recently, and you're acting cagey. I just want to make sure you're okay."

I took a few more steps back and bumped into Brendon, who just grinned. I frowned, wondering why he would be smiling, and then I took a good look at Violet and beamed. Violet looked over at us and rolled her eyes.

"You know, for a brilliant man, one that I love, sometimes you are so dense. I think your brothers understand."

"I know I do," Aiden said as he made his way over to my other side.

"What? What do you understand?" Cameron asked, scowling.

"Let me see. You say I look tired. And that I'm being cagey—meaning that maybe I wasn't feeling very well, and I needed a moment to think. And it had nothing to do with my migraines. Hmm, I wonder what it could be."

Cameron's eyes lit up, and he took a staggering step back, shaking his head. Then he wrapped his arms around her and spun her around the bar.

"I think he got it," I said dryly, and Aiden and Brendon started clapping, Beckham joining in.

"We're having a baby?" Cameron asked and spun her around some more.

"We are. However, I am a little nauseous, so maybe you should stop spinning me."

"Shit," Cameron said before setting her on her feet and pulling out the chair, nearly pushing her down onto it before she had a chance to say anything else.

"I'm not that nauseous," she said, laughing. I just got the results back this morning since I went in for my routine appointment for my migraines. They take a test all the time because of the meds I'm on."

"What? Are the meds going to hurt you or the baby?"

She shook her head. "No, but my doctor needs to be aware. And now we're aware. And, oh my God, this is so weird," she said quickly, and the two laughed before Cameron went down to his knees, cupped her face, and kissed her again.

"Well, kid, it looks like you're going to be an uncle," Brendon whispered from my side.

"Yeah, you're going to be an uncle, too," I answered, my voice low.

Aiden moved forward, gripped his twin's shoulder, then pushed the other man out of the way so he could hug Violet tightly. I shook my head, knowing my brothers would be fighting to get to Violet before I even got a chance. I might be as tall as they were, but I wasn't nearly as muscled yet. I would get there. Eventually. However, seeing how Cameron and Violet looked at each other, I knew I needed to tell them my news, as well. Because there was a reason I was ready to do this, even if they might think I was making another mistake.

"You want to tell me what's on your mind?" Brendon asked, a brow raised.

I shook my head. "It's their time. We can talk later."

"No, tell us," Violet said as she shoved her way through the twins. "I'm not the only one who's been cagey. Although I don't think I would use the word *cagey* when it comes to me because I was hiding the fact that I wasn't feeling well, figuring it was a migraine."

"We're going to talk about that later," Cameron warned.

"Whatever you say, babe. Talk to us, Dillon. If you're worried about the baby changing things, you're right. It will. But you'll always have a room at our place. We love you being there. Plus, you can help with nightly diapers and feedings," Violet said with a wink, and I shook my head, not quite able to smile just then.

"Okay, now you're scaring me, kid." Aiden scowled at me.

He and Cameron were identical twins and looked alike. Although, for some reason, Aiden always looked a little edgier to me. Aiden and Cameron were my half-brothers, while Brendon and I weren't actually blood-related at all.

However, the three of them had been raised by the same foster parents, who had eventually adopted them. I hadn't come along until later and hadn't been given the gift of meeting Jack and Rose. But through fate and circumstance, we'd come together. Cameron had helped me legally change my last name to Connolly, so now it was the four of us—along with the three women—against the world.

Soon, there would be another soul in the world. Another Connolly. It was time for me to move on.

Only I wasn't sure they would let me.

"What is it?" Aiden asked, scowling even harder. I hadn't even thought that was possible.

"Well, I didn't want to steal your thunder, but since there will be a new baby, maybe you could use my room as the nursery, rather than the smaller room you already use as your office," I said quickly.

Violet frowned, shaking her head. Tears filled her eyes, and I wanted to kick myself.

"Don't cry," I said.

"You don't want to live with us anymore? Where are you going?" Violet said quickly.

"You're welcome to live with us," Brendon said.

"Us, too," Aiden added. "Although you'd have to compete with the cats. And there are a lot of fucking cats," Aiden said dryly.

"No. I mean, I love you guys, and wow, I can't even begin to thank you for all the open doors and all that shit," I said, stuttering. My heart filled three sizes, and I wasn't sure I would be able to come up with the words.

"You don't have to leave," Violet said, her voice choked with tears.

Cameron moved forward. "You don't, but don't make my wife cry."

"I'm emotional. You're going to have to let this happen," Violet said.

"Damn it, I'm going about this all wrong," I said, cursing myself.

Brendon stared at me. "You're usually so good with your words. You need to do better right now. Talk to us."

I sighed and pulled my phone out of my back pocket. I flipped to my emails and gave the cell to Brendon. Brendon's gaze moved to the screen, and then his eyes widened before he took a staggering step back.

"No shit?" he asked, and Aiden snatched the phone from his hand.

I met Aiden's gaze, worried.

Two years ago, Aiden had started training me for the career I thought I wanted. Then again, I had thought I'd wanted to be a rock star when I was seventeen and decided not to apply for college. That had led me into my first mess. Now, I was thinking about leaving the idea of becoming a chef alongside Aiden behind. I didn't know what I wanted to do with my life, even after two years of school to get a business degree so I could help run the pub.

"You got into Denver State."

"Yes, partial ride, but if I do well the first semester I'm there, I can get a full ride for the rest of the years I need. I'll be a little bit behind everybody because I was already a semester behind, even with my course load. I'll be able to transfer nearly all of my credits, but...yes. I got in."

"Got into DSU," Violet whispered. "That's an amazing university."

She should know, she had a Ph.D. in chemistry and was brilliant. She knew all about school.

"I did."

"When were you going to tell us you were applying?" Aiden asked, his brows low.

I swallowed hard. "I wanted to see if I could get in. And then, I wrote the essay, and things just worked out. I wasn't sure when I was supposed to make a decision—or even if I would—and then I kept keeping that secret. One thing led to another, and...here we are."

"Here we are," Violet whispered.

"You're going to DSU," Cameron said, shock in his voice. "I'm damn proud of you. But that's not too long of a drive, is it?" Cameron asked. "You don't have to move out for this. Hell, I'm so fucking proud of you."

I blushed, ducking my head. "Well, the thing is, I sort of already made other plans..."

"I think I'm going to need to sit down," Aiden said, sliding onto a stool. "Jesus, kid. You could have warned us."

I lowered my head. "I didn't want you to be disappointed in me. I changed my mind, I think."

Aiden met my gaze, then shook his head. "I used to work at a Michelin-starred restaurant, kid. I did pretty damn well for myself, and I still work at some of those places. One day, I'll have a restaurant of my own," Aiden added, and everyone nodded. "We're allowed to change our minds as we figure out what we want in life and who we are."

He had left his job because of a workplace feud and ended up working at the brewery when their foster father passed. He'd brought the place back, elevated it to a high level where they served more than bar food, but we all knew that Aiden was working with Brendon to open up another Connolly business. One where he could be a true chef and not make wings. We were all working towards a future with the Connolly businesses, and I wanted to be a part of that.

I was just figuring out how.

"I cannot wait to see how you do in school," Violet said. "And wait until the girls hear this! We'll be there for any help you need, too."

"We're going to have to have a party," Brendon said. "New babies and new schools."

"And, apparently, new homes," Cameron said, staring me in the eyes.

I winced. "Yeah, well, I went down to the university to talk with the bursar, and I saw a flyer that seemed perfect for me. One of the houses on college row came up for rent. Five rooms, lots of space. I'm moving in soon with four roommates."

Everyone just blinked at me before Aiden threw back his head and laughed. "You sure don't do things halfway, kid."

"I'll still be working here as much as I can, to help with the family and to pay my rent. But the school loans I already have for the university I'm currently at will work for this one. Everything's going to be fine," I said, adding more about the financial situation.

Brendon shook his head. "I've got money, kid. You have a single loan, one you're going to pay off as soon as you're out of school. And you're going to work your ass off to get a full ride if you can. But it doesn't matter. We're not making you go into debt for the rest of your life if we can help it."

"I'm going to pay my way," I corrected, my back up.

Violet reached out and touched my hand. "You are. With your work with the family, and with the fact that you're going to quit keeping secrets from us," she said wryly.

"I didn't know how to start talking about it, and then I ended up in this big secret cave. And now I'm fucked."

"You're going to have to get un-fucked," Aiden growled. "Because Brendon is going to need help with the conglomerate that is the Connolly family businesses. Therefore, you need to be up to scratch. No more secrets. And, you know, the girls are going to have a hell of a lot of fun helping you decorate the house that you're moving into with three strangers."

I winced. "Please don't help me decorate. I mean, I love you guys," I added, looking at Violet, "but I don't know these guys. I can't just have my three sisters showing up, adding things to the house."

Violet raised her chin. "But you really can't stop us. Sorry, but we're Connollys. And you might think you can just walk away from us for a minute and keep secrets, but you're wrong. We'll keep hounding you, and we're proud of you. Now, I do believe it's time for a drink," she said. "A virgin one for us, and a shot or a beer for everyone else. Because we have stuff to celebrate, new beginnings, changes, and the fact that we're a family. No matter what."

I swallowed hard and hugged her close, knowing the others were either glaring at me or giving me confused looks. I didn't blame them. After all, I'd thrown them for a loop, just like I'd done with myself.

Things were changing, and it was time I caught up. Hopefully.

Chapter 2

Dillon

"Please stop carrying boxes," I said, taking a large container from Violet's hands. She sighed.

"I'm allowed to lift things. I'm not that far along," she said.

Cameron shook his head. "Go sit down on that ugly couch and rest. Think about what you need to add to the house to make it livable."

I winced, looking around at the two-story colonial that I had fallen in love with the first time I saw it. It had large, open-concept living and dining areas, with a couple of rooms off to the sides that were meant for a library and an office, at least I thought so given the built-ins. The kitchen was visible from the front door, and the huge island was made for a chef's kitchen. Part of the area was blocked off by a half-wall, which made the space look nice. At least, I thought. I wasn't an architect, but I liked the place. All five bedrooms were upstairs, each having its own bathroom. Each one was slightly different, and all various sizes. My new roommates—guys I still hadn't met—and I hadn't chosen which rooms we were getting yet. An oversight for sure.

In fact, the only box I had brought in was the one Violet had carried, and it was for the living room—not that I was sure I would put anything in there. I was a little worried about how this was going to end up and look once we were all living there.

I looked across the living room, seeing four guys around my age that I had never seen before. I figured they were my roommates.

And it seemed none of them had come with their families. I had only come with Cameron, Violet, and Aiden, but still, it was three more people than they had. They each gave me a look, the blond one raising a brow, the three dark-haired others giving me odd looks.

I cleared my throat. "Can you guys go back out to the car for a second?" I asked softly.

Violet squeezed my shoulder and nodded, while Aiden and Cameron gave each other a look, shook their heads, and then left, taking the box with them.

That wasn't awkward at all.

"Hey, sorry. My family is kind of big," I said dorkily. That phrase wasn't something I was used to saying. At least it hadn't been before two years ago. And here I was, moving into a home with people I didn't know, leaving the only family I ever really loved behind.

Dear God, I was part of my own made-for-TV movie, and I was already failing.

The blond cleared his throat and moved forward.

"Hello there. I'm Pacey," he said, a posh British accent sliding from his mouth. That made me pause. From the texts we had shared when deciding what day to move in and get the keys, I hadn't realized that he was British. But it wasn't like I could really tell. The guy hadn't talked about biscuits across the pond or anything—or any other stereotypical British things that came to mind.

"Hi, I'm Dillon. And that was some of my family."

"Only some?" one of the guys asked, scoffing.

I held back another wince. Not off to the greatest of starts.

"That's Sanders. Well, his name is Paul, but he goes by his surname," Pacey explained.

Sanders just snorted, giving me a once-over that left me feeling judged. Or maybe I was just reading into things since I felt as if I had no idea what I was doing.

"Tanner," the brooding one in the corner said as if his name were all that was needed. And maybe it was.

"And I'm Miles," the slightly shorter guy said, giving me a slight wave. "We probably should have decided who got which room before this so it wouldn't be so awkward, but here we are. Oh, and sorry about the couch. My mom wanted to help with the new house since it's my first time living on my own outside of a dorm and went garage sale diving. It's a lot comfier than it looks. At least, that's what she says."

I looked at the very large brown monstrosity that I thought was a sectional, not a couch, and grinned. "Looks great to me. I mean, I don't have a couch."

"I've got a TV," Tanner said, shrugging. "Actually, I have two thanks to my dad wanting to get a larger one for his man-cave or whatever. We can put one down here, at least the bigger one. I don't think the smaller one's going to work in any of the rooms but the master, and I never have good luck with that."

There was something there, but I wasn't going to ask.

"Well, I have a bunch of kitchen supplies thanks to my sisters-in-law." I looked at them and shrugged. "When they moved in with my brothers after the weddings, they ended up with a lot of doubles. We can probably fill that entire kitchen—or we will if my sisters have any say in it."

Pacey smiled. "That sounds like a plan. I have a few other things we can make work, too. As long as you guys aren't the labeling sort," he said with a sigh. "I mean, I'm sure we can all remember what's what. Or make a list, I don't really care. But I refuse to live with another person who has a label maker they use on everything they've ever owned, including their pillows."

I blinked at him and then laughed. "Well, I think my sister Violet out there may have a label maker, but I can ask her not to bring it in. Though she might want to use it with the fridge or something."

"That's good," Miles said before leaning back on his heels. "Anyway, we're all parked in the back near the large garage. We probably need to start unloading things. My family was going to help, but work sort of got in the way."

"Yeah, same thing with half of my siblings," I said.

"My parents actually hired a moving company, so my belongings should be here within the hour," Sanders explained.

"Makes sense," Pacey said. "Well, I guess we can draw straws or something, but I don't have straws. I do have Twizzlers," he said and then reached into his messenger bag for an open bag of candy. He pulled out five red ropes and broke them into various sizes. He popped a spare one into his mouth and gave us a look before tossing the other ends towards everyone else. "I guess I could have cut into two, but I really just wanted a Twizzler for myself," he said as he swallowed the plastic-y candy.

I chewed, the strawberry flavor bursting on my tongue. Well, this was a good way to begin living together, I guessed.

"Okay, there are five sizes of rooms. Mostly because I think this was a custom home down this row, much like the rest of them. No two rooms are exactly the same, so we'll go by sizes."

Sanders stared at me. "Here, you go first, new guy."

"You guys got here, what? Five minutes ahead of me? But I guess I can be the new guy," I said, shaking my head.

"Well, you're the only one starting at DSU this semester," Miles said.

I looked around at them. "Yeah, I guess you guys have all been here a while."

"For a couple of years now, but we can show you the ropes if you want. School's hard, fun, and can be intriguing," Pacey said, grinning.

Tanner didn't say much, and I had to wonder if the guy liked me or not. Not that I cared. I had enough friends. Right?

Pacey continued. "Anyway, pick one."

I pulled out a Twizzler and didn't look at it. Sanders went next, and then Tanner reached forward, pulling one out silently as Miles took the next, and Pacey looked down at the last one.

"Well, then. I guess that makes sense," Pacey said, and I frowned.

I looked down at the extra-long Twizzler in my hand and snorted. "I wasn't expecting that," I said.

Sanders glanced at my candy before schooling his face. "No big deal. The third-sized room has the biggest tub. Mackenzie will like that." He winked.

I wasn't about to ask.

Tanner held up his very short Twizzler. "Looks like I drew the proverbial short straw. None of the rooms are tiny, though, so it's not a big deal. By the way, there were two desks in the office, and two in the library. We can just claim which ones we want. There's also a large desk in the alcove for whoever wants the fifth. The other four are the same in size, although I think the view in the library is better."

"Then you can take that one," I said, looking at the others. "Since you kind of got the short end of the stick on the room."

Tanner shrugged. "That's fine with me. Hopefully, we can get some studying done because I actually want to graduate one of these days," he said dryly.

"Same here," I said quickly.

"I'll take the alcove since I'm in the middle of room sizes," Sanders added.

"Okay, on that logical path, I'll share the library with you," Miles said, and Tanner nodded.

I looked at Pacey. "Looks like we're study mates," I said.

Pacey just smiled, a blond brow rising. "Looks like. Do you want to ask the rest of your family in so they can help you unpack?" he asked.

"Oh, I'm pretty sure they have their ears to the wood."

The front door opened, and Violet walked in, her

cheeks red but a smile on her face. "Well, this pregnant woman would really love to know where your bathroom is, if that's okay," she said quickly, blushing even harder.

I laughed and looked up at the guys. "Do you mind?" I asked.

"I am not going to stand in the way of a pregnant woman for anything," Pacey said and gestured towards the door next to the library. "There you go, it's the half-bath, although it has two sinks for some reason. How this house has five and a half bathrooms, I'll never know. It's like a Tardis in here."

"You know *Doctor Who?*" Miles asked, a smile on his face.

Pacey shrugged. "I know a lot of things."

"We've got a lot in the truck, just tell us where to go," Cameron said. "By the way, I'm Cameron, this is Aiden. If you guys need anything, just let us know," Cameron said, and everybody finished introducing themselves as Violet came back out.

She smiled as she looked around. "This place is gorgeous. The fact that everything is hand-carved wood everywhere, it's like we're in the Clue mansion."

"Let's not actually have this be a Clue murder mystery, though," I said quickly, then Miles and Pacey burst out laughing, along with my family. Tanner didn't laugh, but his eyes did brighten a bit. Well, at least I could make the guy chuckle a bit. Sanders looked down at his phone, texting quickly, not paying attention.

We set about unpacking my truck, and by the time Brendon and the other wives arrived, we were helping my new roommates unpack their stuff, too. I seemed to have the most things, but it was probably because I'd had six people helping me pack, constantly giving me things because they were amazing and wanted me to feel loved. I hadn't been spoiled in my life before this, and they were doing their best to help out.

Aiden and his wife went to unpack the kitchen, while I helped where I could. I loved cooking, and according to Aiden, I was a decent chef. But I wasn't the only one helping out. Tanner had come in to watch every place Aiden put something, nodding approvingly at the spices and other things. Tanner had his own array of jars and cookware, and I couldn't help but be surprised. Seemed the quiet and brooding one also liked to cook. Looked like we would all eat well, or he would have some really good food for himself. Either was fine with me. I just didn't want to be the one who ended up cooking for everybody.

Violet went about labeling, and even though Pacey mock-grimaced, I could see the other guys appreciated it. There was a huge chef's stove and refrigerator in the kitchen, way more expensive and fancier than I'd ever had. Violet made sure the two bottom drawers of the fridge were equally separated so each of us could have our stuff, while the condiments and the other drawers and shelves were for staples or other things that we shared. It only made sense, given it was four people who didn't really know each other. At least she didn't bring out her fancy label maker.

"Just in case," Violet said. "When I was living in a home with three other girls and not family members, everybody got catty about yogurt. It was a whole thing. I don't really want you guys dealing with that. You can totally take away the labels later."

I kind of like them," Miles said, shrugging. "I mean, my

last roommate constantly stole my food and my books. And my shoes. He even tried to steal my bed once."

"Really?" Pacey asked.

"Really," Miles answered. "And that was the one semester I lived in the dorms. Before my parents pulled me out. But now I'm here, and very ready not to live with that person anymore."

"I promise I won't steal your books," Sanders said as he pulled out his phone to text quickly. He looked up and shrugged. "Girlfriend. She was going to stop by and help but got stuck with signups with her club."

"A sorority?" Violet asked.

Sanders shook his head. "There are no sororities and fraternities here. No Greek row. However, we are located on college row, which sort of takes that place."

I looked at my siblings, who just raised their brows at me.

"Let me get this straight. You're in the party house?" Aiden asked, laughing.

"I could see the parties happening here," Brendon said, looking around. "Although, if you fuck up this craftsman-ship, the owner will probably murder you."

"Probably," I said, and Pacey laughed along with Sanders and Miles. Tanner simply shrugged, leaning against the doorjamb.

"Oh, these are my parents," Miles said as two older people walked into the room. It was a little awkward since they were far older than my siblings, and my brothers were acting like my parental units in this case. They made intro-ductions and went off with my family to look around after speaking with Miles.

"Well, I guess it's the five of us," Sanders said, glancing

around. "I was a little wary when it came to looking at a flyer for roommates, but I figured…why not? I needed a place, and I wasn't really ready to move in with my girlfriend."

"Is she going to be here a lot?" Tanner asked, scowling.

Sanders shrugged. "Maybe. Is that going to be a problem?"

Tanner shook his head. "No, just don't have sex on the couch," he said.

Miles laughed. "Yeah, we did get it at a garage sale. It's probably already been broken in."

"Okay. So, first thing we're going to do is sanitize the thing," I said quickly, and the others laughed. Even Tanner cracked a small smile.

"I feel like we're overstaying our welcome," Violet said and reached out to pluck lint from my shoulder.

I rolled my eyes. "You don't do that usually. Why are you acting so weird?" I asked, and she blushed.

Cameron reached around and smacked me on the back of my head. "Behave."

"I'll try. You guys go. I know you all have busy days, and I need to unpack."

"If you need anything, you let us know," Brendon's wife said quickly.

"I will. But I'm going to be living…what? Thirty minutes from you guys? It's fine. I've lived away from you before. For years, even."

I saw my new roommates look at one another at that, and I held back a wince. I hadn't meant to mention anything about my past, but I was nervous enough that I'd let things slip.

"We're going to be overprotective. It's what we do," Aiden's wife said quickly.

"And on that note, we're leaving," Cameron said and pulled his wife and the rest out. I waved and closed the door after Miles' parents left, as well.

And then there was just the five of us. I looked around, shoved my hands into my pockets, and held back a grimace. I had no idea what I was doing, and I really hoped I hadn't made a mistake.

"Well, we're at least partially moved in, so I'll count that as a win," Pacey said.

"That's good," I said. "I guess I should finish unpacking a bit before I go and meet with my new counselor to finalize my schedule."

"You haven't finished that yet?" Sanders asked, his eyes wide.

I hoped to hell I wasn't blushing. "Since I'm a new transfer—and a little late at that—it's taken them a bit longer to fit things in, especially with all the credits being transferred. But it'll be okay. I'll make up what I have to next semester."

"You'll be fine," Tanner said, surprising me. "They're really good about making sure you get the classes you need, even if you aren't one of their precious darlings."

I frowned at that. "What do you mean?"

"Just the regular stuff," Pacey answered for him, and I hoped that they were on the same page, at least. "Some people are really good at schmoozing their way into the classes and the grades they want. For those that grade on a curve, it kind of screws the rest of us. But we make do. You just have to decide what kind of student you want to be," Pacey added.

"Yeah, the suck-up, the loser, or the one who gets by," Sanders said, and I froze.

Tanner shook his head. "You can be whoever the hell you want to be. Just get your shit done. And don't fuck anyone on the couch," he added.

Miles nodded vigorously. "Yes, we can make that a house rule. Along with divvying any chores that need to be done. I overheard your sister making remarks about a chore wheel. And while that sounds like it might work, I really don't know if we need that," he said quickly.

"Well, if after a month we completely muck up this house, maybe a chore wheel will be needed," Pacey said dryly.

"You never know," I said. "I should get busy before my meeting since I still need to work tonight."

"You have a job?" Sanders asked.

I blinked. "Yeah. My family owns a bar and a couple of other businesses. I need to pay for rent somehow, right?" I asked, laughing a little nervously.

"I think this guy here is the only one without a job," Tanner muttered and hitched a thumb at Sanders.

Sanders winced. "What? My parents want to make sure I get a good education. Can't really do that if I'm focusing on work."

I met the other guys' gazes.

"You make do with what you have," Pacey said easily. "Anyway, we all have work to do. I guess I'll see you around. Welcome home," Pacey said, and I nodded at the others before making my way to my room, wondering once again what the hell I was doing.

Chapter 3

Dillon

I LOOKED DOWN AT THE RED SOLO CUP IN MY HAND AND frowned. "Well, apparently, my brothers were right about this place," I mumbled.

Tanner just gave me a look and snorted. "Because you didn't want to party? Or because you think you're too cool for a nearly flat beer out of a keg?"

I shook my head and took a sip. "It's not nearly flat, it *is* flat," I said with a grimace, then finished it anyway. Because, hey, beer.

"Pacey and Sanders are working on the next keg. You just happen to come from a family that owns a bar. And from what I hear, knows what they're doing when it comes to beer."

I shrugged and looked around my new place, currently filled to the brim with people I didn't know. "My brothers wanted to make sure they had the best beers available, local and craft, and everything hipster you could possibly think of. I may have tasted some, but I'm going to plead the fifth."

Tanner just glanced at me, his eyes filled with laughter, surprising me since they were usually a little more brooding. The other man took a sip of his beer and grimaced. "I hope the next keg is good. I mean, anything is better than this, unfortunately."

"Do I want to know where Pacey and Sanders got the kegs? Considering I'm pretty sure all of us are twenty."

"Sanders has an older brother who graduated last year. He makes sure Sanders always gets what he wants."

There was something more in that particular statement, but I let it go. We were only a week and a half into living together, and we weren't quite meshing yet. Nobody was rude or uncomfortable, but we were still trying to find our routines. Considering how I wasn't good at finding a system thanks to hating change, it wasn't easy.

"Okay. We've got it," Sanders said, to the cheer of the others in the living room and kitchen.

"I didn't realize this many people wanted to be here before school started," I said as Miles came to my other side. The guy looked even more nervous than I did and kept hunching his shoulders as if afraid someone might notice he was there. Once Miles got to know people, he wasn't as shy—at least given what I'd seen so far. But for now, he tended to hide behind Sanders or Tanner until he got more comfortable.

"I'm pretty sure Sanders knows all of these people. Or knew at least some of them, and they invited everyone else."

"Sanders or Pacey," Tanner added.

I looked at my two roommates, the ones who hadn't invited the rest of the world, and felt like maybe I had found some kindred spirits. Or perhaps I was deluding myself.

"Hey there, Tanner," a redhead with a very low-cut shirt and very short shorts yelled as she came up to Tanner's side. She smiled and leaned against the other man at her side. "We were just talking about you. How about you show us the rest of the house? We'd love a tour."

The guy holding the woman raked his gaze over Tanner, and Tanner shrugged, set his cup on the counter, and held out his arm. The guy and the girl split apart, each going to Tanner's sides as they wrapped their arms around his waist before they left. I could only assume he showed them around the house then—our new home.

I looked over at Miles, whose eyes were so wide, I was afraid they might fall right out of his head.

"Well, I wasn't quite expecting that right out of the gate," I said with a laugh, and Miles shook his head.

"I knew he was bi or pan because I've seen him date men and women throughout the time I've known him. Just didn't realize he did it at the same time. Good for him."

I shook my head, holding back a laugh at the confusion on Miles' face. "A few friends of the family are in poly relationships, even have kids. The idea doesn't shock me. The fact that it's Tanner, the one who usually doesn't even say two words unless he's in the mood, is what does."

"Maybe it's the brooding thing. I should try that on someone." Miles looked around. "Although that would require me talking to people, and I don't know if I'm up to that."

I laughed as a girl with thick glasses, a short skirt, and two shots in her hands came up to Miles' side. "Hey, Miles. I'm going to beat you for the curve this year. But first, we're going to make out. I hope that's okay."

Miles coughed into his hand, looked at the shot glass, and grinned. "I think you're welcome to try. Now, what were you saying about shots? I mean, making out?" He stumbled, and I held back a laugh as the girl and Miles did the shots together, then went off to some corner, presumably to see who was going to beat that particular curve.

I shook my head and realized that I was once again standing alone in a room, even though it was my house. I should probably be better at this.

"Are you going to leave the corner and talk to people? Or are you the quiet guy I wasn't aware of?" I looked over at Pacey as he pushed his hands through his blond hair and shrugged.

"I'm just getting the lay of the land. I kind of went from hanging out with mostly people in their late twenties and thirties, all thinking about marriage and babies and 401ks, to coming back to college like this. I feel like I'm a little behind."

Pacey gave me a look, and I didn't know what it meant. "You know, we're all behind in some things, and yet ahead in others. I would bet amongst all of us, you probably know your way around the world a bit more than someone who might have been under his daddy's thumb for his entire life and is just now learning to live on his own."

I gave Sanders a pointed look, and Pacey's smile appeared. "Wasn't exactly talking about him," he said and grinned as I gave him a look.

"You, then?" I asked.

"Maybe. I like being the mysterious British one, though, so you're going to have to ask later. Now, let's introduce you to everyone. We know most of these people, even if it's just in passing from school. This is the best way for you to learn who to avoid, who to rub up against—figuratively and literally—and who is who amongst our social set."

"I feel like I should be taking notes," I said dryly.

"It wouldn't hurt. Sasha, darling, come over here," he said as a woman with dark brown skin, bright red-and-purple hair, and tight leather pants came towards us. She looked like a goddess, and I nearly fell to my knees. She kissed Pacey hard on the mouth and grinned. "Hello there, Pacey," she said, her accent upper-crust British, the same as Pacey's. "I was afraid you would never say hello to me." She looked at me, her brown eyes piercing. "Who's your friend?"

"This is Dillon, one of my roommates. He's starting his first semester at DSU."

Her gaze studied mine before she lowered them to the rest of my body and backed up. I had a feeling I had just been observed and categorized in every way possible. "You don't look like some eighteen-year-old little boy finding his way."

I coughed. "No, not even a little." *If she only knew.*

"That's good. Pity I'm in a serious relationship with that guy over there," she said, pointing to a large muscular man with dark skin and kind eyes. "That's Jason. We've been together for a year now. If you see him around and you're lost, he'll be able to tell you where to go. I swear he doesn't even need a compass, and he can find his way out of any situation, even on a mountaintop. It's a little annoying, though I'm grateful because I have gotten lost inside my own home before," she said and laughed.

My lips twitched, and I shook my head. "Good to know."

"So, are you looking for something fun tonight? Or just here to get to know everyone?" she asked.

"Our Sasha here is a little blunt. That's why we like her," Pacey said at my confused look.

I nodded, relaxing. "That is good to know. And, honestly? Between work and school and my family, I don't know if I have time for a relationship or anything that resembles one."

Sasha's eyes brightened, and she met Pacey's gaze before Jason came over, and they all laughed.

"Those are the famous last words," Jason said as he tilted his head.

I sighed. "Well, that's reassuring."

"I have the perfect person for you to meet," Sasha said as she took my wrist and pulled me through the horde of people.

Sanders was off in the corner, sitting on a large chair that made him look as if he were on a throne. His girl-friend, Mackenzie, was perched on his lap, laughing at something he'd said, while they held court amid those around them. I actually like Sanders' girlfriend. She was brilliant, very type-A, and knew exactly what she wanted. And I liked Sanders when he wasn't so sarcastic, where I didn't know if he was being mean or not.

I heard Miles' low laugh from another corner and risked a glance over at him and the girl with glasses as they leaned into each other, talking about something I probably didn't want to know about.

Tanner and his duo were long gone, and I had a feeling they were upstairs enjoying the end of the tour.

Pacey was back with Jason, while random groups of people came up to talk to them. Pacey was that magnetic, and it made sense to me that people gravitated towards him. They all wanted a piece of him. And, frankly, I liked being around him, too. He made me feel like I wasn't some lost kid still trying to find his way.

"Mandy, come over here," Sasha said, holding up her hand.

I gave Sasha a look. "You know I was letting you lead me around by the wrist. Not the balls," I muttered. "I don't need you to hook me up with anyone."

Sasha just laughed at my comment, though thankfully didn't take it to heart. "Oh, shush. You're allowed to have fun. You're young, free, and probably have a thousand things you're worried about. Getting laid shouldn't be one of them."

A girl with long hair, bright gray eyes, and swollen lips came over to us. She looked fucking sexy.

"Mandy, this is Dillon. Dillon, this is Mandy. I don't know Dillon's major, darling, but he's new here. It would be great if you could show him around."

Mandy grinned and studied my face. "Well then, Dillon, if you have Sasha's approval, I'd love to show you around campus. Or wherever," she said, a little giggle added onto the end.

I cleared my throat. "It's, uh, nice to meet you. Although I only met Sasha about thirty seconds ago." I turned, and Sasha was gone, presumably off to where Jason and Pacey were. I shook my head as Mandy laughed outright.

"That sounds like Sasha. She'll throw you to the wolves. But I promise, I don't bite. Too hard. Unless you ask."

I shook my head, a smile playing on my lips. "I thought that was a line I was supposed to give."

Mandy just shrugged. "Maybe. But I like to be in control. Got a problem with that?"

"Depends on what you're talking about, Mandy."

"You know what? I think I like you. Let me show you around. Maybe introduce you to a few of my friends."

She waved to a group of girls, who all gave me the once-over and gestured for me to come towards them. I looked around my new home, my friends scattered about with their couples, and I figured...why the hell not? I had responsibilities later, and I would deal with them.

But for now, maybe I would have a little fun.

Chapter 4

Dillon

MANDY STOOD IN FRONT OF ME AT THE COFFEE COUNTER, going through her long order. Mine was probably just as long, but she was meticulous in making sure she got precisely what she wanted. But that was Mandy. She always got what she wanted. Somehow, that included me. I wasn't quite sure how I'd even ended up in a relationship for four weeks with a girl I was still getting to know, but I was happy-ish. Mandy made me smile, laugh, and took my mind off the fact that school was fucking hard, in addition to dealing with work and morning sickness. Not that Mandy had morning sickness, thank God. But I was over at my old place often enough that I had even held back Violet's hair.

That was an experience I never wanted to repeat.

I liked Mandy, but we didn't have much in common, truthfully, and we were only near each other for certain things. Things that I wasn't going to talk about with my brothers.

My sisters-in-law wanted to meet her, and I had no idea why. I mean, I understood why, but Mandy and I weren't like that. She had been very clear about the fact that she did not want serious. She wanted to date around. I was fine with that. It was college. It's what you did.

And, frankly, I was too exhausted to worry about anything but focusing on what I needed to.

"You ready, babe?" Mandy asked. I nodded and held up my phone. She shook her head. "No, I already paid. Come on. You get it next time."

"Sounds good," I said and moved over to the side of the line.

"Pussy," a guy muttered under his breath as he walked past, and Mandy narrowed her eyes.

I shook my head. "It's not worth it. And I just want coffee. Just because he's not enlightened enough to learn that, *'Hey, your girl wanting to pay for coffee is a good thing,'* doesn't mean we need to deal with it."

The guy was already gone, so it wasn't like he overheard me. Mandy just smiled. "You know what, Dillon Connolly? You're a decent guy."

I knew the tips of my ears were bright red, but I did my best to act nonchalant. "Yeah?" I asked.

"Yes. You are. And, one day, you're going to make a girl very happy."

I frowned at that, but then the barista said our names, and we went to get our drinks.

"Not that I'm not happy right now," Mandy said,

seeming to think about what she'd said earlier. "But, come on. We both know this isn't serious. We're having fun. That's what you do in college. And I plan to have as much fun as possible."

"That sounds like a plan," I said, a little weary.

"Plus, while your brothers seem to have finally settled down and are the marrying kind, I wouldn't have thought it possible."

I frowned, feeling as though I should be insulted. "I have no idea what you mean by that or what to say."

She patted my cheek and smiled at me. "Don't you worry. You don't need to think about it at all."

I knew when someone was patronizing and condescending when I heard it, but since we were still in public, I didn't want to deal with it. I had a feeling that whatever fun I was having with Mandy would be over by the end of the afternoon. I could handle being the fun-time guy for a minute. I couldn't handle being the idiot dating the girl with other prospects, who treated me like shit.

A girl with honey-brown hair piled on the top of her head caught my eye, and I blinked for a minute. She looked familiar. Had I seen her before? I wasn't sure, but the look in those hazel eyes made me think there was recognition on her side, too.

Or perhaps I hadn't had my coffee yet, and Mandy had thrown me for a loop.

I pulled my gaze away from those doe eyes and elfish features and told myself it didn't matter that Mandy wasn't in it for the long haul. There were plenty of girls on campus, and since Mandy was done with me, I might be able to find another for myself. Or, I could focus on work and school.

Either way, it was my decision. Because for once, I wanted to live. I had spent enough time hiding. And I would do what my brothers had told me to do from the start. Finally. I would make sure to enjoy life.

Even if I failed along the way.

Chapter 5

Elise

I LOOKED OVER WHERE THE MAN WITH THE BRIGHT EYES AND dark hair had been and blinked. "Earth to Elise, where are you?"

I shook my head and looked over at my best friend and roommate. "Who is *that*?" I asked and could have rightly smacked myself for voicing my thoughts.

Corinne grinned, her eyes dancing. "That, my darling Elise, is Dillon Connolly. He's the new guy."

I stared at her and blinked. "We're at a university. There are lots of new guys. How do you know his first and last name already?"

"He just moved in with Pacey."

"Oh, yeah. Your friend. The one you won't tell me about or let on how you know him."

Corinne rolled her eyes. "It's nothing nefarious. At least, I don't think so."

That made me snort. I loved Corinne, and she loved her little games. They were never cruel, never mean. And they always made me smile. It was more like word games and mystery and magic. That was Corinne, all mysterious. A little pixie.

"Anyway, Pacey mentioned him. He's a transfer student, the same year as the rest of us. He just didn't start here."

"Plenty of people do that."

"True. And he's hot. Too bad Mandy saw him first."

I cringed. "I saw her with him. I hoped he was just standing next to her while my imagination ran in a thousand different directions. But good for them." See? I wasn't a bad person. I just had a little daydream, and now it was over.

"Well, it's been about four weeks, from what I can tell," Corinne said.

"How do you know all this?" I asked, laughing.

"I would tell you that I'm mysterious and know all, but we both know it's because of Pacey."

"Okay, yeah, that's true," I agreed, laughing.

"Anyway, they met at the house party I tried to get you to go to. The one you declined. And they've been together ever since, I guess. It's only a few weeks in, and it's Mandy, who has told us all that she doesn't want anything serious and wants to be free and happy. And more power to her. She should be able to sleep with whoever she wants as long as it's consensual and happy. She shouldn't be put in a little corner of marriage and possibilities. Just because she isn't a man, doesn't mean she can't have sex whenever she wants."

I cringed as other people looked around. Corinne wasn't exactly quiet.

"Good for her, you're right," a woman said from the table beside us.

Corinne waved. "Thank you."

"Seriously, though, it shouldn't just be men who are allowed to go out and have casual sex. Everybody should have the option if they so desire."

"I'll talk all about casual sex if you want," a guy said from the other end of the line.

The woman at the table rolled her eyes. "Nice try, honey."

"Anybody should have as much sex as they possibly can and feel like," Corinne said. "As long as we're talking about consent."

"Amen," four different women in line said, and I knew I was blushing from head to toe.

"I swear, you love putting me at the center of these conversations," I mumbled.

"Just a little," Corinne said, beaming.

"Anyway…" I whispered furiously as the others went back to their original conversations. "I'm glad Mandy seems happy."

"I'm sure you are, and you should also know that Pacey doesn't think they're going to last much longer because Mandy's already thinking about this guy named Jeff."

I blinked again. "Okay, I'm seriously a little worried about how *Gossip Girl* you're sounding."

"X O X O," she whispered, and I laughed. "Seriously, though," my best friend continued, "that is Dillon Connolly. And he seems quite dreamy."

"He's not for me. But he has a nice smile."

"Well, it took us this many years for you to notice a guy's smile. Since you did, I think you're on the right track. By the time we hit our dotage, you may get laid again."

I growled under my breath, even as I blushed harder. The guy in front of us finally turned, his dark hair pushed back from his face, his eyes piercing.

"I was trying to ignore your conversation, but now I can't," he began.

"I'm not sleeping with you," I said quickly and then shut my mouth.

The guy looked at us and then laughed. "Okay, good to know. By the way, I'm Tanner. I live with Pacey and Dillon."

"Oh," I said, mortified.

"I've heard about you. It's nice to meet you. I'm Corinne."

"Hello, Corinne. And you must be Elise."

"Hello," I mumbled.

"We're having another house party in a few weeks, right after the first set of exams. You two should come."

I shook my head vigorously, in desperate need of a rock to hide under in my embarrassment. "I don't think I should."

"No, I think you should come along. You never know what could happen at a party. A night can change everything."

I met this gaze, then looked over at Corinne. I knew I wasn't going to get out of this. Because my best friend had plans, and so did this stranger, apparently. I was screwed.

"What kind of party?" I asked finally.

Corinne smiled, delight in her eyes. "The best. If

Sanders and Pacey are throwing it, it means there will be booze, merriment, exhibition, and dares."

I froze. "Dares?"

Corinne just grinned. "Yes, Elise. Dares. As in… I have a feeling if you let me, Truth or Dare might take on a whole new meaning."

Well, crap.

Dillon & Elise's romance continues in My One Night!
Don't miss their story!!

MY ONE NIGHT

An ON MY OWN NOVEL

By
Carrie Ann Ryan

MY ONE NIGHT

A one-night stand is supposed to end once the sun rises. Only it doesn't always work out that way in this opposites attract and tortured hero romance.

I never expected this.

I didn't want to go to another fraternity party, but when my friend pulls me in, I somehow find myself hiding in a corner with…him.

Dillon Connolly.

The smirking, so-called good guy with the shadows in his eyes.

A single glance, a sweet smile, and I let myself have one night of giving in.

Only I have to promise myself not to fall in love.

No matter the cost.

I never expected her.

Elise Hoover haunts my dreams more than I care to admit. I never thought I stood a chance—until she said yes.

When a single night turns to two, I know I'm in over my

head, but somehow, she makes me believe I can have anything.

Until the sun rises, and my past along with it.

I thought I'd run from the problems that could hurt us both, but now I'm falling for her and I can't stop.

I know I don't deserve her, but now I have to fight to keep her…or save her from myself.

Chapter 1

Dillon

THE HOUSE WAS PACKED TO THE RAFTERS, PEOPLE DANCING to the music, some in corners, laughing, making out, or just talking. And most of the group had drinks in their hands. After all, it was a college party, and our place happened to be party central for the evening.

This was the fourth gathering my roommates and I had put together since school had started for the semester, and I was already tired of it. The other houses on college row held more parties than we did, and that meant most of the people currently under this roof went to one of those places, or to a bar if they were over twenty-one or had a decent fake ID. Others would head to dorm rooms or random apartments around the city for the night if there wasn't a college row party. There was always a place to gather, and even more areas to study—not that I thought most people currently drinking in this house even cracked open their textbooks.

My roommates and I did—we made sure of it. We were all trying our best to graduate on time, so we each studied to various degrees.

The rest of the people in this house? The ones drinking? Partying? I wasn't sure they'd ever actually been to class. I didn't know if they knew how to study.

As I had already almost fucked up my chances the first time I slacked off, even trying to get into college, I wasn't about to make that mistake again. At the last college I'd attended, I'd studied hard, made good grades, and had gotten into Denver State University with a partial scholarship. If I kept up with my classes this semester, I was on track to get a full scholarship. That would mean no more loans, no more saying "no" to my big brothers every time they tried to help me.

Not that I didn't love them, I did. I was grateful for everything that they were doing and had done. I just didn't want them paying for my schooling. Especially when I knew they were all either working on babies or already pregnant—well, their wives anyway. The next generation was coming, and that meant college funds for the new kids.

I didn't need them paying for me. Although it wasn't like our parents would pay.

I shivered at the thought.

No, my mom wouldn't have dropped a cent for me, had rarely done it when she was alive and had been so-called *raising me*. As for Dave, the man who was, apparently, my dad? I wasn't even sure I knew who he was beyond a druggie who scared the crap out of me. So, no, I'd pay for my education and hope to hell that I kept up with my grades to get that scholarship.

"Why do you look as if you are off in another world, all serious-like?" my roommate, Pacey, asked as he came to my side.

I looked over at Pacey and smiled. He shoved his hand through his hair, pushing the blond strands back from his face. They were forever falling over his eyes, and I knew from listening in on many conversations, including those of my ex-girlfriends, that that look sent women and men alike into shivers. And Pacey knew it.

"I'm fine. I don't know why you think I'm acting weird or thinking too hard."

Pacey just raised a blond brow, looking all stiff and upper-crust British. Since he was, it only made sense to me.

"I'm not making up that look. You're thinking hard, and I'd like to know why."

I shrugged and downed the rest of my beer. "Just thinking about exams coming up."

"They are always coming up. That's what happens when you have some classes working on a three-exam schedule, some a midterm schedule, and a…you know what, let's do a surprise exam that's going to scare the shit out of your students schedule."

I laughed outright at that, and the two of us headed over to the keg. I wasn't sure where we'd gotten it other than Sanders usually had connections. I just hoped to hell the cops didn't show up since none of us were of age.

A girl with tight jeans, a low-cut shirt, and bright red lips operated it.

"Hello, boys," she said, reminding me of a character from *Supernatural* as she said it.

"Hi there, Alexa," Pacey said, practically purring. The man was good at that.

"Oh, welcome." She giggled, actually *giggled* and blushed. "Can I get you something?" she asked and held up the tap. "I can get you exactly what you need," she said, and I barely resisted the urge to roll my eyes.

"Just a beer for my mate here, for now, Alexa darling," Pacey answered, grinning.

I had a feeling that Pacey would be leaving me soon for the red-lipped co-ed, and I didn't mind. I'd seen her around a few times. She was friendly, smart, and didn't treat people like crap. That counted for a hell of a lot in my book.

I took the beer from Alexa and had to be careful not to drop it as she only had eyes for Pacey. I shook my head, a smile playing on my lips as I moved away. Pacey nodded ever so slightly, all debonair and magnetic. He was like a spiderweb. Most people got stuck in his wake. However, he wasn't exactly the spider. More like one who convinced those caught in his web that they wanted to be there and were excited by the prospect. I hadn't seen a person walk away from Pacey's bed disheartened, angry, or in any way acting as if they hadn't gotten what they wanted.

"Okay, now I need to know what that look was about," Pacey said as he stared at me.

I snorted and took another sip of my beer. "I was just thinking that you're not an asshole when it comes to sleeping around."

Pacey's brows shot up, and then he threw his head back and laughed.

More than one person turned our way to stare at Pacey —and I supposed at me, as well—but there was just something about my roommate. If I was in any way attracted to

Pacey, I figured the two of us might be a decent match for a relationship. Although we were too busy and focused on school to worry about anything else. Besides, there wasn't even a flicker of a buzz between us. And I was just fine with that.

"Well, that is kind of you. And I do try to satisfy my lovers."

"Dear God," a man said from beside us, practically fainting into another guy's arms.

I met Pacey's eyes, rolled mine, and left to go back to my corner, which was thankfully still empty. Pacey followed me with his gaze, a curious look on his face. "Now, do you want to tell me exactly what you were thinking about before?"

I shrugged. "Just school, focusing on things. About the fact that the cops haven't come in here yet."

"Stop it. Why would you say something like that?" Pacey asked and knocked on the wood beam beside us.

Miles, one of my other roommates, popped out of nowhere and knocked, as well. "I was four feet away and I heard you. You do not call out to the universe for things like that."

I held up my free hand and winced. "Sorry. I'm having an off evening."

"I'd say," Tanner mumbled as he came forward. Tanner was one of my other roommates, and I honestly didn't have a good lead on him. From what I could tell, he was smart but tended to brood in his room or at his desk. He shared the library with Miles for their study area. I shared with Pacey in the actual study. The house was set up like that kids' murder mystery gameboard, and I always found it a bit weird. Our other roommate, Paul, who went by his last name—Sanders—had his little desk area in the foyer. It was a bit more out in the open so we could tell when he was studying or not—mostly not these days—but he had the biggest space. We had all chosen our rooms and study areas courtesy of a bag of Twizzlers the first day we met, in lieu of drawing straws. The Twizzlers were usually in Pacey's hand, as the guy was addicted to them. I didn't see them on him now, but I figured they were probably in the pantry, beckoning him like always.

That brought a smile to my face, and Pacey once again glared at me. "Why are you off in your head again? Now what are you thinking?"

"Just about Twizzlers."

Miles' eyes widened, and Tanner winced.

"What?" I asked.

Pacey straightened, his eyes narrowing. I thought I saw a little humor there—at least I hoped—but I wasn't sure. "Sanders and Mackenzie ate the last Twizzler, and I haven't been to the store to replenish. I was a little busy taking my exam this afternoon and setting up for the party. Therefore, I have not had a Twizzler all day. Let's not discuss it."

I looked between all of them, my jaw dropped. "Sanders and his girlfriend ate the Twizzlers?" That offense was a literal Code Red in this house.

"I cannot blame Mackenzie," Pacey said, holding up a hand. "She didn't know. She will, though, because I will make sure she does. And Mackenzie is usually nice enough to replenish whatever she eats here." Somehow, I had a feeling this was all Sanders.

"Did you put the Twizzlers on the common shelf?" I asked, knowing I was treading on dangerous ground here.

Pacey's eyes narrowed even more. "It shouldn't matter. We all know I'm the one who buys my favorite candy."

"I've never actually heard you sound so haughty before," Miles said, holding back a laugh.

"Very, very British," Tanner said deadpan.

Pacey looked between all of us and lifted his lip in a small snarl. "I hate you all. And I would do better if I had my favorite crutch to get me by. Sadly, I do not."

"Hi," a bright voice said from beside us. I turned to see Sanders' girlfriend, Mackenzie, standing there, her long, brown hair hanging in curls and waves down her back. "I didn't realize they were yours when Sanders offered them to me," she said, and I met Pacey's gaze.

He winced and then did his best to school his features. "It's okay, I understand."

"Well, then I hope this will help." She reached into her large bag, the one that all the girls around here seemed to carry with them these days, even to house parties like this, and pulled out a family-size bag of Twizzlers. "It's the least I can do. I'm so sorry," she said.

Pacey looked down at the candy and then at her, a smile slowly crawling over his face. "I do believe you're my favorite." He took the red licorice from her and winked.

"Oh, well, I was kind of a jerk to help finish it. And I felt bad. However, here you go."

"You macking on my girl?" Sanders said as he put a proprietary hand on Mackenzie's waist. She rolled her eyes but leaned back against him. According to Mackenzie, the two had been dating since the cradle, and Sanders usually went along with that idea. I didn't know how someone could be with another person for so long, but I thought it was kind of nice. The two seemed to suit each other and got along. Mackenzie was a little uptight sometimes. Things always had to be a certain way, and her making sure of that could come off as kind of rude, a bit stuck up, but then she did things like this. I didn't really understand her, but I liked her. That seemed to be my go-to these days.

Sanders was a bit of an oaf sometimes, kind of a jerk, but he did his best not to act like one with us. He was considerate and didn't keep music too loud at night when we were studying. I liked all of my roommates. I just happened to get along with Pacey the best. Maybe because he reminded me of a British version of my brothers for some reason—not that I would ever tell him or my brothers that.

"Who uses the word macking?" Tanner asked, rolling his eyes.

"It's probably back in the new slang," Miles said, defending Sanders. Tanner didn't really get along with Sanders, and Miles was always the mediator. I usually stayed out of the way. I had enough family drama when it came to mine. I didn't need to add the cross-section of five guys who didn't know each other, trying to live with one another.

"Anyway, it was none of the sort," Pacey remarked, his tone formal. "She was just replenishing the stores you seemed to have forgotten were mine," he said, holding up the bag of Twizzlers.

Sanders blushed and then shrugged. "Sorry about that. I would have taken care of it tomorrow. Thanks, babe." He kissed her hard on the cheek, and she just smiled.

"It's what I'm here for. I have lists of lists. And I'll be sure to bring my own snacks next time. Again, sorry." She tugged on Sanders' hand. "Now, come on. There's someone I need you to meet. Bye, boys." She waved at us and then sauntered off, Sanders right behind her.

"I have a feeling those two are going to be married by the end of the semester, and we're going to be one roommate short," Pacey said dryly.

"I hope not," Tanner grumbled, and I looked up at him.

"Really? I didn't think you liked Sanders."

Tanner shrugged. "It's not that. I don't mind him. I don't mind any of you guys," he added, and we all laughed. "It's more that I don't know if you need to get married when you're twenty years old. And I'm pretty sure the only people they've ever slept with are each other."

"That could be something they like, though. If you find the right person, why do you need to keep searching?" I asked.

"I never took you as a romantic," Pacey said, studying my face.

I quirked a lip. "I've watched my brothers fall in love, one after another, and in spectacular fashion. I can't help it." I looked down at my beer and took a sip.

"Well, that's nice to know," Miles said. "And I'm sorry that Mandy wasn't it for you." Tanner slapped Miles upside the back of the head, and Miles just grinned. "What?"

I laughed. "Mandy was never going to be forever. Remember? She told me flat-out that I wasn't her forever and that she wanted fun. I like fun." *I guess.*

"I have a feeling you're going to like a whole lot of fun," Tanner said as he looked over my shoulder.

I followed his gaze and narrowed my eyes at the girl across the room. There was something familiar about her that I couldn't quite place. "Why do I feel like I know her?" I asked.

"Oh, you don't know her, but she and her roommate know *you*."

I gave Tanner a look. "What?"

Tanner grinned, looking as if he were having more fun than he had in years, and leaned forward. "Quick, that one right there? She's on her way over here to talk to you. I have a feeling you're going to like what she has to say."

I looked over at Tanner. "Why are you acting so weird? Like the man behind the curtain."

He shook his head. "Don't look at the man behind the curtain." He laughed. "But they seemed interesting when I met them a few weeks ago at the coffee shop. You should talk to her."

Coffee shop? And why did *that* sound familiar? "Talk to who?" I asked but looked over at the girl with the light eyes, the pointed chin, and the soft face. I swallowed hard.

Suddenly, the guys were gone as if shadows and ghosts had swallowed them up.

The girl in front of me couldn't be taller than my chin, even in heels, and she had her shoulders hunched forward for a moment. She met my gaze, but nearly tripped over her feet as she rolled her shoulders back.

"Hi," she squeaked and held out a hand. She blushed and nearly lowered her proffered palm, but I quickly reached out and took it. Her hand was warm, a little clammy, but I squeezed it before letting go.

"Hi," I said, confused yet intrigued by this girl with her wide eyes and pouty lips.

"I didn't mean to try to shake your hand just then. I'm not very good at this."

I looked around, wondering if anyone was paying attention. I couldn't see my roommates, but her friend was watching us, warmth in her eyes—not abject terror or snarkiness so I had to count that as a win.

"Well, hi. I'm Dillon."

"Oh, I know," she blurted before groaning. "At least, that's what my roommate said. Anyway, I'm here for a reason."

"And that reason would be?" I couldn't keep my gaze off her.

"I am on a dare. I'm not good at them, but I'm going to do my best on this one."

My brows shot up. "What on Earth could I have to do with your dare?" I asked, fascinated.

"I need you to kiss me," she said quickly. "Preferably without everybody watching. Is that okay?" she asked. I looked down at her and then up at her friend, only to see that she wasn't alone anymore. No, Tanner was there with her, along with Pacey, all three of them smiling and raising their drinks in cheers.

"What?" I asked, confused.

"My friend thinks I need to get out more. And she dared me to kiss you. I thought I would ask first because… hello, consent."

"Yeah, consent is good," I said, truly confused.

"Anyway, my name is Elise by the way. It's nice to meet you. I guess. I sort of saw you around the coffee shop before. Well, not like today before, but before-before." I felt like I couldn't catch up, and she kept rambling. "Anyway, this is the most insane—insanest?—thing I've ever done in my life. But I came up to you, I told you about my dare, and now I'm going to go home and hide under a blanket.

That would probably be good. I'll be back after the semester's over."

She turned on her heel, and I reached out and gripped her hand before she could leave. She froze and then turned to me slowly, looking like a deer in headlights.

"It's nice to meet you, Elise."

She blinked. "Oh, it's nice to meet you, too."

"So I take it that you consent?" I asked, not knowing why I was doing this but knowing I needed to.

Her eyes widened. "Consent? You mean for the dare?"

"Yes," I said slowly.

Her mouth parted, her eyes getting even wider, if that were possible. "Oh. Well, yes."

I didn't let her say anything else. I simply lowered my head and kissed her, living in the moment for the first time in a long while.

Chapter 2

Elise

I HONESTLY COULDN'T BELIEVE I WAS DOING THIS. BUT there were lips on mine, and I felt as if I were drowning. Who was this person, and why was he doing this? Why had I been the one to dare him?

No, that wasn't right. Corinne had dared *me*. She had said that I needed to have a little fun and see if I could best my nerves and kiss the guy I hadn't been able to stop thinking about for weeks—not since I had seen him in the coffee shop. And now, here I was, standing next to him, his hand on my cheek, his thumb brushing across my skin, and his mouth on mine. I could hear someone cheering, knew others were looking at me. It wasn't like I could hear them looking at me, but I could feel their gazes on my skin. And I hated it. I didn't want to be the center of attention. And yet, I couldn't stop what I was doing. And so, I parted my lips and let him kiss me harder.

He pulled away, his breath a little choppy. And then he smiled at me. A sweet grin that spread over his entire face and brightened his eyes, making him look like the sexiest guy I had ever seen in my life.

What the hell was I doing?

"Did that satisfy your dare?" Dillon Connolly asked. I blinked before mortification set in. My stomach dropped, and I took a step back.

"Oh. Maybe. Anyway, I should go."

I turned on my heel again, but Dillon reached out and gently touched my wrist. "Don't."

"I really should," I mumbled.

I looked over at him as he stared at the people staring at *us*. Suddenly, everyone looked as if they had something else to do.

What would it be like to have that kind of power? To be the big man on campus. The one who didn't know it.

I saw Dillon around now that I knew to look for him. Everywhere he went, he acted as if he might not have a care in the world, but he also didn't push people away. Didn't think he was better than them, even though he *was* better than most guys on campus. Yet it was still weird because I felt like he didn't understand the power he wielded, the magnetism that brought people to him like a moth to a flame.

"I really should be going."

Dillon shook his head, a smile still playing on his lips. "You're just going to leave me after kissing me like that?"

I raised a brow, doing my best to look my most haughty. "You're the one who kissed me."

"Only because you asked."

Shame crept up my spine, and I lowered my head. "I'm sorry," I mumbled.

Dillon cursed under his breath. "That's not what I meant. I was just trying to play along. Come on, let's meet this friend of yours who dared you. And talk. I don't usually kiss strangers."

I looked at him then, raising a brow. "That's not what I hear."

"You're hearing things about me?"

I could have kicked myself. "That's not what I meant. Forget I said anything."

Dillon shook his head. "No, we're going to talk about that. Plus, I just had my mouth on yours. I think that gives me the right to maybe a little conversation."

"Fine," I mumbled, aware that others were still staring. I hated when people gawked.

We made our way to where Corinne stood with the guy from the coffee shop and another guy with blond hair. I could feel Dillon behind me, his warmth at my back. He didn't touch me, didn't leave me with his hand on the small of my back like sometimes happened in my dreams. It wasn't necessarily Dillon in my dreams, but you couldn't always see the other person's face in those kinds of dreams. Still, you were happy and finding your place. But then you woke up and realized that, once again, you were alone. But that was okay. I didn't really have time for a relationship or need.

And yet, my hormones seemed to have other ideas.

"Hi, Corinne," I grumbled. My best friend and room-mate grinned, her hair piled on the top of her head.

I loved her so much, even though I hated her a little right then.

"Hi. I didn't expect you to kiss him in the middle of the party, but good going." She gave me a thumbs-up, and Tanner laughed from beside her.

"I do believe you two are my favorite people ever," Tanner said, and the other guy just shook his head.

"I think we need an introduction," the blond interjected, his British accent startling me. It was sexy. In fact, the whole package was. As was Tanner. But for some reason, it was Dillon who had been on my mind recently—and I hated it.

Or maybe I hated myself for liking it too much.

"Corinne, this is Dillon. Dillon, this is Corinne. And I don't know these guys."

Dillon snorted. "It's nice to meet you, Corinne. I don't know whether I should thank you or run away from you."

Corinne beamed.

"That's usually the case when it comes to people these days."

Dillon just shook his head, smiling. "Tanner, Pacey, what are you guys doing over here?"

"I have no idea, but I'm quite enjoying myself. Hello, I'm Pacey," the blond man said as he stared at me.

"I'm Elise," I said, confused. "How do you guys know each other?"

This time, Tanner spoke. "We're roommates. Along with a couple of other guys around here. This is our home."

I swallowed hard. "Oh. Small world."

"Well, this has been interesting. Where did you guys meet?" Pacey asked, and I could still feel the heat of Dillon behind me. I didn't look up at him. I didn't move slightly back so I could lean against him. All I wanted to do was hide, and I wasn't sure I could do that.

But then I met Corinne's gaze and remembered my promise.

Tonight was about fun. About remembering that this was college, and I was allowed to be who I wanted to be— or who I wasn't.

I could be anyone. I could do anything. I was allowed to have fun.

I wasn't an innocent virgin who'd never even touched a guy before. But I wasn't good at the whole human-interaction thing.

Maybe if I let myself, though, I could have fun tonight. And I saw all of those promises and memories in Corinne's gaze as she looked at me.

Treasure every moment, I thought to myself.

Our motto.

Something I needed to do better about remembering.

"I met the girls at a coffee shop," Tanner said. "They were having a lovely conversation behind me, and I just had to invite them to our party. I didn't know there would be this dare involved, but this is the most exciting thing that's happened recently. Anyway, I'm delighted that I met up with them at that coffee shop."

I looked up at Dillon as he frowned at Tanner's words.

"When was this?" Dillon asked as if trying to remember something.

"That would be the day that you and Mandy broke up," Tanner said, clearing his throat.

"Mandy?" Corinne asked.

I moved to the side a bit so I could face Dillon and the

others. I wasn't really happy with him behind me where I couldn't see his reactions. Not that I could read him even if I could see him. He usually had a smile on his face, and I felt like I couldn't get a bead on him. Not that I wanted to. It wasn't like I wanted to be with him or anything. Right?

And now I was losing my mind. Half a beer, and I had lost all sensibility.

"Oh," Dillon said and then cleared his throat again. "That was an eventful day," he said. Then he looked at me, narrowing his eyes. "I think I saw you. You guys were a few people behind me in line. Right?"

I blushed, feeling like a stalker for some reason, even though we had been invited to this party.

"Yes, we were there," I said, my voice trailing off.

"I know that, but I think I saw you there, didn't I?"

"Yes. And you were a topic of conversation, hence why Tanner invited us tonight," Corinne said, smiling at him.

I could have hit my friend just then, but I didn't.

Mostly because I wasn't the violent sort, and it would have only made me a spectacle I wasn't ready for. At least, not yet.

"Anyway, we came tonight because we wanted to see what all the fuss was about," Corinne said, rolling her shoulders back as she looked at the guys.

Tanner's eyes danced with laughter, something that surprised me. I didn't know him well, but he usually seemed to be glaring off into a corner somewhere when he wasn't talking with a co-ed. Not that I thought he was a womanizer, but people seemed to be drawn to him. And from the looks that others gave Dillon and now this Pacey, Tanner wasn't alone in that.

"Anyway, I'm glad you came," Tanner said after a

minute. I blushed. "I'm pretty sure Dillon is happy, too," he said, and I didn't duck my head this time. Instead, I met his gaze head-on. He just raised a brow and smiled. *Jerk.*

"So, I take it there was a dare involved," Pacey began, and I sighed. "Yes, I was told to ask Dillon to kiss me. And then he proceeded to do so in the middle of the room, rather than in a corner where nobody could see. But it's fine. It's done. And now I no longer have to do dares for the rest of the evening."

Corinne shook her head. "Is that how we're playing the game, then?"

"You're my best friend. And yet, I want to hit you right now."

Corinne just laughed. "I don't blame you for that. I didn't think you'd go through with it at all. But I'm glad you did. You need to get out sometimes."

I let out a sigh. "I am out. Didn't you see? We are out. At a party. On a school night."

"You don't have classes tomorrow," she said dryly.

"I could," I said, and the guys laughed.

"You sound just like my brothers and sisters-in-law," Dillon said, and everybody looked towards him, seeming to want to know more—me included. Why did I want to know more about this man? Why did having a single inkling of who this man could be make me want him more?

What the hell was wrong with me?

It must have been the kiss. Maybe it had altered my brain cells or something. Although it had been good, could it be *that* good?

"Anyway, I see someone I need to talk to," Tanner said before looking at all of us. "You guys should stay. Don't go. Another couple just had a big fight in the back, and I'm sure everybody's already forgotten about this little rendezvous."

He shrugged and then moved off into the house, blending in with the crowd as if he had never been there.

Pacey just shook his head and smiled. "I do believe I need another drink and to go meet with Alexa."

"Really?" Dillon asked. I had to wonder who Alexa was.

"Maybe. We'll see." He turned to Corinne. "Would you like to join me?

Corinne sputtered and then laughed. "You mean to get a beer? Sure. But I'm not getting into bed with you and another girl. Sorry."

"I promise not to dare you on that. But I should at least dare a kiss, shouldn't I?" I asked, teasing. Well, it was maybe teasing. I was a little flustered.

Corinne just grinned. "No, you wanted to end the game. So now you don't get to dare me. Sorry." She gave me a little finger wave, hooked her arm with Pacey's, and the two blended seamlessly into the crowd, leaving Dillon and me alone in the corner. Is this what they had wanted? To leave me behind, wondering what the hell I was doing?

"So, should I ask you what your major is? Or your sign? I don't know, something to start a conversation that doesn't begin with a dare?" Dillon asked, and I let out a soft laugh.

"I'm usually better at conversation, but I didn't actually expect you to kiss me. I thought I would just go along with the dare because my friend asked, and then I'd run away and hide and never have this conversation again."

Dillon tilted his head and looked at me. "Do you do this often? Play Truth or Dare or whatever the hell you guys were doing?"

"I've known Corinne since we were five years old. Our

mothers joined a Mommy and Me group and we grew up together—only three houses down. But the neighbors we grew up with when we were kids were great, and we were allowed to climb their fences if we wanted. Not that my parents let me too often." My parents rarely let me do anything I wanted to do, but that wasn't a subject I would get into with him—or anyone, for that matter.

"Corinne is a daredevil. She went skydiving as soon as she turned eighteen because her parents wouldn't let her do it before then. She got a tattoo and has gone scuba diving, horseback riding, anything you can possibly imagine. She likes to live life to the fullest because that is our motto. Treasure every moment."

"It's a good one," he said. "You didn't do any of that stuff?" he asked, leaning against the wall as he looked at me. He made it seem like he was interested in what I had to say, and I couldn't help but relax a bit. I didn't know this guy, and yet I was speaking to him. I wasn't hiding. It was odd.

"We started playing Truth or Dare when we were little, and it escalated into fun things—sometimes dangerous but never cruel," I put in, wanting him to understand. Not that I even understood. "Corinne dared me to have fun tonight."

Dillon grinned. "And kissing me was fun?"

"I'm pretty sure you already know it was. No need for me to inflate your ego."

He put his hand over his heart and took a staggering step back until he bumped against the wall.

"Ouch. What did I ever do to you?"

Haunted my dreams and made me wonder what the hell was wrong with me. Of course, I didn't say that aloud.

"And, yes, she dared me to kiss you. But as I said before, I planned to ask before I did it. It only seemed right."

"Well, I'm glad you asked. It made this evening a little more fun."

I looked around the full house. Saw people laughing, drinking a little too much, and others kissing in dark corners. More made out right in the open. "You weren't having fun?"

He shrugged. "I guess. Just having an off evening."

I flinched, and he cursed under his breath.

"That's not what I meant. Sorry. I was having an off night before you showed up. And I swear that's not a line. Thank you for asking me to kiss you. I enjoyed it."

"And *that's* not a line?" I asked dryly.

"It could be. However, let's just forget lines and dares and everything. It's nice to meet you, Elise. I'm glad you came tonight."

"I guess I'm glad, too. I'm really not good at this sort of thing."

"And what sort of thing is this?" he asked. I could have punched him.

"You know what I mean. Talking to other human beings."

He laughed. "Sometimes, I feel like that, too. Although my siblings would say I never shut up."

"That's the second time you've mentioned them. Am I allowed to ask you more?" I inquired, eager to know, even though I knew I shouldn't pry.

I was only setting myself up for failure.

Dillon smiled. "I have three brothers, but they're all a bit older. They each recently got married and are now working on the next gen."

"So, you're going to be an uncle. That's sweet."

"I hope so. Somebody needs to spoil the kids."

"And that's going to be you?"

"Okay, maybe the other brothers will do the spoiling, but I can be the fun uncle. And then once I get a full-time job after school, I can start saving money so I can spoil."

"So, the reason you're going to college and working on a career—whatever that may be—is so you can spoil your nieces and nephews? Good priorities."

"Exactly. I'll be sure to write that down on my senior thesis. You know, when they ask you where you see yourself in five years? I'll be covered in Play-Doh and flour, or whatever other sticky things the kids are into, and all of my money will go to them. Sounds like a plan."

"You're ridiculous, but I kind of like it."

"Me, too." He cleared his throat. "Do you need something to drink?" he asked. "It doesn't need to be liquor. We have other things. I promise."

"Honestly, I think I could use a beer. Is that okay?"

"We're not carding here," he said. "After all, I'm only twenty. Don't tell anyone," he whispered.

I smiled.

"Same. I promise I won't blab."

"Well, good. I like that I'm not hitting on a younger girl."

"Hitting on?" I asked as he slowly led me towards the kegs for a drink. This time, he set his hand on the small of my back, and I felt the heat of him again.

What was wrong with me?

"Well, you did kiss me first."

"I thought you were the one who kissed me."

"Only because you asked. And I say 'only' because I would typically ask the girl more than her name first."

I smiled as we made our way to the kegs. I didn't recognize anyone in the kitchen.

He got me a cup, and I watched him pour then hand it to me directly. I kept my eyes on his hands, and he gave me a tight nod. "I'm glad you're being safe. Though if I or any of my roommates see somebody putting something in a girl's drink, they're going to have to answer to both us and the cops. We don't play that shit."

"I'm glad you're watching out for people."

"I'm not getting drunk tonight, and neither are Miles or Tanner. It's our turn to watch the rest of the party. Not that Miles or Tanner ever get drunk, but whatever."

"You guys take this whole party house thing seriously."

"Maybe. Sometimes. We try. Anyway, tell me more about yourself."

"Why?" I asked, staring at him, wanting to know why he cared.

He blinked, nonplussed. "What do you mean?"

"Why do you want to know more about me?"

"Because I think you're interesting?" he asked. "That was a question, not a statement." He laughed. "I don't know, it was a nice way to meet somebody, a dare that led to a kiss. I want to get to know you a bit more."

"Well, like I said, I'm not really good at this. And I don't have time for a relationship or getting to know somebody like that. I'm a double major, and I rarely leave the house. I don't want you to be disappointed when I leave here tonight and the only thing you got was that kiss."

Dillon stared at me and then shook his head.

"I'm only a single major, but I also work. I'm not good

at the whole relationship thing either. And, honestly, I was just asking you a little bit more about yourself."

My cheeks heated. "Oh."

"However, I get it. And it's good to know where I am upfront."

"I'm not usually such a jerk. I'm just a little flustered, I guess. I didn't expect Corinne to dare me like that. But I should have been ready."

"What else did she dare you to do?" he asked point-blank, and I froze.

"What?"

"She dared you to do something else, didn't she?"

I swallowed hard, mortification sliding over me. "Maybe."

"And what was it?" he asked softly.

I met his gaze and licked my lips. "To have fun tonight. To lower my inhibitions and do the one thing I've never done before."

Dillon looked at me, tilting his head. "And what is that?"

"I don't know if I should tell you," I said quickly.

"You really can't leave me hanging." He looked around the empty kitchen. "People are heading out, and nobody can hear you but me. What did she dare you to do?"

I met his gaze and swallowed hard. "She dared me, that if the occasion arose, to do the one thing I've never done before. As I said." I paused. "To have a one-night stand."

Dillon blinked, and I bit my lip.

"Oh," he whispered. "Is that something you want?"

"I don't know," I said quickly. "I'm not against it," I said, lowering my head. Then I raised my chin again until I met his gaze.

I saw that his eyes had darkened, and his mouth had parted ever so slightly. "Well then, I think it's time to see exactly what kind of dare we're dealing with. A one-night stand, you say?" he asked, and I nodded, my cheeks flushing.

"Is that something you would be interested in?" he asked, his voice very careful.

I bit my lip, studied his face, and knew I needed to tell the truth.

"Yes."

I only hoped to hell there was a path through the crowd later so I could run as quickly as I could.

Chapter 3

Dillon

"I DIDN'T THINK YOU'D SAY YES," I SAID, BLINKING DOWN AT
Elise. Her eyes widened, and she blushed again, that pale,
pretty skin turning pink.

"Well, if you don't want to... I mean, I guess I could
find someone else," she said quickly, and I growled. Actually growled.

"No, you don't get to find someone else."

"You got a little possessive and growly right then. I
think I kind of liked it. What was in that beer?" Elise asked,
looking down at her cup.

"You had four sips. And you watched me pour it.
There's nothing in that beer. And we can pretend we didn't
just say any of that, if you want."

"Um, that's not what I'm saying," she said softly,
leaning forward.

"Okay, what *were* you saying?" I asked, my voice low.

"I'm saying it would be nice to act like a normal college student for once. At least, for the evening."

"And you think normal college students have one-night stands?" I asked incredulously.

"Maybe? I told you I'm not good at this."

Though nobody was around, I still looked over my shoulder, making sure.

"You're not a virgin, are you?" I asked, even if it was invasive. Then again, these were the kinds of questions I needed answers to.

Her eyes widened, and she laughed. "No. I'm not. I'm not as innocent as you may think, Dillon."

I wasn't sure about that, but I still smiled. "Really?" I asked. "Not innocent?"

"Okay, maybe in some things. But I've had sex before. And not just once." Her eyes widened again, and she put her hand over her mouth. "I can't believe I just said that," she mumbled between her fingers.

I laughed. I couldn't help it. "Come on, let's get out of the kitchen where anybody can eavesdrop."

She blushed again, then looked around frantically. "Okay, that sounds like a plan."

I held out my hand, and she looked down at my palm before slowly sliding her fingers into mine. "We don't have to do anything you don't want to do. But you intrigue me, Elise. And you make me laugh. I think I could use that."

"Oh?" she asked, and I shook my head. "Forget I said that. About the needing. Let's just see what happens tonight and have fun."

"Deal. Nothing serious. No deep talks. No promises."

"I can do that," I said, wondering what the hell I was

doing. This wasn't necessarily unlike me, but I wasn't usually so upfront about it. Having a conversation about a one-night stand seemed odd.

And yet, with Elise, it made a weird kind of sense.

She needed to be open and honest, and I couldn't help but be the same way. There were things I didn't want to talk about, didn't want to deal with. So, I wouldn't.

And maybe, just maybe, I could have fun for the evening. Make a connection, ever so brief. It would be nice not to worry about random shit. Not to focus on the things surrounding me and reaching in, not ever letting me go.

"Come on, then," I said, clearing my throat.

"Where are we going?"

"The only place I know where nobody can overhear."

We passed Paccy, who seemed to have found Alexa, but I didn't see any of my other roommates. The place was slowly emptying out, and Pacey gave me a nod and then raised a brow as I passed.

In that gesture, I knew that he would take care of closing up the house, but that raised brow told me that he would ask what the hell was going on later. And I probably would have to tell him, just as soon as I figured out what this night was. We walked up the stairs, Elise's hand in mine as she followed me.

A couple of people were still on the stairs, just talking, and they didn't pay us any mind as we made our way up the steps and down the hallway to my room.

I pulled out my keys and unlocked the door. Elise laughed.

"Is that how you keep people off your bed?" she asked and then turned bright red.

"A guy has to be careful. Pacey warned me. He didn't

lock his door once in his old house and walked into the room with the girl he was seeing, only to find somebody already enjoying his bed."

"Oh, hell," she said with a laugh.

"Exactly. Anyway, here's my home." I shrugged and took a step back. When we had chosen rooms, thanks to Pacey's Twizzlers, I'd ended up with the master. Each room had its own bathroom and was each a different size. Somehow, I had the largest room in the house with the most massive bathroom—though not the biggest tub. And while I might love it, I still felt terrible that I had all this extra space. I even had a little seating area, one where it was nice to get some work done when I didn't want to study downstairs with the rest of the guys.

It was like a tiny apartment up here within the big house, and I knew I was blessed. I still paid the same rent as the other guys, even though I didn't think it was fair, but they had all agreed that it made no sense to go by square footage when the rest of the house was so big. Everybody had the space they needed. Mine just happened to be in my bedroom.

"This is a bigger room than I thought you'd have," she said, looking around. "It's like three times the size of mine."

I chuckled, my shoulders tensing. "It was a big statehouse back in the day. And since this is the master bedroom, I have all the space. I didn't ask for it," I said quickly at her look. "I just got lucky when we drew straws. Or Twizzlers, in that case."

"You drew candy and got the biggest room?" she asked, laughing.

"Yeah, sometimes fate works out pretty weird," I said,

meeting her gaze. It was a bit awkward now. It had been a little strange before, but now it felt as if we were on the brink of something that could change everything. Still, I needed to stop worrying about being so serious. I didn't know if we would go through with what we had talked about, but maybe we would. Or perhaps we would just sit in my little seating area and talk for the night. I didn't know what I wanted, but I did know that I would be happy with either outcome. It was so weird that I would think that after just meeting this person.

But then again, I remembered her from the coffee shop. I remembered looking at her, remembered that first glance. Even then, I'd wondered who she was. Later that evening, I had broken up with Mandy, though not because of the girl with the bright eyes and the intriguing face. Still, she had haunted my dreams a few times and made me want to know more about her. But I had broken up with Mandy because she hadn't wanted to be with me and had called me less than. She had said that I wasn't worth dating for long. That I wasn't the forever type. I might not have wanted forever with Mandy, but I had thought we had at least been on the same page. I hadn't known I was just her boy toy for the afternoon while she waited for someone better to come along.

I had been a stand-in for most of my life until my brother Cameron took me in. I had been less than in my mother's eyes for her entire life, and even less than that in my father's—a man I didn't even know.

I hadn't wanted to be that with Mandy.

I felt a soft brush of fingertips on my skin and looked up into Elise's eyes.

"Why are you frowning? You look so sad."

I shook my head and pushed those thoughts from my mind. "It's not important."

She tilted her head. "Maybe it is."

"Maybe. But not for tonight." I let out a sigh. "I want to talk about happy things. Nothing important. You know?"

She nodded and leaned into the cushions as we sat down on the small loveseat in my room. "Yeah, I constantly have to talk about important things with my friends and my family. They're always wanting to know what I'm thinking or doing. And while I love them, I sometimes just want to pretend that nothing's wrong for the moment. You know?"

"Exactly," I said, relieved that she understood.

"Not that we need to do anything tonight," I repeated.

"Totally. We don't need to do anything," she whispered and then licked her lips. I couldn't help but follow the gesture and lick mine in response.

Her eyes widened, and her mouth parted slightly.

"What are we doing?" she whispered.

"I have no fucking clue," I said, shaking my head. "But I kind of want to find out."

I leaned forward and gently brushed my lips over hers. She let out a shocked gasp and then opened for me, sliding her tongue against mine.

I groaned and deepened the kiss slightly before moving back, needing to catch my breath and gather my thoughts.

"We don't have to do anything, but if you want, I think we could have a little fun," I said, knowing that wasn't the best line. I didn't even want to use lines. I wanted to be open and honest. And, hell, I wanted to taste her again. Something about her called to me, and there was probably something wrong with that. A temptation and an addiction that I needed to stay away from. But I didn't want to. Not then.

Maybe not ever.

"You taste so sweet," I whispered, and she looked up at me.

"Oh?" she said, her voice breathy.

"Yes, and I want more," I said softly.

"Good. Me, too."

I loved her contradiction. Sometimes, she was all fire and directness. Other times, she was the exact opposite as if she were still trying to find out who she was and determine what she wanted. I didn't mind. I was pretty much the same. And for the evening, it felt like we fit together.

At least, I hoped so.

I kissed her again, brushing her hair away from her face as I did. She tentatively slid her hands down my arms, squeezing my biceps, and I leaned into her, wanting more. She tasted slightly of beer and toothpaste. An odd combination but it worked. I kissed her harder, running my hands across her face and then down her neck to her collarbones. She shivered at the touch, and I grinned before backing away slightly to nibble at her lip.

She groaned, and I moved a bit, kneeling with one leg on the loveseat to slightly push her back against the side of the cushion. Her eyes widened, and then she slowly trailed her fingers up my ribs, over my shirt. I hovered over her and then kissed her again, this time gently placing my hand on her side, under the softness of her top. Her skin was warm, so fucking silky, and I groaned as she let out a breath. She kissed me deeper, and I moaned, slowly lowering myself so I knelt between her legs. I kissed her again, then slowly moved my hand up, cupping her ribs just below her breast. She groaned, and I kissed her harder.

But when I wanted more, I knew this angle wouldn't work. I lowered my hands, reached for her hips, and moved to sit down. She let out a gasp and straddled me as I sat, her heat right above my cock. It didn't matter that we both wore jeans and there were enough clothes between us that we shouldn't be able to feel this much friction. All I could do was feel the heat of her. She pushed her hair back from her face, and I cupped the nape of her neck, bringing her closer to me. Her breasts pressed against my chest, her hands moving to either side of me on the couch as she rocked against me. I groaned, my cock pressing hard against the zipper of my jeans. I kissed her again, needing more. She increased the friction, and I wrapped my other hand around her hip, squeezing. She didn't stop moving. Instead, she ground down harder. I moaned and pulled away, needing to breathe.

"You keep doing that, I'm going to come in my pants like a teenager."

She smiled at me. "You're young. You could probably go again right after," she teased.

I growled and bit her lip again. "That's not very nice," I said and tugged on the bottom of her shirt. "Okay?"

"Yes," she panted and lifted her arms. I pulled the blouse over her head, tugging the tank that she wore underneath with it. That left her in a pale, rose-colored bra, her nipples peeking through the lace.

"Jesus Christ," I muttered. She blushed and went to cover herself, but I moved her hands. I pulled them gently behind her, capturing her wrists with one hand. The movement pressed her breasts closer to my face.

"I didn't know you had all this delicate lace under your clothes."

"It made me feel brave for the evening."

"Did you know about the dare before you came?" I asked, wanting to know more.

She shook her head. "No. And I don't think that Corinne would've actually made me complete the dare. It was just a passing joke. And yet, here we are."

I lifted my hips slightly, pressing against the heat of her core. "Here we are."

I lowered my head, capturing one lace-covered nipple with my mouth. I sucked, and she groaned, but she didn't remove her arms from my grip. It left her completely at my mercy, yet I knew she had all the control.

I moved to her other breast, kissing before I let go of her wrists to reach my hand up. I undid the clasp of her bra, and she helped me pull down the straps. When the lingerie was tossed to the side, her breasts were right in front of me.

They were the perfect size for my palms—not too big, not too small—with dusty rose nipples that hardened with the attention of my gaze.

"Jesus," I whispered again and moved to lap at her. She moaned, tangling her fingers in my hair as I sucked on a nipple, biting down gently. "Dillon," she panted.

"That's it, keep saying my name," I teased, chuckling roughly against her as she laughed, tugging on my hair. I didn't let go, didn't stop. Instead, I kept kissing, lapping, leaving gentle bites along her skin as I moved back to her collarbone and her neck, sucking hard.

My hands were at her hips and then cupping her

breasts, before I slowly slid them down her belly to play with the seam of her jeans.

"I want to see more," I whispered.

"You first," she said, tugging on my shirt.

A smile played on my lips as I pulled my tee over my head from the back and tossed it beside her bra.

Her eyes widened, and she looked down at me and grinned.

"Whoa."

"Well, then. I like the sound of that."

She kissed me again while I played with her nipples. Somehow, I lifted her, undid the button of her jeans, and pulled them down slightly. We scrambled off the loveseat, both of us panting with need, no words needed. I tugged off her jeans, bringing her panties with them, and then knelt in front of her.

She was all wet and swollen, and since I was already kneeling between her legs, I leaned forward and took her clit into my mouth, slowly rubbing her swollen folds with my thumb. She moaned, her knees buckling, but I kept her upright with my hands.

I sucked and lapped, and then looked up at her, saw her gaze darken as she panted.

I thrust one finger into her, curling it so I could find that bundle of nerves inside, and she let out a shocked gasp before coming on my face as she nearly fell to the floor with her orgasm. I groaned and stood, moving her slightly so she was steady.

"I just...wow."

"Yeah, wow."

She looked at me and then rubbed the long, thick line of my cock through my jeans. I groaned, undid my belt, and shoved the denim and my boxer briefs down. I toed out of my shoes and my pants and then stood naked in front of her. Her hand moved to the base of my cock, gripping.

I put my hand over hers, squeezed harder, and met her gaze. When she slowly ran her hand up and down my length, my hand remained over hers, pressing harder and yet letting her set the pace.

I almost came right there, right over those beautiful rose-tipped breasts, but I stopped myself, knowing that I needed a moment.

I met her gaze, swallowed hard, then slowly sat down, reaching for my pants. "Need a condom," I grunted.

She nodded, then took the foil packet from my hand before ripping it open. I groaned at the sight, nearly coming again. Then, before taking the condom from her and rolling it down my length, she licked her lips again, and I held out a hand.

"Ready?" I asked. She met my gaze before smiling sweetly and climbing onto the loveseat. She knelt, her knees on either side of my hips, her wetness grazing the tip of my cock. I groaned again and slid my hands over her hips, meeting her gaze.

"Ready," she whispered, and then she slowly lowered herself atop me. She was so tight, far tighter than I expected for some reason, and I closed my eyes and counted to ten. She was fully seated on top of me, my dick inside her to the point I was afraid I might break her, but she just met my gaze after I opened my eyes and slowly pushed my hair from my face.

"Wow," she breathed, and I grinned.

"That's a good word for it," I whispered and slowly

rocked my hips. Her whole body shook, and I licked my lips, slowly rotating my hips ever so slightly.

"Whoa, need a minute," she said, pressing her hands to my shoulders. I froze, sweat trickling down my spine. "Anything you need," I said, my body shaking.

"You're just really big, and I, uh, need time to acclimate."

I grinned. "Well, that's a very nice thing to say."

She groaned, rolling her eyes. "You must think very highly of yourself."

"I can't help it. You're tight around me like a fucking vise, and your breasts are right in front of my face," I whispered, then reached up and licked a nipple before looking back at her. "I'm in fucking heaven."

"Same. Now move," she groaned, and I nodded.

"Anything you say," I said and then moved as requested. She did, as well, rocking her hips and swiveling. I couldn't help but look at her eyes and wonder who this woman was. Wonder how exactly this had happened. But I wouldn't regret it. I couldn't. Because there was something here. Something I couldn't quite name. We kissed, and we touched, and the two of us moved against one another, our bodies pulsating. I couldn't help but want more, even though I told myself I shouldn't. This shouldn't be more. Couldn't. And yet, I wasn't sure how else to feel. I swallowed hard and then kissed her again, slowly sliding my hands between us. I flicked my thumb over her clit, and she shook, her whole body bowing as she came. I pumped into her again, this time harder, and when she met my gaze, I thrust into her one last time, slamming into her, and then I came, too, groaning her name into her mouth as she kissed me again.

After, we were both sweat-slick, shaking, and I held her close, not wanting this to end.

I stood up on shaky legs, and she let out a little squeal. She wrapped her legs around my waist, and I carried her to the bed, my dick still inside her. I kissed her again as I lowered us, lingering in the moment. I didn't want her to tell me that this had been a mistake. That we shouldn't have done this. So, I kept my mouth on hers, kept her busy.

In the morning, I'd watch her walk away.

But I couldn't do it now.

Even if I knew I should.

Chapter 4

Elise

I slowly opened my eyes and sank into the warmth behind me. Strong arms tightened like a band around my waist, and a very hard, very thick part of him pressed against my backside.

I froze, but the person holding me didn't tighten their arms, didn't move. Instead, he just breathed a little deeper along the back of my neck, sending shivers I didn't want to think about too hard down my spine.

I had just had my first one-night stand.

And now we were creeping into the morning, and I would have to do that walk of shame pretty soon. If I didn't, it would end up being a full-day stand, and that wasn't what I had signed up for. Besides, I didn't think a one-day stand existed.

I let out a breath and tried not to let the memories of

the night before slide to the forefront of my mind. And yet, there they were, coming full force.

Much like I had the night before.

I held back a groan at the horrible joke. I knew that if I was making silly puns, even in my head, I was well on my way to a nervous breakdown.

I tried to move, knowing I needed to get up, find my clothes, and get home. I had texted Corinne the night before so she knew where I was. But she would come to find me if I didn't get out of here soon. There were reasons you checked in with your friends, and though Dillon seemed like a nice guy and knew how to bring a woman to orgasm not once but *four* times in a row—maybe it was seven, I couldn't remember—that didn't mean he wasn't a serial killer.

He might just be an excellent, people-pleasing murderer.

That time I did groan, knowing I needed to get out of bed. Dillon's arm tightened around my waist.

"Elise?" he whispered, his breath warm against the back of my neck. I swallowed hard, not liking how I wanted to sink into his hold. We'd made no promises, and I would not let myself get all starry-eyed over a cute guy who happened to sleep with me after treating me with respect. He'd probably done this with more girls than I could count, and I was just another on a long list that I didn't care to dwell on. The first time I had seen him, he had been with another girl. He was allowed to be a player or whatever the hell he wanted to be. I wasn't asking him for promises, and I didn't have time for them. I just needed to get out of here before I looked him in the eyes and found myself wanting more.

"I need to head home. I have to study, shower, and make sure Corinne knows I'm okay."

Dillon kissed my naked shoulder. I shivered and bit my lip. I could not do this. *This* had just been one night. I didn't know what came next. This was my first time having a quick fling, but I knew that wanting more would break the spell and complicate things. And, as all evidence had shown, I wasn't good at complicated.

"Sounds like a plan." He cleared his throat and kissed my shoulder again. "I can help you get ready. Do you want coffee or anything?" He sat up, and I looked at him as the sheet fell, showing off his waist and naked hip. He rubbed the sleep out of his eyes and then pushed his dark brown hair away from his face. He looked way too damn sexy with the slight beard coming in since he hadn't shaved for at least a day. I needed to stop looking at him, or this would become a problem.

"No, I can get coffee at home. Or pick it up along the way."

"Did you drive here? Hell, I didn't even think about that last night."

I winced and then sat up, tucking the sheet under my armpits to cover myself. He raised a sleepy brow, but I tore my gaze away from him. Even though he'd had his mouth on every inch of my body last night, it still felt awkward this morning, and I wasn't sure I wanted to show him everything from the night before. We might not have been drunk —far from it, actually—but there had been an intoxicating mix of something else. Lust? Need? Bad decisions? All of the above? I didn't know.

But this had been my one night with Dillon, and now it was over. It was time for that walk of shame.

"I was just going to call a ride."

"I can drive you," he said and looked around the room. "Let me just grab my jeans. And a shirt. A shirt would probably be good."

I let out a hollow laugh, feeling as if I needed to run, but I wanted to maintain some dignity. "No, it's okay. I think it'd be best if I just called a rideshare to get home. It was my plan last night anyway. That's how Corinne left."

He frowned at me, studying my face far too hard for my liking. Or maybe it was exactly to my liking, and that was the problem. "You don't regret last night, do you? Shit, Elise. I'm sorry. Did I hurt you?"

My heart broke just a little, and I softened. I reached out, made another mistake in doing so, and brushed a lock of hair off his forehead, away from his eyes. "Last night was wonderful. I had a great time. And you didn't hurt me. But we both said this would be our one-night stand. All cliched and the like. That means I get to go home alone. And we don't have to deal with a potentially awkward car ride where we say we'll see each other, maybe be friends, and then never actually see each other again."

"So, we're going to have this conversation when we're both naked in my bed?" he said dryly.

I stilled. "Or we can say we'll see each other around. Maybe at the coffee place again. I had a great time, Dillon. But you explicitly said that you didn't have time for a relationship."

He met my gaze, searched my face. "You said the same thing," he said softly.

I swallowed hard, hating myself a little, but knowing it was easier to just rip the Band-Aid off. "You're right. Now, I am going to go make use of your facilities and get dressed. I hope that's okay."

He snorted and then smiled softly. "I had the perfect time last night," he whispered and leaned forward, brushing his mouth across mine. I didn't pull away. Instead, I parted my lips and soaked in his taste. It might be morning breath and all the other things that came with waking up, but none of that mattered. Because this was Dillon.

I was me.

And I had no idea what that meant.

He pulled away, searched my face again, and I quickly pulled the sheet off him. He laughed, then tugged the comforter over himself so both of us maintained some semblance of modesty. I wrapped the sheet around me, picked my clothes off the floor, and practically ran to the bathroom, shutting the door behind me. My heart raced in my chest, and I looked at my reflection in the mirror, wondering who I was.

I hadn't been a virgin before last night. I'd had sex before. With more than one person. And yet, I felt different. My hair was a tangled mess but looked sexy, haloed around my head. My eyeliner had smudged a bit, but it gave me the perfect smokey eye that I could never attain when I tried. My lips were swollen, and I had a little bit of beard burn on my chin.

I looked sated, pleasured, and scared out of my mind.

I let out a deep breath and whispered, "You're fine. Just get home."

And as Cinderella had to deal with a pumpkin and losing her glass slipper, I needed to get my business done, get dressed, and leave.

When I came out of the bathroom, Dillon stood near

his loveseat where we'd had sex the first time, and I blushed. He seemed to know exactly where my mind had gone, and a smile crept over his face. A knowing grin. One that made me want to press my thighs together until I told myself I needed to stop thinking about things like that.

"Anyway, thank you," I said, and closed my eyes. "You know what I mean."

Dillon shook his head as I lifted my lids again and stepped forward. He brushed my hair away from my face before handing me a hair tic. "It belonged to one of my sisters-in-law. It's new, but she left it here when they were unpacking and helping me move in. You look gorgeous, but...just in case."

I blushed and took it from him.

"Thank you. Having sex-head hair probably isn't a great thing."

He laughed, shaking his head. "I think you look fucking sexy, but what do I know? I'm just a guy."

I blushed again. "You're making it hard for me to walk out of this room, Dillon Connolly."

"I think I want you to feel that way."

I met his gaze and shook my head. "I should go."

"I think you should give me your number first," he said slowly.

I froze. "Wouldn't that negate the whole purpose of what we did last night?" I asked, oddly terrified.

He tilted his head. "I don't know. We don't have to have sex again if you don't want to, but I like you, Elise. And you're welcome to take a rideshare home so we don't have another awkward conversation, but I'd really like your phone number. Even if it's only so you can text me when you get home, and I know you got there safely. But I'd still like a way to reach you."

I relaxed marginally, knowing this was probably a bad idea, even if it sounded good in context. "Okay, so that you know I'm safe."

"Okay," he said, though I had a feeling that wasn't exactly what he had been thinking. But I would ignore that for now. It was safer for my sanity and anxiety if I did.

I pulled out my phone and noticed I had another message from Corinne after I'd checked in when I was washing my face. She told me that I would be answering a few thousand questions when I got home. I ignored that text and looked up at Dillon.

"Okay, I can text you now. How's that?"

He rattled off a number, and I texted a simple emoji, just a smiley face, not knowing what else to do. His phone dinged, and he looked down at it and smiled, then looked at me before cocking his head as he studied me. He didn't lean forward, didn't kiss me again.

And for that, I was grateful. I honestly didn't know what I would do if he had.

Instead, I awkwardly waved, winced, and then turned towards the door. Dillon let out a rough chuckle and reached over to open the door. Thankfully, his roommates weren't in the hallway, and I crept down the corridor and then the stairs. No one was in the house that I could tell, though the smell of coffee wafted from the kitchen. I inhaled and let out a sigh, and Dillon laughed again. "I can get you a to-go cup."

"No, my ride's here." I nodded towards the sedan in front of the house. "Well, have a good day, I guess," I said quickly.

Dillon just shook his head, his gaze still on mine. "You, too. Text me when you get home."

"I can do that," I said, knowing that I needed to leave. If I didn't, I wouldn't, and then it would be a thing. A terrible, horrible, awkwardly overdone scene.

I gave another self-conscious little wave and finally noticed Pacey standing in the kitchen behind Dillon, wearing only flannel pajama bottoms, his very built and naked torso gleaming under the lights.

The blond man winked, and I turned on my heel and fled.

I heard Dillon grumbling something at his roommate, but I ignored it.

I nearly ran to the sedan, knowing that I was making that scene I didn't want to create, and opened the back door. "Josh?" I asked, looking down at my screen to make sure the picture on the app matched the face.

"Elise?" he asked, doing the same.

"Okay, good," I said and slid into the back seat, putting on my seatbelt and closing the door as quickly as I could.

"Have a good night last night?" the driver asked, leering a bit. I ignored him, pulling out my phone and pretending to text Corinne. I checked social media, looking at photos from last night, but I didn't see myself or anyone that I knew in them. Not until I got to Corinne's photo, one where she leaned into Pacey, another girl on his other side, the three of them smiling broadly and laughing.

Maybe something would happen between Pacey and Corinne. They would make a cute couple. I'd have to see how she felt about that. Or I could not think about that at all, because if my best friend and practically sister got into a relationship with Dillon's roommate, it would make things even more awkward.

Josh seemed to get the idea that I didn't want to chat and remained silent after that until he pulled up to my house.

"Thank you," I said, making sure I left him a tip as I got out.

"No problem. Sorry about the comment. I think I need more coffee."

I froze as I slid out of the car and looked at him. "What?"

"I made a jerky comment. I just wanted to say I'm sorry. I do hope you had a good night. If you didn't, and you need me to do something about it, you're welcome to tell me that, too." I just looked at him.

A small smile played on my face, and I wondered how I kept ending up in these situations. "No problem. I'm doing great. Have a wonderful day."

"You too, Elise." I shut the door, and he drove off, presumably to another person either needing to get to campus or leaving a party a little late as I had.

"Get in here. We have coffee," Nessa called from the porch of the small home I shared with her, Corinne, and Natalie.

The boys' house was ridiculously large and felt like a mansion from the east coast rather than something in Colorado.

The girls and I shared a modest home with four bedrooms, but Nessa was pretty sure hers used to be an office since the closet seemed to have been added on later.

It didn't matter, though. Because unlike my first year of

college, I didn't have to share a room or a bathroom with anyone else.

Everything was small, old, and sometimes broke down, but it was ours for the year. And that was perfect.

"Do you really have coffee?" I asked and then paused. "Though I could use a shower."

"Well, you should have thought about that before you came home," Natalie said, smiling.

"I have no idea what you're talking about," I mumbled, and Corinne laughed. "Oh, you know plenty well what we're talking about. You probably smell like sex and that very sexy Dillon. I honestly can't believe you went through with it," she said, and I winced.

"I'm sorry. That was stupid, wasn't it?"

"Hey," Corinne snapped. "I was kidding." She bit her lip. "You didn't feel forced into that, did you? Did you at least have fun? It was all consent and everything you wanted, right?" she asked, and I found myself sitting in my living room, my three roommates staring at me. Nessa handed me a cup of coffee, and Natalie sat next to me. Corinne just looked at me, her eyes suddenly filling with tears. "Did I pressure you? Oh my God, I'm so sorry."

She sniffed, and I cursed under my breath.

"You didn't pressure me at all. It was an awesome line, though. So, thank you for that," I said with a laugh, trying to ease the tension.

She blinked at me and then threw back her head and laughed. "I love you so fricking much, Elise."

"Well, I love you, too," Natalie said, kissing the top of my head. Nessa squeezed my knee.

"Now, why don't you tell us exactly what happened?"

"And we're going to need details. Because at least somebody got laid last night," Natalie said with a laugh, and I shook my head.

"You are beautiful, hilarious, and brilliant. Usually, I put brilliant first, but I felt like saying beautiful this time."

"Well, you're right, I am all those things," Natalie said and laughed. "And yet, no man. Still a virgin. I may die one. It will be horrible."

Corinne snorted as she sat on the chair opposite us. "You're not going to die a virgin. I mean, I might die a virgin, but at least half of our house knows how to get laid."

I narrowed my eyes at Corinne.

"You could have slept with Timmy, Tommy, and Danny, all in high school."

"Could you have any more small-town names?" Nessa said, snorting.

"Maybe," Corinne said. "But now, Tommy and Timmy are getting married. At twenty. And Danny is in jail. Aren't we glad that I didn't sleep with any of them?"

"You still could have slept with Tommy or Timmy. They're both pansexual," I said.

"And completely in love with each other since like the sixth grade. Once they finally let themselves feel that and got to know those emotions, I would have just been in the way. I didn't need them. And we have done a great job of moving the conversation from your fulfilled sex life to my lack of one. Good job," Corinne said, narrowing her eyes.

I blushed, then took a sip of my coffee. "Great coffee," I said, and Nessa beamed.

"Thank you. I like the fact that I know exactly how you like it. You would think after a couple of semesters of being your roommate, I'd be good at it, but I still sometimes get it wrong."

"You got it right this time. Thank you." I let out a breath. "Okay, what do you want to know?" I groaned as they all talked at once.

"Was it good?"

"Did he treat you right?"

"How big was it?"

I looked over at sweet and innocent Natalie and widened my eyes. "*That* is your question?" I asked with a laugh.

She looked just about as shocked as I felt.

"I can't believe those words just came out of my mouth."

"But I want to know that, too," Corinne said, laughing.

"I'm not talking about that. I will say that it was nice, hot, the best sex I've ever had in my life. And the only time it will ever happen."

They all stared at me.

"Why?" Nessa finally asked.

I shrugged. "We both said that we didn't want a relationship, that we didn't have time for one. And it was kind of fun with the whole one-night stand thing on the table."

"You told him you just wanted one night?" Natalie asked, aghast.

"I think this is my fault," Corinne said, cringing. "One-night stands never end up as one-night stands. Not if they're good."

"Well, this one will."

"Are you sure?"

"Yes, of course. Shit." I pulled out my phone and texted quickly.

Me: *I'm home. Sorry. The girls ambushed me.*

A moment passed, and the girls just stared at me as I looked at my phone.

Dillon: *Glad you're home. I was about to send out the National Guard to check on you. That or me and Pacey and my truck. I had fun. Will I see you at coffee?*

I blushed, then bit my lip.

Me: *Maybe. We'll see. Bye.*

Dillon: *LOL Okay. Have a good day, Elise.*

I let out a sigh and set down my phone as the three girls continued staring at me.

"You are such a goner," Nessa said.

"A complete goner," Natalie agreed.

I looked up at my best friend, and Corinne just smiled. "Oh, I'm going to start taking bets on a two-night stand."

I narrowed my eyes and tossed a throw pillow at her.

"Don't spill your coffee. I'll be really annoyed if I have to get coffee stains out of the fabric."

I kept glaring at Corinne. "No bets."

"Oh, there will be bets," she said, laughing. "Now, do we go two nights? Three? Or do we just go straight to wedding bells?"

The girls all started laughing, talking over one another, and I slumped into my chair, sipping my coffee and ignoring them.

My phone was warm against my thigh, and I suddenly wanted to reach out and text him. To say something.

I didn't. It was important that I didn't.

But I had no idea what I was supposed to do next.

Chapter 5

Dillon

"And now we're going to focus on what Dickens was truly trying to convey in *Great Expectations*."

I barely resisted the urge to growl. I had thought we'd spent the past forty-five minutes of class trying to convey what the content meant. But I guess I had been wrong. Apparently, we were going to dive deeper, at least in the last five minutes of class. And then I had a feeling our assignment for the evening would be to find the rest.

I was exhausted, couldn't focus, and already hated this class.

The annoying part was that I *wanted* to like this one. It was my last English-focused track. Sadly, the creative writing class I had wanted to take had been full by the time I was able to sign up. I would be able to register my schedule on time like everybody else next semester, rather than a little behind like I had this time thanks to late enrollment. Either way, it wouldn't help me this semester. I'd be taking a couple of additional science classes and labs for the rest of my college career, and then I'd move to the business and accounting track.

I was going for a business management degree specialization with an operations management minor. I had thought about going with project management, but I wanted to stick with what Brendan had done so we could work together when adding onto the Connolly businesses. I'd had my name changed legally over a year ago now, and it was nice to think that I was a Connolly in truth, rather than the last name my mother had given me. It had taken longer than Cameron or I had wanted to get it done, but I'd had to become an adult rather than his ward to make it happen, thanks to legal issues that made my brain hurt.

I'd always thought life was a little unfair with the way I hadn't gotten to meet my brothers' foster parents. Jack and Rose Connolly had built their bar and brewery and had made it brilliant. When Rose died, Jack had ended up alone in the bar, getting older and unable to handle it all. My brothers had had a huge fight over me, though they hadn't known it at the time, and had ended up leaving Jack alone to run things. When Jack died, my three brothers came back, each bitter and angry. Still, they had somehow found a way to communicate with each other and make the brewery even better in Jack's and Rose's names.

And, along the way, they had added me to the group, a true brother rather than a tagalong. It'd taken me a long time to realize how I fit in, and now that I had, I was trying to find my way on my own, as well. This was a road I had never known before—one I had never thought to be on.

But I needed to find how to be the man I needed to become without my brothers helping me every step of the way. It was as if they wanted to put an entire childhood of being a big brother into one area, and it could sometimes be overwhelming. I wanted to prove that I could do this and make them proud of me. And to make that happen, I'd had to move out. I'd had to work on not having them pay for everything. Hence the scholarship, the new university, and trying to find a major that I liked.

At one point, I'd thought I wanted to be a chef like my brother Aiden. And while I loved cooking, and I loved to cook with him, I wasn't as inventive when it came to recipes. The kitchen's high anxiety and heat was exhilarating for a little while, but I didn't see myself doing it long-term. I had initially gone for a business degree at a different university and had taken cooking classes while learning with Aiden so I could one day be with him in the kitchen. However, it hadn't worked out, and I was still afraid that Aiden wasn't completely satisfied with how I had left things. I hoped he would be eventually. I just wasn't sure exactly how he would ultimately feel.

Our professor kept droning on, mostly about the wonders of all the authors on the reading list.

As every single one was a so-called classic author, meaning there wasn't a single diverse author on the page— let alone a female—I wasn't putting too much stock in this. The other class I had wanted to take had a very complex reading list with books from this century, with a focus on things other than what my grandfather might have learned in school.

But here I was, and I would get a damn A, even if it killed me.

The professor ended class, assigning a paper we had to write over the weekend. I held back a groan but knew I had no choice. The assignment was on the syllabus, though the timing of the papers wasn't. There was just a list of ones we would have to write. When we got to them, that's when the professor assigned them. I wasn't a massive fan of that, but then again, I wasn't teaching the class.

I stuffed my book and notebook into my bag and headed out. Some people had brought laptops into class, but our professor hated the sound of clicking keys. So, I wrote everything down by hand and then transferred it onto my computer later for focus. In the end, it helped me study better, so I couldn't get mad about it.

My phone buzzed, and I looked down at the screen. My jaw tightened, and I swallowed hard.

I hit end and told myself it was nothing. The call didn't need to be important.

But I knew that number and the name associated with it. I might not know the man, nor had I even known his name until recently, but he had been a part of my creation, and therefore, he thought he needed to be a part of my life.

I had no idea what my birth father wanted other than to annoy the fuck out of me and probably ask for money. That's what he had done to Cameron the one time he had deigned to reach out—and he wasn't even Cameron's or Aiden's father.

So, I had lied to myself when I said that I didn't know who my father was. Oh, I knew him. And, apparently, he wanted to get to know me. I didn't trust the idea of that, though.

I stuffed my phone into my pocket and headed towards the coffee house. There were three coffee shops on campus, as well as a smattering of little cafés, but this was the one that Elise had been to when I first saw her across the way. It was a silly thing, and she probably had a class or wasn't even on campus right now. Surely, my luck wouldn't hold out that I could see her again. Not that I was sure I wanted to. But I would probably be lying to myself if I said that I didn't. I wanted to get to know her. She was fun, smart, and I wanted to see her again—and not only to see her naked.

I shook my head, telling myself that train of thought was trouble. She didn't want more from me, yet I couldn't help but wonder if I could change that.

There was something wrong with me, but I couldn't change things right now.

I moved towards the coffee shop, and a girl stood in front of me, stepping into my path. I looked up and blinked at Mandy. Mandy and I had gone out for a few weeks, but it hadn't been serious. We had both said it wouldn't get complicated. That we were just having fun. And then I found out that Mandy *really* didn't want anything serious with me. Her goal really was only fun. To have a good time with as many people as she could. And I didn't mind that. If that was what she wanted, I didn't judge her. However, when she told me I wouldn't ever be the forever type, and that she was only looking for sex, I realized I didn't want that. I wanted to be worth more than that. So, I walked away. She hadn't seemed to mind, and since she was currently walking away from a guy who stood there glaring at me, it appeared she had landed on her feet.

"Dillon," she said, smiling at me. "It's good to see you."

"Hi, Mandy," I said.

"You're looking great."

The guy behind her growled, and she rolled her eyes and looked over her shoulder.

"I'm not flirting, just saying hi. This is Jeff," she said, pointing to the man behind her. "We've been seeing each other for a little bit now, and things are going great. I hope things are going great for you."

I shrugged. "Busy as usual. You look happy," I said and meant it. Her eyes were bright, and she was grinning. She did look good.

"Things *are* going great. School, Jeff, I just...well, I hope you find happiness, too. You know?"

I tilted my head at her and nodded. "Finding happiness would be nice. I'm glad you found yours."

She gave me a somewhat uncomfortable shrug. "Well, I need to be off. I've got class in ten. We just needed some coffee." Jeff held up two paper cups.

"Have a good day, Mandy," I said, and she gave me a little wave before skipping off with Jeff. She took a cup from him, tangled her fingers with his, and kissed him hard on the mouth. The big, hulking guy relaxed marginally yet still glared at me over his shoulder as the two of them left.

I honestly didn't have time for jealousy or whatever the hell Jeff's problem might be, but it was nice to see Mandy happy. I had honestly liked her. We hadn't parted on particularly bad terms, even though I hadn't been too pleased by the way she saw me. But we hadn't fought or gotten angry with each other. It had just ended.

She had probably been the most serious girlfriend I had ever had, and that was a sad state of affairs if that was the case. I didn't have time to dwell on that, though. Between working at the bar on the nights and weekends I could, school, and figuring out my new way of life because I'd changed universities, I didn't have time for a relationship at all.

At least, that's what I kept telling myself.

When I finally walked in, I saw Pacey at the coffee shop, sitting at a small table in the corner as he typed on his laptop. The place was huge, three stories, and had tons of space for people to work. The second and third floors were a little quieter than the first, and Pacey was currently on the second, focusing on his course load. The campus had hundreds of places to get work done, and we had a decent house, too, but I knew that Pacey had class in thirty minutes so it only made sense that he would try and get some work done closer to his lecture.

I picked up my coffee, headed upstairs, and cleared my throat near his table.

Pacey looked up and smiled. "Hey there, Dillon. Take a seat."

I gave him a small nod, smiled, and then sat across from him. "Thanks, I was going to ask."

"You could have just sat down. I might've growled at you, though. Because, damn it, this paper sucks."

"When's it due?"

Pacey looked at me and shrugged. "In three days. And we're turning it in online, so at least I don't have to print it out, but it's still pissing me off."

"What's it for?"

"My government and politics class. It's ridiculous, and they want us to take a both-sides observation approach." He rolled his eyes. "I'm not even from America. I don't know why I have to learn all this rubbish."

I laughed. "I'm pretty sure most Americans say the same thing. And wasn't your mom American?"

"Yes, but she raised me with my father across the pond. So, here we are."

"You've been here for a few years now, right?" I added, enjoying poking fun at him.

"You're not helping the situation."

"And wait, aren't you a dual citizen?" I asked, and Pacey flipped me off.

"You're not being a very good mate. I want to lament over this paper, and you're not helping."

"I can help you lament over the assignment and the fact that we have to do any work at all since we're tired, but I will mention the fact that you should probably learn a few things about the country, especially since you're a dual citizen."

"Believe me, I know enough," he said dryly, and then leaned back against his chair and smiled. "So, are we ever going to talk about what happened a few nights ago?" he asked, and I sighed.

"What do you mean?" I asked, lying.

"You're a terrible liar. How is Elise?"

"I don't know," I said, suddenly uncomfortable. "I haven't texted her."

"Why not?"

"Because I don't think she wants me to," I replied.

"I think you should at least text her to see if she's okay."

"Why wouldn't she be?" I leaned forward, slightly alarmed. "Did you hear something?"

Pacey sighed and closed his laptop. "I didn't hear anything, but she seems like a nice girl. Smart, funny, and not an asshole. You should talk with her."

"She didn't want anything beyond what we had last night."

"Texting doesn't necessarily have to change that. She could be your friend. I'm just saying."

"There's nothing *just* about it," I mumbled.

"Text her," he pushed.

I pulled out my phone and sighed. "What do I say?"

"You know, I usually start with something like…hello. Although texting doesn't get my winning accent, so then I have to add a very stereotypical 'love' or other things to it so they're reminded I have this sexy British poshness."

I met his gaze and laughed. The table next to me shushed me, and I winced.

"You're going to get me into trouble," I whispered.

"You say that. Or am I going to push you into a situation that you'll love?"

I narrowed my eyes. "Excuse me?"

"I've met your brothers and your sisters-in-law. They all mentioned that you are the family's touchstone when it comes to relationships and communication. Funny how you can't seem to take your own advice. So, here I am, throwing it back in your face."

"I don't think I like you right now," I mumbled, looking down at my phone.

"I don't think you have to," he said, laughing. "Text her."

I sighed. "Okay. But only because you're forcing me."

"Whatever it takes," he said with a laugh.

Me: *Hi.*

"Hi? That's all you're going to say?" Pacey asked quietly.

I scowled at the other man. "Give me a second. I thought I was better at this."

"We all thought you were."

Elise: *I'm headed to class soon. Is everything okay?*

I winced. "This sucks. I'm really not good at this."

"Maybe tell her that. Not me. She can't hear you. Hence why you're texting."

We were whispering, but the table next to us kept glowering. I lowered my head and began typing again.

Me: *I have class again too. I was just getting coffee with Pacey. Anyway, I'm at our coffee shop and thought of you.*

That made me smile. *Our coffee shop.* That was nice. Not creepy. Right?

Elise: *I just missed you then. I needed more caffeine to focus today.*

Me: *That's what I was thinking. I had the most boring lecture ever, and now I have to go to an accounting class that's already making my head hurt.*

Elise: *I thought you were good at accounting.*

Me: *I am, but the class is hard.*

Elise: *They're going to get harder as we move on.*

Me: *That's so helpful.*

Elise: *That's me, a ray of bright sunshine. Hey, I've got to go. But thanks for texting.*

Elise: *It was nice to hear from you.*

My heart warmed, and I let out a breath.

I knew Pacey was looking at me, but I ignored him.

Me: *Maybe we can get coffee sometime.*

Elise didn't text for long enough that I was afraid I'd fucked up.

Elise: *Maybe. I think I'd like that. I really have to go now. I'm not ignoring you. Promise.*

I smiled, and Pacey let out a slow chuckle. I flipped him off and ignored him.

Me: *Have fun in class, if you can. I'll talk to you soon. Promise.*

Elise: *Okay. Sounds good. Bye, Dillon.*

Me: *Bye, Elise.*

I set down my phone, and Pacey sipped the last of his coffee, grinning at me. "Told you."

"I hate you sometimes," I grumbled.

But that was a lie. I didn't hate him. I just didn't know if I owed him yet or not.

Chapter 6

Elise

I WAS FLIRTING WITH DILLON CONNOLLY. THAT WAS probably a mistake, but I couldn't help myself. And I was doing it by text as if we hadn't said that it would just be the one night. But I really couldn't help it. I was enjoying myself. I was enjoying *him*.

I looked down at my phone and grinned, laughing at the silly meme he'd sent. It made no sense that I would be laughing so much when it came to him. I shouldn't be, but he made me smile. However, it was a delusion. I couldn't let myself want him more than I already did. We hadn't even seen each other since I ran from his house—and that wasn't even an exaggeration. I'd *run* from him and any future desires he may spark.

It made no sense that I was talking to him now, and yet,

here I was, looking down at a text from him, my lips still twitching.

"Is that Dillon again?" Corinne asked, a smile on her face.

"I have no idea what you're talking about," I said, and she just laughed.

"You say that, and yet I think it's him. And I think you're happy."

"Stop," I said.

"Stop what?" Nessa asked as she made her way into the room.

"Elise wants me to stop acting like this is normal," Corinne said, and I blinked.

"What? What do you mean by normal? Are you saying I'm *abnormal*?"

"Keep pretending that you don't want to get to know Dillon. That you don't want to see him again. Just sit there texting him and not talk to us about it." She mock pouted, and I chucked a throw pillow at her again.

"Will you please stop tossing throw pillows?" Natalie said as she made her way into the living room, a charcuterie board in her hands. "They might have the word *throw* in the title, but that's not a direction. More an idea."

I stood up and cleared off the coffee table so she could set the tray down. Nessa gave me a grateful smile and placed it in front of us. The large wood board was filled with four types of cheese, two kinds of meat, various nuts, peppers, olives, pepperoncinis, and a few other yummy things. My mouth watered, and I knew I was about to chow down on one of my favorite meals. I'd grown up on cheese and crackers, and now I got to play with the seemingly grown-up version.

"Ladies, she is texting with Dillon and not telling us about it," Corinne said, pouting again.

"For shame," Natalie said with a laugh.

"You know the rules," Nessa added. "You like a boy, you fuck the boy. You text the boy afterward. Then, you tell your friends. It's one of the commandments of living with us."

"I wasn't aware there were commandments for this situation," I said dryly.

"Now you know," Nessa said. "And if I ever have sex again, you can make sure I'll follow them, too."

I rolled my eyes. "I don't know why you said it like that. Besides, I'm never having sex again with Dillon, so it's a moot point."

Corinne sighed. "Is it? Or are you just planning to pretend that you're never going to sleep with him again? Because you're texting him, even after you said you wouldn't see him anymore."

"I haven't seen him," I said, wincing.

"Well, texting is close enough. Unless he sent you dick pics. That would count as *seeing* him." Nessa paused. "Has he sent you dick pics?"

"I want to know, too. And if he has, why haven't you shared?" Corinne said with a laugh.

"First, no, ew. And if Dillon were sending me dick pics, I wouldn't share them with you."

"Spoilsport," Corinne said, shaking her head. "But I'm glad you didn't. He wouldn't have consented to that, and that would be rude."

"More than rude. But no, no dick pics. Thank God."

"Oh, is there something wrong with his dick?" Nessa asked, her eyes filled with laughter.

I flipped her off and took a cracker with cheese and a little mustard. "There is nothing wrong with Dillon's dick, and I'm not talking about this anymore."

Corinne grinned. "You say that, and yet I have a feeling I can get you to speak. In detail."

"Anyway, what did he text you if it wasn't a pic of his dick?" Natalie asked, leaning forward to look at my phone on the table.

"It went back to a blank screen," I said dryly. They couldn't see what was on my cell. My three friends looked at me, and I sighed.

"All it was, was a stupid meme. It was funny and reminded him of a conversation we had, I guess."

"Oh, that's so sweet. You guys are sharing memes and having conversations. *And* not sleeping together. Everything you're doing can be part of a relationship," Natalie added. "A true one based on the foundation of trust."

"Or it could just be that we're texting because we're bored, and it's nice to have someone to talk to when we're thinking about coffee," I stated.

The three girls laughed. "Sure, whatever you say. However, we all know that you don't text randomly. There's got to be something there."

I cringed. "There can't be. I'm focusing on school. Dillon has school and work and a huge family. There's no time for things like a relationship or anything we could have together on top of that for him. *Or* me. He's a nice guy, and maybe we can be friends. But that's it."

"You know, those are famous last words," Corinne said dryly.

I grimaced. "Maybe, but they won't be my last words."

"You totally just jinxed yourself," Nessa added, taking a

bite of a pepperoncini. She scrunched her eyes and winced. "Oh, those are spicier than I remember," she said.

Natalie shrugged. "We accidentally bought the hot kind rather than the medium or mild. I didn't even know there were different heat variances with a jar of pepperoncini."

"Well, now my mouth is on fire," Nessa said, drinking a glass of water. Her eyes watered, and she cursed. "Now I need milk. Or bread or something."

"We have little crostinis here. Try that."

I handed her the breadbasket, and she took a big bite of a crostini and sighed. "I am such a wimp."

"Maybe, but we love you."

"You're a jerk," she said, and I smiled.

"I could be, but it's fun to tease you after you've been teasing me for most of this conversation."

"We love you, and you seem happy when you're texting Dillon. We just want to know what's going on."

"Nothing is going on. We're just texting. Like friends. People do that."

"Maybe, but you've never done it before."

"It's just that's not what Dillon and I agreed to. It may be construed as flirting, but we're busy. It's only texting. I text all of you guys, and none of you expect me to sleep with you."

"And it's a great shame that we haven't yet," Natalie said dryly, and I laughed, surprised.

"You are gorgeous. I'm just saying," Corinne said, batting her eyelashes. "I do find it odd that we haven't slept together. I mean, we've known each other forever. It's only natural that we would turn from friends to lovers."

I scrunched up my nose and filled my plate with cheese and other goodies. "You guys are such jerks," I said.

Natalie smiled softly. "Maybe, but we're your jerks. You love us."

My phone buzzed, and everyone looked down at it. I let out a breath and read the name on the screen. "It's just my mom. Not Dillon." They all leaned back in their chairs, disappointment on their faces. "I love my mom. She's allowed to call and text me. Don't look so sad."

Corinne pouted. "We just wanted it to be Dillon."

"I was just texting Dillon, and he's working. He's not going to want to text me at all hours of the night."

Natalie gave a dreamy sigh. "He should. You guys are so cute together."

"You haven't even seen me with him," I said dryly.

"Maybe not, but Corinne said you guys were adorable. I don't see what the problem is."

"The problem is, we are just texting. Like people do. It doesn't mean we're going to sleep together again." For some reason, voicing that annoyed me, urging me to the edge of sadness. I hated that feeling, so I ignored it. I simply looked down at my phone and read the text message.

Mom: *Will you be coming over for dinner this weekend? We have a few things to talk about. And your father and I would like to discuss your grades.*

I crossed my eyes and groaned.

"Your parents wanting to talk about your grades with you like you're in middle school again?" Corinne asked, taking a sip of her soda.

"Yes. I don't know when they're going to realize that they don't need to know everything I'm doing."

"They will never get that. Not if you keep letting them butt in."

I narrowed my eyes at Corinne. "I do not let them."

"Yes, you do. All the time. You probably planned to go over there and show them your grades so you didn't have to deal with confrontation."

"I'm not a pushover."

"No, you're not. Which is why I don't get why you do everything your parents say. Even if it doesn't make sense."

"It's not like that."

"It seems like it," Corinne said, shrugging.

Natalie leaned forward. "I don't know your parents, and mine are always checking on me. They're even more overprotective than yours."

I shook my head. "My parents aren't overprotective in what I'm doing outside of school. They just want me on a set path, and since I'm not exactly going down that path, they want to know every little thing. I got a full-ride here, and I've been paying for school. The student loan I got pays for rent and food. Therefore, they don't have to give me any money."

"You're right. That means you don't owe them anything but your love and appreciation," Corinne added.

"Maybe, but I still want to make them proud. It's stupid."

My phone buzzed again.

Mom: *I hope you're studying and not just ignoring me. We need to discuss your future. We can't do that if you're not telling us everything.*

I sighed and began typing.

Me: *Sunday works. However, I would only like to come for dinner if that's okay. Grades aren't even final yet.*

I hadn't meant to add that part. I didn't need to qualify what I was doing. But she was my mom, and I hated disappointing her.

Mom: *We'll see you Sunday. Bring your grades.*

I sighed, knowing she would ignore me. She was good at that.

"Sunday dinner with a report card?" Corinne asked dryly.

"That's what we do."

"Whatever you say," Corinne said, and Nessa and Natalie shared a look. I had been friends with Natalie for a few years, Nessa since we started college, but they didn't understand the dynamics between my mother and me like Corinne did. Not that Corinne or I understood what my mother wanted. Other than for us to do exactly what she desired.

My phone lit up again, and Corinne snatched it.

"I don't want you dealing with your mother right now. Tonight's just for us." She looked down at the phone as I held out my hand, and a small smile crept over her face. "Oh, it's not your mother."

"Is it a dick pic?" Nessa asked, and Natalie laughed.

"Give me the phone," I snapped, oddly worried.

"It's just Dillon. He says he's just getting home." She handed over the phone, and that was indeed what Dillon had said.

I let out a sigh as the three girls stared at me.

"Answer him," Natalie said.

"He didn't ask me a question," I retorted.

"Maybe not, but text him back. Don't keep him waiting. Please? Let us live vicariously through you."

"I hate you," I grumbled but began typing.

Me: *I'm glad. Was it a good day at work?*

Dillon: *It was. Good tips. I'm not old enough to be behind the bar yet, but I do okay for myself. My brothers needed an extra hand* *since one of their waitresses got sick, so I had to work a couple of hours later than planned. But now I get to start working on that paper that's due.*

I cringed. The girls stared at me.

"Just a paper. Everything's fine."

"Well, that's not exciting," Nessa grumbled, and the girls laughed. I shook my head.

Me: *Is the paper due tomorrow?*

Dillon: *No, but I don't know what I'm going to write, so it's going to take me a while just staring at the screen.*

Me: *I'm the same way sometimes. I mean, sometimes I get the paper right away and it takes me half an hour. Other times, I stare at a blank screen for two hours and pretend that I know what I'm doing.*

Dillon: *That sounds like how I work. Anyway, I was wondering, are we ever going to get coffee together? Or is texting all you want?*

I blinked at the abrupt change and realized that all three girls were standing behind my chair now, looking over at my texts. I glared at them, but...they might as well look. I would tell them anyway.

Me: *Um, I could do coffee.*

Dillon: *Or maybe dinner? It doesn't have to be coffee. That way, we don't have to wake up too early for our morning classes.*

My hands froze, and Natalie and Nessa each squeezed one of my shoulders as Corinne came in front of me, clasping her hands in front of herself. "Do it. Say yes."

I met her gaze and then glanced at the others. "This isn't what we signed up for."

Nessa waved me off. "Who cares? Just because you said you wanted a one-night stand doesn't mean that was guaranteed to happen. Enjoy yourself. You're already texting. You're way past the idea and concept of a one-night stand."

I sighed and looked down at my fingers. I knew what I wanted. It just worried me that what I wanted might not be the best thing for me.

"Do it," Nessa said.

"Please?" Natalie added.

I winced, looked down at my phone, and typed.

Me: *Dinner might be nice. On a day that you're not working. That way we can just relax.*

Dillon: *Sounds like a plan. I'd like to see you again, Elise. Just to make sure I remember what you look like. It feels like it's been ages.*

"Aww," Natalie whispered, and Nessa giggled.

I glared at them and went back to my phone.

Me: *Well, I guess it's a date.*

Dillon: *I guess so.*

I cringed, my hands shaking.

Dillon: *See you soon.*

I had a date with Dillon Connolly. One I had told myself I didn't want and wouldn't have.

And yet, I was falling into the abyss.

And I was afraid I would never find my way out again if I weren't careful.

Chapter 7

Dillon

I WAS GOING TO BE LATE, AND I KNEW EXACTLY WHY. IT WAS always the same reason these days—that damn text.

Unknown Number: *You owe me, boy. I'll be seeing you soon.*

I knew who it was, and I ignored it just like I had all the others. I had to. It'd end up hurting those I loved if I didn't. But it still didn't help me relax so I could go out on this date, thinking about the fact that my deadbeat sperm donor was still out there. Waiting.

And now I was running late. If I weren't careful, I would miss the date with Elise altogether. And considering that I wasn't sure if she wanted to be out with me tonight at all, I was terrified it would scare her away if I didn't show up on time. I didn't know how she had become so important to me so quickly, at least in the sense that I wanted to get to know her, wanted to find out more about her. Yet, there was no changing it. I couldn't go back to the way things were before, and I wanted to know Elise. To find out what made her tick and to just be with her. In whatever way she let me.

But that wouldn't happen if I ran late.

"Knock, knock," Pacey said from the doorway. I looked up to see my friend giving me an odd look.

"What's wrong?" I asked, and he cleared his throat.

"Nothing. I was checking to see if you were ready for tonight. Big date."

I narrowed my eyes at him. "I don't know if you're being sarcastic or not," I said, studying his face.

Pacey shook his head. "I'm sarcastic often, but not about this. I'm excited to see you out with Elise. She seems nice."

"She is nice. I really hope I'm not late, and I don't fuck it up, though."

"Well, then don't fuck up."

I snorted. "That is such a great pep talk, thank you."

Pacey just smiled. "I do my best."

"Anyway, where are you going?"

"I was thinking of that café across campus. Though it's not really a café, is it? More like a place to go and get dinner. But it sounded good."

"Yeah, it's a good place for a first date. Not too fancy since you don't need to spend too much money. But it's also not a Denny's, or someplace you would take your high school girlfriend."

"I didn't have time for girlfriends in high school," I said dryly.

"Boyfriends?"

"Those either," I said with a laugh.

"Well, I'm sure you can catch up now."

I frowned. "I don't know if I want to catch up per se. But going out with Elise tonight is a start." I slid my shirt over my head, the sweater a decent cut that looked like a fancy Henley. Pacey looked at me and tilted his head. "Yes, that will do."

I snorted. "Thank you for your acceptance of what I'm wearing for the evening."

"You couldn't do it without me," he said dryly.

I rolled my eyes. "Seriously, though. I said I would meet Elise there because she had class and wanted to head home first and didn't want to be late. So, I should probably get there before she's sitting and waiting for me, thinking that I stood her up."

"That would be good. And have Elise tell her friends I said hi."

I paused, looking at him. "How well do you know her friends?"

"I know Corinne and Nessa. We had a class together last year and studied well. They're good people. I like them."

"Like them, like them?" I asked, teasing.

"Since I'm not in primary school, I'm not going to demean myself to answer that question. However, I do like them, and I was the one who mentioned my roommates— therefore *you*—to Corinne. And because of that, she introduced you to Elise. So, this date tonight is kind of all because of me."

I shook my head and laughed. "That's good to know. Well, I'm headed out."

"Sounds like a plan. Have fun. And use protection."

I flipped him off, a smile playing on my lips, and made sure I had the condoms in my back pocket. Not that I expected to go there tonight, but it was always important to be prepared. Cameron had drilled that into my head as soon as I started looking at girls and guys that way. Cameron had come into my life when I was younger, but not at the beginning. The Connollys hadn't known that I existed until Cameron was forced to help raise me. And that had caused a rift between my brothers because he had kept me a secret. I hadn't known the actual reasons for it until later, but I understood. Things were complicated in our family, and that was an understatement. We had all been through different forms of hell, some worse than others, but now we were all together, in a different state, learning and growing.

At least, that's what I hoped.

I headed out to my car, grateful there was a paved driveway in the garage area. My truck was older than the rest of the guys' vehicles, so I tended to park outside of the garage or on the street because I didn't mind if it got rustier. I knew I should probably replace the damn thing, but that would cost money, and I wasn't really in the mood to say goodbye to the first thing I'd bought with my own earnings. My siblings had all offered to help me buy a car or even buy this one outright. Brendon had a lot of money. However, I had wanted to put as much down as possible on my own. They each had paid for part of it as a birthday present, but most of the payment had been mine.

And I loved that fact. Just like I had been paying for my own college as much as I could and was now using a scholarship to get through most of this semester. I knew that my siblings would drop everything and help me the moment I asked—and usually without me asking, pushing my need to take care of myself out of the way.

But I wanted to do this on my own. I felt like I earned whatever I worked toward more. I was probably biting off my nose to spite my face, but I couldn't change that. At least, for now.

Going out on my own wasn't easy, but I was finding my path. I didn't want my brothers to feel as if they needed to drop everything and take care of me again. Cameron had done it more than once in his life, and it had irrevocably altered everything about him. He had almost lost Violet because of it, more than once. And I didn't want that to happen again, even though deep down I knew it wasn't the same. Still, I needed to find my own way.

I pulled into the parking lot of the café and got out, watching Elise get out of a rideshare vehicle. My brows rose, and she shrugged.

"I honestly didn't want you to have to wait on me, so I said I would just use a rideshare. Sorry if that makes you feel weird."

I shook my head, walked up to her, and smiled. "No, I get it. It's sometimes a good idea to make sure you have your way in and out of a situation. And I get you not wanting me to know where you live."

She cringed. "Sorry. It's one of those things that women have to do to keep safe." She shrugged.

"Anyway, I haven't been here before," she said, and my brows lifted. "Really? The guys and I have been here a few times, though mostly to celebrate a good grade or something. It's not too expensive, so that's why we like it," I said and then winced. "Not that you don't deserve to go someplace nice. But you know…college."

She smiled. "Oh, I get it. I only have my student loan to pay for food and board and things, so I understand."

"I have my job."

"And where do you work again?" she asked as I took her hand. She blinked a bit and then wrapped her fingers around mine as we walked towards the door of the café.

"My brothers own the Connolly Brewery in downtown Denver."

"Oh, I think I've heard of that place."

I smiled. "I hope so. They're trying to make a thing of it. Eventually, we're going to open up an actual restaurant where my brother, who used to work at a Michelin-starred restaurant, can once again cook what he wants to rather than adding unique things to a bar menu."

"Your brother is that good of a chef and works at a bar?" she asked dubiously.

"It's a very long story," I said.

"We're going to have time with dinner, right?"

"I guess we will." I wasn't sure I would tell her everything, but I could mention how my three brothers and I had come together. My phone buzzed in my pocket, and I almost ignored it, but it was a call rather than a text.

I frowned and paused before we walked inside. "I'm sorry, it's my sister-in-law. I have to take this."

She nodded. "Of course."

"Violet? What's wrong?"

"Everything's okay. It's going to be okay."

"What happened?" I asked, dread filling me. Elise

reached out and took my hand, squeezing it. I looked at her then and nodded, my shoulders relaxing marginally. I wasn't alone. She might not be able to hear the other side of the conversation, but she was here for me. It was weird, but I liked it.

"Cameron had a little accident."

Ice speared me. "What happened?" I asked again.

"It was more his appendix than an accident. Sorry. I'm a little off."

"Are you okay?" I paused. "Is Cameron okay?"

"Everything's going to be fine. It literally just happened, and I was busy making sure I got Cameron to the hospital and then calling your other brothers because of work and everything. And now I'm calling you. I'm sorry I didn't do a group chat or something. It honestly didn't occur to me. I'm running on fumes here."

"A migraine? Is it the baby?"

I could feel Elise's attention on me, but thankfully, she didn't press. At least, not yet.

"I'm getting a migraine, but my sister is on her way here to take care of Cameron and me. He's going to be fine, just had his appendix removed. The surgery went wonderfully. He just can't work tonight, and with me here waiting with him and my sister, that means we're shorthanded. Beckham and Meadow are out, using their vacation days. I'm really, really sorry to do this, but can you come in and cover?"

I was nodding and then realized that she couldn't see me. "Of course."

I looked over at Elise and cringed. "I just need to deal with a few things, and then I'll be on my way. Anything you want. Do you need me to come to the hospital, too?"

"Maybe later. Or you can come visit him at the house. He's not going to have to stay long because everything was pretty routine. It was just a little scary at first," she said, her laugh a bit hollow.

"What else can I do?" My heart was racing, and I felt like I needed to reach out for something, but my family wasn't there. And I wasn't there for them. But I would be.

"I just need your help with work. And you're doing it. We'll all meet with the family and annoy Cameron to death later when we make sure he sits down and doesn't hurt himself."

"We're going to do the same thing with you and the baby," I added dryly.

"Perhaps, but that's fine."

She smiled. "I'm sort of used to it at this point. Now, I need to head out. I see Sierra," she said, speaking of her sister, Aiden's wife. "I'll talk to you soon."

"Of course."

I hung up and looked at Elise.

"Is everything okay?" she asked, searching my face.

"My brother Cameron had to have his appendix out. And while he's going to be okay, his wife is pregnant and gets severe migraines. She needs to relax. That means her sister, my other sister-in-law, has to be with her. It's all very confusing, but in the end, I have to cancel tonight and head to the bar to help out. I'm so sorry."

Elise shook her head, and my hopes dropped. "Do not be sorry," she said quickly. "Do you need an extra pair of hands? I'd love to see the bar that you grew up in." I didn't correct her on that. "I can help out where I can. We can make it a date that's a little different," she said, laughing. I just smiled, wondering who the hell this girl was and how I could stop myself from falling too quickly.

"You know, I think I'd like that."

We headed to the car and talked about school and majors and nothing too important because I think Elise knew that I needed to focus on driving and not on the fact that my brother just had surgery and I hadn't known. I didn't blame Violet for not contacting me sooner. She had been a little off and had contacted everyone individually as quickly as she could. It'd all happened so fast, and I understood. But I was still a little scared. And I would be until I saw Cameron for myself.

It didn't take too long to get there, and we pulled into the parking lot behind the bar. Real estate space was hard to come by in downtown Denver, but we took advantage of a small employee parking area.

"Okay, here we go," I said with a laugh.

"Why do you sound like you're sending me to the guillotine?" she asked dryly.

"You're about to meet some of my family, and this might be a little bit of an awkward first date."

She blinked, her face going pale. "You know, I didn't think about that. I was thinking more about the bar, not the fact that your family works here."

I cringed. "I can get you a rideshare home right now if you want."

"No, we'll make this work. It'll be unique. After all, we sort of already slept together, so I guess we're starting whatever we're doing backward."

I laughed. "There was no *sort of* about it, Elise."

"Touché."

The Connolly Brewery looked like an Irish pub in

downtown Denver. The family had started it years ago, and it was slowly becoming a staple again.

The family had put money, time, and love into everything. And, thankfully, people were coming back in droves. I loved it. I just hadn't expected to be here tonight.

"Oh, this is wonderful," Elise said as we walked into the brightly lit dining area. Everything was shiny wood and a little classier than a stereotypical pub, but it was still great.

It was like a second home to me. Or maybe a fifth at this point.

Brendon was hiding behind the bar, scowling, and I held back a smile.

"Why are your lips twitching?" Elise asked.

"That would be my brother, Brendon. He hates bartending, and according to our regular bartender, Beckham, he's not very good at it."

"I heard that, asshole," Brendon muttered.

"Aiden's in the back. Harmony will be helping me."

"Oh, thank God," I said, and he flipped me off. The regulars at the bar laughed, as did Elise.

"You're lucky I like you, kid. And who's this?" he asked, his gaze brightening.

"Hi, I'm Elise," she said, waving. Brendon nodded.

"I'm Brendon. I know Violet called you in, but we didn't know you were out on a date. Sorry about that."

"It's okay," Elise said, and I nodded. "I'm here to help. Just let me know what you need."

"We need a waiter."

"I can help carry food or something," Elise said, shrugging. "I may as well. I don't want to sit around doing nothing."

Brendon met my gaze, smiling.

"Okay. That sounds like a plan. We could use the help."

Elise smiled at me, and something twisted inside. I thought I knew what it meant.

Hell, this girl surprised me at every turn. While this wasn't exactly what I had imagined for our first date, it seemed there was no going back.

And I liked it.

Chapter 8

Elise

My feet hurt by the end of the evening, but it was the most unique and enjoyable date I had ever been on.

"That was busy," I said, and Dillon winced as he looked over at me from the driver's seat.

"I'm sorry about tonight. It wasn't exactly what I had been planning. I promise there was supposed to be an actual dinner where we sat down at a table we weren't also serving."

I shrugged. "It was entertaining. I've never actually waited tables before. I don't know how people can do that every night, but I had a good time with you." I blushed. "I mean...a good time in general. And I only dropped one plate, so I can count that as a win."

"I didn't think you did too badly," he added and laughed.

I mock scowled. "I would hit you, but you're driving. I'll just have to do it later."

"That sounds like a plan," he said and chuckled. He paused then, letting out a breath. "By the way, where am I taking you?"

I looked over at him, anticipation churning in my belly. "Oh. I guess I didn't give you an address or, I don't know..."

"I'm sort of on my way to my house because that's where the campus is, but if you want me to take you home, I can do that. Or I guess I could take you to my place and you could use a rideshare again. Or...I don't know."

I looked at him then, the strong line of his jaw, his very sexy forearms as he turned the steering wheel. "We already ate at the bar, but maybe we can still hang out?" I asked, blushing.

He looked over at me as he stopped at a stop sign, smiling. "Yeah?"

"I mean, I'm not actually propositioning you," I said with a laugh.

He snorted. "Well, shucks," he said.

"I know. How horrible of me."

He just drove, a smile playing on his lips. "How could you?"

"But, yes, it's still decently early since you didn't have to work the whole shift—or I guess *we* didn't have to work the whole shift."

"Thank God, I wasn't prepared to work tonight. And I do enjoy taking time off."

"I can see that," I said with a laugh. "So, yes, let's go steal some Twizzlers from Pacey."

That made him grin, and he turned off the street,

headed towards his place. He parked in the back, and we got out. As we did, my stomach clenched.

I didn't know what I was doing. Was I here for something more? Or just to hang out with him? This wasn't what I'd expected. I kept telling myself I didn't have time for this, and yet here I was, figuring it out.

At least, I thought so.

We made our way inside through the back door and into the kitchen. Pacey and Tanner were there, Pacey cutting up fruit for a glass container while Tanner made coffee. It was after nine, but we were in college, so it didn't faze me. They both looked up at us as we walked in, and I blushed. A small smile played on Pacey's face, while Tanner just narrowed his eyes.

"Hi," I said softly.

"Hello there. How did the date go?" Pacey asked, looking at me rather than Dillon.

Tanner just snorted, and Dillon let out a groan.

"You're not supposed to ask her that when the other person's in the room," Dillon grumbled.

"I do believe I can do anything I want," Pacey corrected.

"That sounds like Pacey," Tanner said, laughing. "Anyway, I'm headed back to study. You two have fun. Just not too much because then I'm going to get all grumpy." Tanner took a sip of his coffee, winced—presumably at the heat—and made his way out of the kitchen.

"That wasn't grumpy?" I asked, knowing Tanner could still hear me. He didn't turn back, but he did shake his head, his shoulders bobbing slightly, and I smiled. He seemed to be the most serious and scowly of the bunch, and the fact that I could make him laugh like that made me smile.

"Anyway, the date didn't turn out exactly as we'd planned," Dillon said, catching my gaze. I smiled, shrugging.

"But it was still enjoyable," I said quickly.

"What's going on?" Pacey asked.

"Cameron needed to have his appendix out. He's okay, thank God, but I had to go in and cover his shift at work. Elise joined me, and our date was spent waiting tables and eating at the bar with my family surrounding us. It was interesting," he said dryly and looked at me. "I *am* sorry."

I shook my head. "No, don't be. I really did have a good time tonight. I know, I know, that doesn't seem like it would be fun to anyone else since it was work. But it was different. And I've never been there before so…yay. And the food was divine. I had tapas."

"At a bar?" Pacey asked.

"Yes, at a bar," Dillon said. "I told you, Aiden is changing up some of the things on the menu and will continue to do so even as he opens his own restaurant."

Pacey shook his head. "A restaurant in this day and age. I don't know how people can do that. It's a little terrifying."

Dillon shrugged. "True, and that's why we're taking our time and making sure we get it right."

I cleared my throat. "But if the food is anything like he made tonight? You guys are going to be a hit."

Dillon's smile was slow to form but wide in the end. "Really? I'm going to have to tell him that."

"I told him that to his face," I said with a shrug at Dillon's look. "He came out to check on me when you were in the back, getting something. I think he wanted to see who you would dare bring into your family's precious bar."

"No, he's just as growly as Tanner is. That's his normal look."

"I heard that, asshole," Tanner said from the other room.

"That's why I said it so loudly," Dillon called out, and I just smiled.

"Anyway, you two kids have fun," Pacey said with a shrug. "Mackenzie and Sanders are in their room. The music is on, thankfully, so we're not going to have to hear much this time."

I winced. "Oh, that's not good," I said, doing my best *not* to look at Dillon.

"Sanders' room is the least soundproof," Dillon said comfortably, his expression purposely blank.

I knew what he was thinking, considering I hadn't been that quiet when I was here before. And now, I just wanted to crawl into a hole and hide.

Pacey continued. "Miles is out with his study group. Sadly, I don't think that is code for a date."

"Why are you so sad about that, considering you're at home alone tonight and not on a date?" Dillon asked, his eyes bright.

"Because I have plans with my time, thank you very much." Pacey looked between us. "Have fun, you two. I'll be sure to keep the tele up loud."

Dillon flipped him off even as I winced, lowering my head. "So, do you want some coffee? A beer? I think we have tequila somewhere, but that seems a little much. I don't know."

I just smiled. "I will take some water. I know, boring."

"No, water's good. You worked hard today. I can't believe we had to work on this date. I'm sorry. This wasn't what I had planned."

"Your brother had an emergency, and not only did they need help at the bar, I think they just wanted you where they could see you, just in case. They wanted family close."

"That was my thinking. We have a couple of other waitresses they could have called, but they wanted family. And I get it. And I'm not resentful about it. Okay, maybe a little bit because it did cut into our evening."

"Not really. We had food. We hung out. I got to know you. And now we're drinking water together in your home. Or at least talking about it. I still think this counts as a date." I hoped those were the right things to say. I wasn't good at this whole flirting thing, but with the way his smile slowly spread across his face, maybe I was doing okay, after all.

"Let's get some water and then head up to my room. Not that we need to do anything," Dillon added quickly and then let out a low chuckle. "But that way, Tanner and Pacey can't sneak up on us and do whatever they want to do. Miles will probably be home soon, too, and I'm sure if Sanders and Mackenzie come down, it'll be a whole thing." He paused, then looked at me. "Unless you want it to be a whole thing."

I shook my head, rose on my tiptoes, and pressed my lips to his. "Let's go upstairs so it's just the two of us. You're right. People have surrounded us for most of the day."

"Oh, thank God," he mumbled, then kissed me harder, squeezed my hip, and handed me my glass of water after he'd pulled away. We made our way upstairs, and I indeed heard soft music coming from Sanders' room. I tried not to think about the fact that if I could hear them, they had possibly heard what'd happened in Dillon's room. But if they told me that the soundproofing was good enough, I would have to believe it. That was a lie that I would gladly and readily tell myself.

We made our way to his room, and I swallowed half my water in one gulp as I tried to think about what we were supposed to do or say. I hadn't had a steady boyfriend before, nor had I had sex often. It had been smaller dates that had led to intriguing evenings, but I wasn't good at this whole human-interaction thing.

"Me, either," Dillon said and shrugged. I looked up at him.

"Did I say all of that out loud?"

"I don't think all of it because you sort of started mid-sentence, but I'm the same as you with human interaction."

"Oh," I said, mortified. *Dear God.*

Dillon looked at me then. "I'm glad you're here. I had fun the first night we were together, and had a blast tonight, even though it felt weird. Not weird to be with you, but weird that we had a date while working."

"As I said, it was unique," I reiterated, and he smiled.

"It was, wasn't it? Anyway," he said softly.

"Anyway," I added.

He smiled. "I don't know what I'm doing here. I wasn't expecting this."

I sipped my water, swallowed hard, and tried not to choke. "I wasn't either. I'm not good at this, just like you."

"I know you said you didn't have time for a relationship..."

I cringed. "I don't. But..."

"Yes. But... We're both busy. We're both in school and

focused on a hundred different things, but I enjoy spending time with you. And I'd like to continue doing that. You know? To see where it goes."

"But nothing scary," I added.

He met my gaze. "I hope to hell not."

And then he lowered his lips to mine. I groaned, sinking into him as he pressed in. He smelled of sandalwood and a little like the bar. It was something that was all Dillon.

I swallowed hard as he pulled away and slowly wrapped his arms around me. I settled my hands on his hips, squeezing slightly, and he smiled against my lips.

He kissed me again, this time adding more pressure. I parted my lips for him, needing him, craving all of his taste. He rocked against me, the rigid length of him hard against my stomach. He had stretched me before, almost to the point of pain, but it had been perfect. Bliss unlike I had ever experienced before.

And now, here we were again, and I couldn't help but want more.

He tugged on my shirt, and I smiled against him as I lifted my arms. He pulled my shirt and tank top over my head, leaving me in my bra. And then he kissed me again, before slowly dragging his lips along my jaw and down my collarbone. He nipped and licked, and I groaned.

When he kissed me again, I tugged on his shirt, and he smiled against me before pulling it over his head.

"How do you do that?" I asked.

He frowned. "What?"

"You tug your shirt over the back of your head. It's so sexy. I thought only movie stars did that."

He blushed, and I couldn't help but notice that he

turned pink all the way down to his very firm, very ripped chest and eight-pack.

"I don't know. It's just something I do. I didn't realize that it was a movie-star thing."

"I like it. You should keep doing it."

"I think we can arrange that," he said softly.

He kissed me again, this time leading me towards the bed. I tugged on his pants, and he did the same with mine. Suddenly, my pants were off, as were his, and I stood in nothing but my bra and panties with him in his boxer briefs.

"Damn, did I tell you how much I love your curves?" he asked, squeezing me.

I shivered. "I think you might have mentioned it. But wow." I hadn't meant to utter the last part, but he kept touching me, and it was hard to think. Hard to breathe.

"Wow is a good word." He kissed me again.

I was falling, falling so hard I wasn't sure what I was supposed to say, what to do. I hadn't expected this. Didn't expect him. And I shouldn't have. This could be a horrible mistake that led to temptation and pain, but I wasn't going to stop. At least, not right now. College was about finding who you were and making choices. Discovering your path. And if that road led to Dillon, then I would let myself fall, at least for the time being.

I just hoped I didn't break when I landed.

Soon, I was on the bed, Dillon hovering over me as he kissed my naked flesh. We had both lost what remained of our clothes. The condom packet lay next to my head. He kissed along my collarbone, then between my breasts. He paid particular attention to my nipples, biting and sucking to the point that I almost came. I rubbed my thighs against him, needing the friction, needing something, anything, but he refused to lower himself, wouldn't press himself against my heat.

"Dillon," I whispered.

"I'm not done yet."

And then he lowered himself, kissing across my stomach, my hips. He nibbled, nipped. And then his head moved between my thighs, and it was the most erotic image I had ever seen. He kissed, sucked, took in my heat. He laughed at me, blew cool air on my warmth, and then spread me. I covered my face, embarrassed, and he just chuckled against me.

"You're so pretty and pink. So wet and ready for me." He licked at my clit. "Are you going to come for me, Elise?"

"If you keep touching me, the answer's going to be yes."

He kissed me again, this time spearing me with two fingers. My hips shot off the bed, and he curled his fingers, finding that tight bundle of nerves that nearly sent me over the edge. And when he latched on to my clit with his mouth, fucking me with his fingers, using his other hand to play with my breasts, I was lost. I came, an agonized shard of bliss slicing through me as I fell from the cliff of wherever I had been. I orgasmed so hard, I was afraid I would break, but then he was there, holding me tightly, and I couldn't catch my breath.

He pulled away, and I panted, putting my hands over my breasts to calm myself. He smiled at the look, and I quickly sat up, getting a bit dizzy and lightheaded.

"What's wrong?" he asked.

I shook my head and went to all fours.

"There's something I need to do." And then I slid his

cock into my mouth. He was wide and far too long for me, so I used my free hand to grip his base. My other hand was on his hip, keeping me steady.

Dillon let out a groan, slid his hands through my hair as I sucked his length. I hollowed my cheeks, humming along him as the tip of his dick pressed against the back of my throat.

"Elise," he whispered.

And then his hips began to move as he slowly fucked my mouth. I kept humming, needing him more.

His body tightened, and I felt him twitch, then he pulled away and twisted me around. I was still on all fours, and I heard him slide the condom over his length. He had one hand on my hip, and I felt the tip of him against my core. He lowered his head, kissed the back of my shoulder, and then slid home.

We both groaned, my pussy so tight and swollen from my orgasm that it was hard for me to even breathe with him inside me. He whispered sweet nothings against my neck and across my shoulders, and then he began to move. I shoved back into the thrusts, and he fucked me hard, both of us trying to catch our breaths but unable. And when he pulled on my shoulder slightly, I sat up so I knelt in front of him, on my knees only as he continued fucking me.

I could barely breathe, but this was worth it. It was all worth it. He continued thrusting deeply, moving in and out of me, one hand on my breast, the other on my clit. He kissed my shoulder, sucking hard, and I came. Shattered. He shouted, his whole body shaking as he came hard deep inside me. Both of us let out gasping breaths and then fell to the side, his cock still deep within as the two of us fell down from our orgasms, trying to find our footing. But it was no use. I was still cradled in his arms, his cock still deep inside me. It was no use trying to return to reality. Or any semblance of normalcy. This was it. This was what I had been missing.

The thought took my breath.

I could not fall for Dillon Connolly. It would be a mistake of epic proportions to do so. And yet, I didn't know how I would stop myself.

I didn't know if I could.

Chapter 9

Dillon

I WANTED TO SCOOP MY EYES OUT WITH A SPOON. MAYBE IT would make this whole study thing easier. Pacey had his head bent over his book, his eyes narrowed as he read. I leaned back in my chair and rubbed my temples.

"Do you think rubbing your temples will help the words stay in your mind?" Pacey asked dryly. "Because if so, I'm in. You just let me know."

"Why is this so boring?" I asked, groaning.

"Because they force you to take other classes outside of your major so you're not only well rounded but also because it sometimes sparks a need for what you could be in the future. And, apparently, learning helps you become a better person. Who knew?"

I snorted and glanced over at Pacey. He was now leaning back in his chair, the wheels squeaking as he did.

"I thought you liked school."

"Don't say that out loud. People will find out, and it'll ruin my credibility."

"Your credibility at what?"

"I don't know. Being that mysterious British guy?"

"I'm pretty sure given the accent, most Americans think you go to a secret wizarding or boarding school and that you're brilliant anyway. Sorry."

"It's the cross I have to bear. Handsome, wickedly brilliant, and an accent that makes anyone around me fall to their knees."

"Whatever you say."

"I can't help it. It's just me."

"You're an idiot."

"This class is making me feel like an idiot. And while I've enjoyed my electives and don't need to focus only on my major courses—if I did, I would either get bored or frustrated—my professor sucks."

"I feel you. Mine's not much better. I wish I had been able to get into the class I wanted. But sadly, signing up after most of the students already registered kind of screwed me."

"Well, I couldn't get into the class I wanted because it happened to be at the same time as the physics class that I needed. So now I'm lost in the abyss of this class with a syllabus that doesn't make sense."

"I still don't get how you can understand that physics class."

Pacey shrugged. "I'm a physics major. With an applied mathematics minor. It's sort of what I do."

"You're a little too smart for me."

Pacey snorted. "I'm not. I just happen to like science

and math more than you do. Because you've got a head for business, people, and you're usually really good at studying. Could it be you're too busy thinking about Miss Elise rather than focusing on university?"

I flipped him off. "I can handle more than one thing."

"You say that, and yet I could've sworn you were the one who said you wouldn't even try dating because neither of you wanted to focus on anything but school. In addition to your work and your family, of course. Was I wrong?"

"I hate that you remember things I say that well."

He shrugged. "Another cross to bear, it seems."

"Must be heavy under there," I said slyly.

"You have no idea. Come on, I'm feeling peckish. Let's get a snack or a pint. Anything so I don't have to focus on this stupid assignment."

"What are you writing?"

"I need to read a play and write a paper describing it without adding my feelings to it. They want us to dissect it analytically. You would think I would enjoy the idea, but you can't go into drama and imagine something completely analytical. It makes no sense."

I shook my head. "That doesn't. My paper's giving me a headache, as well, but I think that's because I can imagine my professor's voice droning on as I'm reading. It's his textbook, by the way. The one he wrote."

Pacey snorted. "That becomes a problem once I get into next year's classes and whatever grad school I get into. If the professor happens to have written a textbook, they need the royalties, so that's what you end up buying in addition to whatever other books go along with the class for that semester. It's a racket."

"I want to believe they deserve to get royalties for the book they wrote, but it seems a little self-serving."

"Maybe it wouldn't feel so bad if we didn't both hate our professors. If we liked the guys, it might be different."

"That is true," I said, shrugging. "Twizzlers for you?"

Pacey shook his head.

I paused in the act of reaching for the bag of candy. "Are you okay?"

He laughed. "I don't eat Twizzlers every day. Sometimes I even go a week without them."

I staggered back, putting my hand over my heart. "No."

"Yes. I always have to have them on hand if I want them, but I don't want them now. I was thinking grapes. Or maybe some carrots."

"Really?" I blinked.

"Hey, we're not going to be twenty forever. We need to work on that metabolism now. I want to use the body I have now, rather than clogging my arteries when I think I don't have a care in the world."

"You sound like my brother."

"Which one?"

"Brendan. Aidan and Cameron both eat decently well, but Brendan is a little more anal-retentive. Aidan and Cameron love to needle him about it."

"Aidan's the chef, right?" Pacey asked as he started piling fruit and veggies onto my tray. I added some cheese, and Pacey didn't seem to mind.

"Yes, Aidan's the chef and doesn't usually fry the food we eat as a family. However, he will add egg rolls or wings just to piss off Brendan, especially if Brendan pissed him off first." I shrugged. "It's a brother thing."

It was odd for me to say that since I was still new to the

whole *brother thing*. Yes, Cameron had been in my life since I was eleven, but the others hadn't. I had known they existed somewhere on the periphery, but I hadn't truly known them because of things out of my control. But now I did. And here I was, trying to prove myself to them for some reason.

The doorbell rang, and I frowned, looking at Pacey. "Did we order something?"

"Maybe Miles did."

"I've got it," Miles called out, and I shrugged, eating a piece of cheese. Pacey took one too, and I grinned. Cheese is healthy. At least, I thought so.

"Hey, Dillon, it's for you."

I frowned again and then made my way to the front of the house. Pacey followed, leaving the veggie tray behind. If Sanders or Miles ended up in the kitchen, it would probably be gone by the time we got back. But that was fine. We could just make another one.

Once I reached the front door, I froze, staring at the man in the doorway, wondering where I had seen him before. He didn't look familiar, and yet I knew those eyes and that jaw.

Who the hell is that?

My heart raced, and my mouth went dry.

"You okay?" Pacey asked, his voice low.

Suddenly, Sanders and Tanner were there, all standing beside me as Miles stood near the open doorway, his eyes wide as he looked between us.

"Hey there, son. I figured it was time we met."

Son. So that's how I knew those eyes. Because they were mine. As in, this was my fucking father.

The man I had never actually met. Unless he had been

there when I was an infant, and I didn't remember. But the guy at my door was Dave. My sperm donor.

"How the hell did you find me?" I was surprised that my voice was so steady and that I wasn't shouting. Or maybe I was, and the screaming in my head wasn't only into the void.

"Found you on Instagram. They had a picture of the house at one point or another. Pretty nice digs you got here. Figured you and I should talk. These your friends?" Dave lifted his chin at my roommate even as he rubbed his arm as if he were jonesing for a fix. "These can't be your brothers, right? They'd be older."

"What's going on?" Miles asked.

"How does he not know what your brothers look like?" Sanders asked and let out an *oof* as Tanner elbowed him in the gut.

I cleared my throat. "I don't know who you are. You need to go."

Dave's eyes narrowed in rage. It was just a slight shift, but I caught it.

And I knew my roommates did, too.

"Now, son, I thought we could talk about what you owe me. You sitting here in this nice house. Going to this fancy school. You owe me a few things. I just thought we'd catch up. Make sure we put everything on the table. You don't want to have to deal with what's going to happen if you say no, do you?" He began to pace as if unable to stand still for longer than a few seconds, and I tensed, worried what he'd do. Hell, I worried what the others thought, too.

Jesus, my roommates did *not* need to see this. They didn't need to know what kind of loser my supposed father was. I didn't even want to know who he was. Let alone what drug he was on.

"You need to go," I repeated with a growl, my voice stern.

Miles straightened, blocking the door with his body. "Yes, you should go."

"You really think you can close the door on me, little kid?" he asked, and Miles rolled his shoulders back. Miles wasn't short, nor was he a skinny beanpole. But the way he hunched in on himself sometimes, most people didn't notice that he was actually above average in height and muscle.

The man who had left me widened his eyes a fraction as he noticed Miles, and I let myself take a little pleasure in that.

"Come on now, son."

"Please don't call me that."

"I see. That asshole brother of yours has been spreading lies."

"That's enough," I growled, moving forward.

Before my dad could say anything else, though, Paccy stepped up, Tanner and Sanders with him. I moved as well so I wasn't left behind, but embarrassment filled me. Here my new roommates were, watching me interact with my so-called father. They probably all came from completely different backgrounds than I had, even though I didn't know precisely what or how. But it didn't matter. They would likely think less of me now. And I would deserve it. I was some kid that nobody wanted until I was forced to stay with Cameron. And though I was still trying to deal with that, I couldn't really focus on anything with my dad standing here in front of me.

I cleared my throat. "Go. Before I call the cops."

"You think you can do that?"

"I think you need to go."

"Or we can handle this ourselves," Tanner said.

Sanders grinned. "Oh, yeah. I'm pretty sure five of us young kids—as you called us—could kick your old ass. We could take you in a minute. You want to try it out, pops?"

I'd never loved Sanders more than at that moment, even as I hated myself that this was happening at all.

Dave narrowed his eyes again, then huffed away, his hands fisting and un-fisting as he stomped down the stairs to where he'd presumably parked his vehicle. I growled, followed him out onto the porch despite Miles' protest, and looked to see where Dave had double-parked his old truck. I committed the license plate to memory, just in case. I had probably seen a few too many movies.

"You okay?" Pacey asked from behind me. I shrugged.

"Yeah. Shit."

"That was your dad?" Sanders asked.

"Not really." I didn't know that man and didn't want anything to do with him. I didn't know what he was on or what he'd do to get the drugs and money he thought he was owed. The farther he was away from me, the better. It wasn't safe for him to be around me or my family.

"I'm sorry," Miles said. "He said that he was your dad, and I don't know anyone but your brothers and your sisters-in-law. I'm sorry. I would've headed it off at the pass if I had known. If he comes back. I'll do just that."

I shook my head and turned to look at all of them, heat creeping up my face. "No, you didn't do anything wrong. I don't even know that guy. For all I know, he was just saying he was my dad. I've never actually met him."

"Seems to me you lucked out having never met him before," Tanner said dryly.

I snorted, surprising myself that I could laugh. "Yeah, I guess I did."

"We'll all make sure he doesn't bother you again. At least here," Sanders said, shrugging. "Nobody needs to deal with that. And, hell, I'm pretty sure we could've taken him. Even Miles here could."

Miles flipped the other guy off. "Thanks for that."

"Sorry, I'm just saying."

I shook my head, my temples pounding. "Okay, I can't focus right now. I guess studying's out."

"Go see your brothers," Pacey said softly, and I met his gaze. The others started nodding. "You need to tell them what happened. Is he their dad, too?" Pacey asked.

I shook my head. "We don't think so since we don't know who his and Aiden's dad actually is. How come my family's so fucked up?"

"Preaching to the choir," Tanner mumbled, and the other guys just nodded.

I didn't know their families or where they had come from. We weren't there yet.

"You should head to the bar," Miles said, bouncing on his feet. "We can go with you if you want."

I shook my head. "No, I'll go tell them so they're not surprised. And I think bringing you guys to the bar for the first time tonight might not be the best idea. But I'll make it happen. Though you're still not going to be able to drink there," I warned.

Tanner just shrugged. "That's fine. I like your family. Well, most of them."

I snorted again, really grateful that I could laugh. "I'm going to grab my phone. Shit, what a day."

Pacey studied my face, and I did my best to school my features. I had no idea what I was feeling. How was I supposed to work it out now?

Pacey just kept staring, as did the others, and I quickly moved off to the office, put away my things, and grabbed my phone.

"You mind that I'm not going to be able to clean up the kitchen right now?"

"I'm sure we can finish the snacks without you," Pacey said dryly.

"Did you say snacks?" Sanders asked and headed towards the kitchen with Miles on his heels.

Tanner just rolled his eyes and followed. Pacey met my gaze, and I sighed.

"I'm fine."

"You're not, but that's okay. Talk to your family. They'll help. Or I guess you can talk to a certain girl you've been trying not to think about."

I flipped him off, feeling a bit lighter, and headed out the back door towards my truck. I should've called or texted, but I needed time to get my thoughts in order. I'd recognized that chin, those eyes. That man was my father. I supposed he could be a weird uncle or a cousin or something, but I didn't think so. The texts that had started to come only solidified that fact. I just didn't know what he wanted from me. I didn't have any money. Brendan and Aidan did, and so did Cameron after selling the bar that he had built from scratch back when we were living together before we left California.

But I didn't have anything. I was working on it. But I was just starting out.

I pulled into the back lot of the brewery but didn't see any of my brothers' cars. I cursed but hoped that maybe they were all parked somewhere else, or perhaps they'd had one of the girls drop them off. I wanted to see my family. I needed to talk to someone. I knew it couldn't be my roommates, not when they all probably already wondered what the hell had just happened. I needed to figure it out for myself first.

I walked into the brewery through the back entrance since I had a key and waved at the line chef. I didn't see Aidan. Well, shit, there went one.

I looked up at the bar and noticed Beckham, his wife Meadow working beside him. She didn't always work with him, but she sometimes liked to spend time with him at the bar and helped pick up the slack. I looked around more but didn't see any of my family.

"They're all off today. It's a slow night, and they were working this morning. Unless you were here to see my smiling face," Beckham said.

Meadow hit him in the arm. "Be nice. I'm sorry, honey, were you expecting to see them?"

I swallowed hard, wondering why I was so fricking emotional. "No. Well, yeah, but it's not a big deal. I was in the area," I lied. "I'll head back home since that's where I was going anyway." More with the lies.

Beckham tilted his head, stared at me. "Kid," he began, and I shook my head.

"I'm fine. Really. I'm going to go."

"Off to meet your girl?" Beckham asked, clearly fishing. This time, Meadow didn't tell him to stop.

I thought of Elise and the fact that I needed someone to talk to. Hell. Maybe I should.

"Yep. On my way."

Beckham grinned. "Well, then. That's good to hear. The romance connoisseur and guru, finding something for himself. I like it."

"Beckham," Meadow chided.

"Okay, I'm off," I said and headed back out. My heart raced, and I knew I probably shouldn't pick up my phone. So, I wouldn't. I just needed to figure it out for myself. Or call one of my brothers and head to their place. Anyone would welcome me with open arms. They all had lives of their own, and I didn't want to intrude, but hell, I didn't know what else to do.

My phone buzzed, and I looked down at it, the display giving me the answer I needed.

Elise: *I just got out of my late class, and I could use coffee or something hard to drink. It was the worst exam ever. What do you say?*

I swallowed hard. "Shit," I whispered.

Me: *How about I bring you some coffee? And a baked good. Meet you at your house?*

I knew she was having a shitty night and probably didn't need to talk. Maybe I wouldn't. Perhaps I would listen to her complain about the test, and then we could talk about nothing at all.

I just didn't know what else to do.

Elise: *You know what? That sounds wonderful. I'll text you my address. See you soon. Wait, you know my coffee order?*

I smiled.

Me: *I do. Unless you've changed your normal order.*

Elise: *No, I kind of want to see what you come up with.*

I couldn't help but smile, even after the shitty altercation with my dad.

Me: *Deal. See you soon.*

I set the phone down and headed to our coffee shop, wondering why it could be *ours* after such a short time.

And wondering if I would open myself up to a girl I had told myself I couldn't fall for.

Chapter 10

Elise

I RAN DOWN THE HALLWAY, INTO MY BEDROOM, LEAVING Corinne and Nessa in my wake.

"Is there a reason you're running?" Nessa asked as she followed me.

"Dillon's on his way here. With coffee." I looked around my room frantically, straightened my comforter, then looked at my reflection. "Crap. Why did I say he could come here?"

"Because you like him? And you're sort of dating him?" Corinne asked, and I looked at her reflection in the mirror as she nodded pointedly at Nessa.

"We're not dating." I paused. "Are we dating?"

"Well, let's see," Nessa began, holding up her fingers. "One, you go out to eat with him."

"Two," Corinne continued, "you've slept with him. More than once."

Nessa nodded. "Three, you guys constantly text and talk about your days. I've even heard you talk to him, gasp, on the phone."

I glared at them both. "You are not helping."

"Your room is pristine," Corinne said, looking around the place. "You look great. You even washed your hair this morning, so it's not like you're going to cover him in dry shampoo."

I sighed. "Oh, come on."

"What's he coming over for?" Nessa asked, walking towards me.

"I don't know for sure. But he said he's bringing coffee. And I think I might've asked *him* over. Or to go out for coffee, at least. I don't know. My test sucked."

"Oh, I'm sorry. Do you think you didn't do well?" Corinne asked.

"No, I think I did fine. I was just stressed, and it wasn't what I expected. But whatever. I have more important things to worry about, like the fact that Dillon's on his way here."

"Okay, he's on his way over. With coffee. Even though it's evening, but okay," Corinne said.

I sighed. "I like coffee. And Dillon didn't even have to ask me what I wanted."

"Ooh," both girls said.

I laughed.

"Right? I mean, he could totally be wrong, but at least he's trying. And I think I accidentally made it a quiz for him, and that's not right. I'll have to make it up to him later."

"Yeah, you will," Corinne said.

I flipped her off again. "Okay, am I dressed?"

They looked down at me and nodded. Nessa tapped her lips. "Tight jeans, cute boots, double tank tops under a sweater with one shoulder showing. Your hair is done. You have some makeup on but not too much. That way, it doesn't look like you added more for him. Maybe a little bit of lip balm or gloss and call it a day."

I blinked at Nessa. "That was quick. And spot-on."

She smiled. "You look great. Now, come on, plump up those lips, and make sure you put a sock on the door."

I cringed. "None of you guys share a room with me. Why do I need a sock on the door?"

"Please do not put a sock on the door. Play music or something. Or always play music so that way I don't know what you guys are doing in there," Corinne added.

"Wait, did someone say put a sock on the door?" Natalie asked as she walked in. "Oh, by the way, this is Mackenzie." She gestured to the girl at her side. "We're doing a group project together. What's going on?"

"Oh, hi," I said, wanting to die from sheer mortification. "Hi, Mackenzie. Nice to, uh, meet you."

Mackenzie, a girl with gorgeous hair and eyes, tilted her head and smiled. "Wait, you're going out with Dillon, aren't you?"

I blinked, then recognition hit. "I think so. Oh! You're Sanders' girlfriend, right?"

Mackenzie grinned. "I am. This is nice. I didn't realize you were roommates with Natalie. Small world. Or, I guess, small campus." She grinned again. "And if you're talking about socks on the door, I guess Dillon's on his way over?"

"I'm not putting a sock on the door," I said with a laugh.

"I'm just saying," Nessa began, and I groaned.

"Stop it. Go act natural. Or away from here."

"Is this his first time here?" Mackenzie asked, and my roommates all nodded.

"This is his first time here. And he's bringing coffee. Apparently, he already knows her order," Nessa stage-whispered.

Mackenzie's eyes brightened. "Oh, that's so sweet. Dillon seems like a great guy. I know the guys just moved in with one another, so I don't know them all that well, but he's always very respectful. And I've never seen him with more than one person at a time, if you know what I mean." She paused, blushing. "I'm sorry. Was that too much information? I was just saying that he would never cheat, and he's a great guy. And even though he's super handsome, and I know that other girls and guys have all commented on it, he totally only has eyes for you. And I'm going to shut up now because I was trying to be helpful and warm and all that, and I feel like I'm just digging a hole. Does anyone have an extra shovel? I could use it." She put her hands over her face, and I just laughed.

"I think that was actually kind of helpful. I know Dillon's hot," I said.

Corinne laughed. "Hell, yeah, he is."

"Anyway, I'm still trying to get over the fact that I think I'm dating him. I wasn't really ready to use that term, yet here we are. But the fact that you just said that about the whole not-cheating thing and everything means maybe I need to have a conversation about who we are to one another. But that's something for another day. You did make me feel better, though, even though I'm still nervous. Now I'm just going to pretend that everything's not tumbling around in my head, and I don't want to throw up."

The doorbell rang, and my phone buzzed.

"He's here!" Corinne said, clapping her hands. "I'll go get him."

"No, it has to be her," Natalie said, pulling Corinne back.

"But doesn't she need to make an entrance?" Nessa asked.

"Not necessarily. If it's a date in which he's just coming over, maybe it needs to be her so he doesn't realize we're all here waiting and watching in the wings," Mackenzie explained.

"I really think I'm going to throw up," I said. "Also, please don't wait and watch in the wings."

"Don't leave him waiting," Mackenzie said and pulled at my hand. "It will be fine. I'll go study with Natalie in her room. If you need a buffer, we can come out and have a conversation. But he doesn't even have to know we know he's here."

"You sound like you know what you're doing."

"Sanders and I've been dating since the cradle. And he always has tons of either school friends or work or family friends that date a lot. That means I've *always* had to watch the girls with the guys figuring out what they're supposed to do. I've taken some notes."

"We need to talk sometime," I said.

"You'll take her help but not mine?" Nessa asked.

"I always take your help. I think that's how I'm in this situation."

"No, that was *my* help," Corinne added helpfully.

"He texted again," Natalie sing-songed. I groaned, grabbed my lip gloss, and ran towards the door. Somehow, I had my phone in my hand, redid my lip gloss, and made it to the door while stuffing everything back into my pockets and was only breathing a little heavily. I looked behind me and saw that the girls were gone as if they hadn't been there at all.

I opened the door and smiled, trying not to look like I was out of breath. "Hey there."

"Are you okay? You look flushed."

I closed my eyes and let out a curse. "It's a very long story that means nothing. But I'm great. Hi." I went to my tiptoes, kissed him softly, and took the coffee from him that had an E on it.

I took a sip and groaned. "It's perfect."

"Nonfat sugar-free caramel latte with actual caramel on top to negate the sugar-free."

I cringed. "I like caramel. But I try to be good. It's just like asking for a double burger with extra cheese, extra-large fries, and a diet Coke. But it makes sense in my head."

"I don't mind. I go full-on sugar. Although Pacey reminded me that I'm not going to be young forever and that I should probably start watching my figure now or will end up with a beer belly before I'm thirty."

"Do you even drink a lot of beer?"

"My family owns a brewery, and I'm probably going to be working at it or something like it for the rest of my life. It could happen."

I tilted my head. "I've met your brothers. Well, at least two of them. They didn't have beer bellies."

"It is my hope that I at least have Aiden's and Cameron's genes."

I frowned. "But not Brendon's?"

A look crossed Dillon's eyes, and I frowned harder, pulling him farther into the living room. "What did I say? I'm sorry. Is there something I'm supposed to know? I forgot."

He let out a breath, his gaze going dark for a moment. "No, it's just…I wanted to talk to someone, and then I realized later that I didn't know who I was supposed to talk to. And now I don't know. Let's just talk about your test."

"No, let's not." I pulled him past the kitchen, the living room, the closed doors of everyone else's rooms, and into my bedroom. I locked the door behind us, aware that even though my friends wouldn't come in if they were all leaning against the door trying to listen in, they could end up opening it by accident. I had to trust that they wouldn't do that, but tonight was a weird night."

"Talk to me."

"I don't know. It might be too much. I don't want to put all of this into your head or add to your burdens."

I set my coffee down and pulled him onto the bed with me. We sat cross-legged facing each other, and I just stared at him. "I think we're doing this whole one-night-stand thing completely terribly."

He smiled softly. "I don't think you can count it as one anymore."

"True. And while I'm not great at labels because they scare me, I think it's okay if we talk to each other about what's on our minds. I would like that. I don't know if I'm good at the whole just-casual-sex thing."

Dillon shook his head. "I'm not either."

Relief flooded me. "Oh, thank God."

His lips quirked into another smile. "Yeah, same. I think I tried it once and ended up feeling like shit afterward."

"With Mandy?" I asked softly, not knowing if I wanted the answer.

"Yeah, though I thought we were something more. She only saw me how she wanted to. And I didn't like it."

"That's not nice."

"No, we had our roles laid out before us, and I didn't fall into line. But I don't want to talk about her."

"Then talk to me about what's on your mind. For real."

"Shit. Okay, so about the whole genes thing… Brendon isn't actually my brother."

I blinked. "What?"

"It's a long story."

"If you're up to telling it, I'd like to hear it."

He met my gaze, then looked down at his hands. I slid mine into his open palm, and he squeezed it, but I didn't do anything else. Didn't say anything else. I just let him think.

"I guess I'll start at the beginning. My mother liked drugs, selling herself for drugs, and was the worst possible mother ever." He didn't look at me, but I still froze, my hand on his. "Don't say anything until I'm done, okay?"

He looked up at me then, and I nodded. "Of course. I don't know what there is to say to that anyway."

"Nothing, really. Mom was a terrible mother. She was worse, I think, when Aiden and Cameron were born. They're twins but have a different father. Mom ended up getting in trouble with something or other and lost Aiden and Cameron to the system. They bounced around for a bit and finally ended up with Jack and Rose Connolly here in Denver. Brendon was in the system as well, and the

Connollys started with a foster program with all three. When they were able, they adopted them all formally."

"Wow," I whispered.

I nodded, swallowing hard. "Aiden and Cameron were even split up for a bit when they were younger, but Rose and Jack did their best to get them back together. And it worked out in the end. Except for, somewhere along that path, my mom decided to get pregnant again. This time with a different dude, another lowlife. And she had me."

I met his gaze, and he shrugged. There was such sadness in his eyes, with a little bit of anger mixed in.

"She wasn't the worst mom at first. She tried. I got cereal—the off-brand stuff, but that was what we could afford, and that was fine. We didn't have lunch or dinner on most days. I ended up getting myself to school when I could, at least at first. Mostly because the elementary school was a block away. But then she found a new dealer, and he ended up becoming her pimp." He cringed at that. "It was easier for her to keep the lights on if she had a job. And that was the job she liked. And while I have a whole idea in my head, I can't judge sex workers for the jobs they do. Though I can't help but judge my mom. Because she was only doing what she did because she wanted drugs. And she wanted to keep the lights on in the house. For her. I was barely a thought."

He let out a breath. "I was eleven years old when she asked for help. She couldn't do anything anymore, and Cameron came out."

My eyes widened. "Cameron?"

"We were out west by then. Cameron was twenty-one. He ended up raising me out there. Aiden and Brendon didn't come, but that's not my story to tell, you know?"

I nodded.

"When I turned eighteen, it was just Cameron and me. Mom was long gone. Dad never contacted me. I had no idea who he was, other than a name on a birth certificate and the fact that he was my sperm donor. But when I turned eighteen, I made a couple of mistakes. Didn't apply for college and lied about it." He groaned.

"What?" I asked finally, confused since that didn't sound like the boy I knew now, the one sitting right in front of me.

"Yeah, I thought I'd be in a rock band. I play guitar," he added, shaking his head. "And drums. Not that great, though. The guys in my band all promised that we'd stay in LA and make something of ourselves. Their parents weren't working two jobs, and didn't own a bar, and weren't working themselves to death like Cameron was. And their kids didn't lie to them." Dillon groaned. "I told Cameron point-blank that I had applied to college. When he found out that I hadn't, that my dreams of making it big in a band were in place, he just looked at me like he didn't even know me. I was an idiot. I still have no idea why I even followed that path. It's not like I actually see myself as that person."

"I can't see you as that person."

He smiled then. "I don't know. I think it was just a little too much. Cameron and I were barely speaking at that point. We didn't really know each other. Yeah, I lived with him, but I didn't *know* that he was there because he loved me. I thought it was just because he felt like I was some responsibility. And then I wanted to know who his brothers were and why they weren't my brothers and why they weren't there, and it turned into this whole thing where I didn't understand anything. My friends ended up going to college, and I haven't spoken to them since. They thought I was a fucking idiot. And I was, but they were willing to push me in that direction. Honestly, I think they just wanted to see what would happen when the deadbeat kid didn't make it."

"Where are they? I can beat them up for you."

Rage filled me, but Dillon squeezed my hand.

"Don't worry about them. I don't care what they do with the rest of their lives. I figured out what I wanted to do. It took Cameron and me moving to Colorado, but after Jack Connolly died and the will was read, he left the bar to the three of them. They had to work together and somehow become a family again. I won't bore you with the details of that, but they all ended up doing pretty well, and I somehow got three brothers and three sisters along the way."

"Wow," I whispered. "I didn't know that. I mean, my family is pretty normal. Or as normal as you can be with two hyper-attentive doctors who expect the most out of you. But it's not the same at all."

"Everybody has their problems. Mine just tend to be a little more dramatic," Dillon said dryly. "I went through my version of hell, but my three brothers? They went through so much more. In the end, though, I always had Cameron. Even when I thought I didn't, I did. And it took me a long time to realize that. But today, things got a little extra complicated."

"What happened?" I asked, nervous now.

He sighed. "I need to tell my brothers this. I should have done so before, but I don't know... I thought maybe if I just ignored it, it would go away."

"What? Dillon, you're scaring me."

"My dad, Dave. He's been texting me."

My eyes widened. "Are you serious? Just out of the blue?"

Dillon cringed. "He somehow figured out where I was, and he's been texting me—hounding me for money and crap. I don't have anything to give him. My brothers do, but I don't. I'm in school, for fuck's sake. But he found me and has been hassling me. Today, he showed up at the house. Where all the guys were. And they got to see my dad in his deadbeat glory. Threatening them—mostly Miles and me. And wanting money." He paused. "I think he's on drugs. And not the kind that keep you laidback. The kind that makes you tweak and get fucking dangerous if you aren't careful."

Dillon was practically growling at this point, and I just looked at him and then leaned forward on my knees to kiss him softly. "Dillon," I breathed against his lips.

"Thank you," he whispered, his shoulders relaxing. "I needed that."

"Anything. What happened at the house?"

Dillon shrugged, and I remained kneeling in front of him, keeping my hands on him. "Dear old dad—or Dave... whatever the fuck I should call him since calling him a sperm donor feels crass—"

"We can call him fuck face if you want. Would that help?"

I was trying to lighten the mood, and when Dillon's eyes brightened, some of the darkness leaching away, I counted it as a win.

"Thank you," he whispered. "I'm going to call him that from now on. Maybe just in my head so I don't get in trouble with my sisters."

I smiled, though I knew it wasn't full. Not when Dillon was hurting.

"Anyway, he threatened. Wanted money. Growled a bit. But the guys helped me get him out. They all stood behind me and were on my side. It was kind of nice."

"They seem like good guys."

"Yeah. They are. You know, fuck face—as you called him—thought they could have been my brothers. He doesn't even know what the fuck they look like."

"Really?" I didn't know what else to say about that. Dillon was hurting so much, and there was nothing I could do but sit and listen and try to be there for him.

"Maybe. I don't know. He said he found me and the house on Instagram—and that's not scary at all."

"They hashtag each of the houses on college row," I said. "There's no privacy anywhere. Anyone can find us. It's creepy."

"Tell me about it. I'm careful about what I put on social media, but since nobody else is, it makes it kind of difficult."

"It's why you're not on my socials," I said, wincing. "And mostly...well, it's because of that, and because as soon as I put you on social media, my parents will never let me hear the end of it. And then they'll growl and take me away from school or some shit."

I hadn't meant to say that, but Dillon just blinked at me. "Excuse me?"

"First, we were really good about lying about what label we were using," I said softly, trying to laugh, but Dillon didn't. "And my parents are strict about what they expect from me. I'm paying my own way with my scholarship, but it's all a bit confusing. They're really pushy about what I'm supposed to be focusing on. And boys are not it."

"And yet, here you are, with a boy in your room," Dillon said softly, teasing. He was smiling then, though it didn't completely reach his eyes.

"Yes. The audacity." I let out a breath. "I'm sorry you had a rough day."

"I'm sorry you had a tough test. We can still talk about that if you'd like."

"I'm pretty sure your day kind of puts mine into perspective. And I think I did okay on the test. I was just being overdramatic."

Dillon leaned forward, kissed me on the lips, and I sighed. "Good job, then. Now, let's drink some of our coffee before it gets cold. We can talk about silly things. Like the fact that I'm pretty sure I saw Sanders' girlfriend's car in your driveway."

"Oh, yes, she's studying with Natalie."

"Are they all sitting at the door? Just wondering."

"I don't think so." We both froze, trying to listen, but I didn't hear anything. I relaxed. "Now, tell me something good."

"What do you mean?" Dillon asked.

"Tell me something good. Something that makes you smile. I think we need that."

Dillon looked at me then, and I swallowed hard, my chest tightening.

"You. You make me smile. That might be cheesy to say, though I could always say that cheese makes me smile. But I'm going with you. Thank you. Thank you for listening. Thank you for not making me feel like a freak. Just thank you."

"You're not a freak, Dillon. I mean, if you are, then I totally am. But thank you for talking to me about it. I feel like you trusted me with something big, and I want to make sure I earn that. You know?"

He leaned forward, kissed me again. "I know. And I'm happy that I came here tonight."

I leaned into him. We talked about the rest of our respective days, and I knew if I wasn't careful, the tightening in my chest would become something more. Because I was one step away from falling.

And I didn't know where I would land if I did.

Chapter 11

Dillon

AFTER THE SECOND SET OF EXAMS FOR ANY CLASS ON A three-exam schedule, Sanders decided it would probably be best if we had another house party. And since the rest of us had agreed, the exams having been difficult, and most of us in need of a night off, it was our turn to host. That's how we ended up with a house filled to the rafters once again, people making out, laughing, arguing, and just having a good time. There was beer, some liquor, and a lot of food. The food was thanks to Pacey's contacts, and I did my best not to think about exactly how he had ended up with those. Pacey seemed to know everybody, but then again, so did Tanner. However, Tanner didn't seem to talk to anyone. I wasn't sure how that worked out, but if it got more food for the house that I didn't have to pay for or make, I was happy.

"I have no idea how you can stand having so many people in your house," Elise said, standing next to me. I wrapped my arm around her shoulders and kissed the top of her head. I ignored the looks of some of the partygoers. This was our first time attending a party as a couple, and we were still trying to figure out what that meant. Others would talk, they would nose around, and I planned to ignore them. I just hoped Elise could.

"I don't know. It doesn't bother me all that much. Maybe it did at one point. But I pushed those thoughts from my mind. They can't get into my room, so it's not like I feel as if they're in my space. It's sort of like we're at the bar. This is just where people hang out. I guess you get used to it after a while."

She nodded. "I suppose that makes sense. You have your family brewery, and now you have a place where people come to drink and have a good time. It just happens to be right under your bedroom."

"We can always leave. Either go back to your place or lock ourselves in my bedroom. Or maybe even go to a café or something if this is too much."

She shrugged and took a sip of her beer. "No, this is good. I don't mind. I mean, I did get to meet you here."

"I thought you met me at the coffee shop."

"No, I saw you from afar, and it started the whole dare thing." She winked, and I fell even harder.

"I, for one, am glad for the dare." It's as much as I would go into actually voicing my feelings, and she seemed to get that.

"Is that Miles?" she asked, and I looked over to where she pointed and then nodded. "Yes. I think he's dating that girl, Tiffany. Or at least they hang out a lot."

"I don't know her. I think I saw her with him last time, though."

"Yes, they're very competitive when it comes to school, though I don't know if they're actually dating or if they just use fighting as foreplay." I froze and then shuddered. "Forget I said that. I don't want to think about that ever again."

Elise laughed. "No problem. I don't want to think about that ever again either. Where are your other roommates?"

"Mackenzie and Sanders are in the kitchen. Mackenzie always helps make sure the food is all set out correctly. I don't mind because that means I don't have to do it, and she's great at making lists and shit, so she gets it done. Pacey was helping them, but then Sanders got all possessive for some reason. Now, Pacey is off hanging out with his friend Sasha, and I think two of *your* roommates." I pointed to a corner, and Elise's eyes widened.

"I am ninety percent sure that both Nessa and Corinne either have a huge crush on Pacey or want to be his best friend. They all seem to get along really well."

I looked over at the group in the corner and nodded. "I don't know about the crushes, but they do seem to get along. And I'm pretty sure Pacey has known them for a while."

"Corinne said that she's known him for a bit. I don't know if there are romantic feelings on her end or even his, but I will have to make sure that Nessa doesn't get her heart broken."

I looked down at her and frowned. "What do you mean?"

She winced and shook her head quickly. "I said too much. Pretend I didn't say anything."

I squeezed her shoulder. "Okay, but if you want to talk about it, I'm here. That could get complicated, I guess. Pacey isn't looking for anything steady."

Elise shook her head. "I'm not going to discuss it. I really shouldn't have said anything at all."

"You're right. So, let's talk about something else."

"Let's discuss how Tanner just showed up with a guy, and now he's talking with a girl."

That made me laugh. "I think the three of them are together, honestly. Or are at least together for parties. I don't know, and I don't ask. It's none of my business. And even if I did ask, Tanner would probably just growl and not answer me."

Elise snorted. "You're right. He likely wouldn't answer you."

Someone cleared their throat beside us, and I looked over to see Mandy. I froze. I did not want to talk to my ex-girlfriend. Not that she was my ex-girlfriend as she hadn't wanted that label, but labeling her as the girl I used to fuck because that's all she wanted from me when I thought maybe I wanted something more didn't make sense.

"Hey, Dillon. Fancy meeting you here," she said. She looked over at Elise. "Hi, I'm Mandy. You look so familiar."

Elise stiffened a bit, and I lowered my hand slightly so it rested on her hip, giving her a gentle squeeze. Mandy caught the movement, and she narrowed her eyes slightly before putting on her usual bright smile.

"Hi, I'm Elise. I think we've seen each other across campus a few times."

"Must be. This is Jeff."

The guy nodded. "Hey," he grumbled.

"Hi," I said, feeling awkward as hell.

"Anyway, I won't be here for long. I'm just meeting a few friends before we go out clubbing. I'm twenty-one now," she said, waggling her fingers.

That made me smile. "That's right. Happy birthday."

She waved it off. "I would've invited you, but it would've been weird. Don't you think?" She wasn't asking me but instead looking at Elise. "Anyway, I just wanted to say good luck. I mean, he may be good with his words and his dick, but he's not going to love you. And you seem like the type who needs to be loved. You deserve it. All women do. He's just not going to be that for you. I want you to know that there will be a man out there for you when it's time. So, you have fun with Dillon Connolly. He'll make you have the most fun ever, but when it's over, you come and find me. I'll find you your forever. Just like I found mine." She smiled as if she hadn't just cut us to the quick and then turned on her heel and walked away.

"Wow," Elise said, drawing out the word.

"She said that all so quickly, I couldn't say what I wanted to. Like, what the fuck?"

"That sounds about right. What the hell happened between you two?"

I shook my head. "I have no fucking clue. It wasn't that bad when we were together. And she wasn't a mean person. But, apparently, she hid it pretty deep beneath all her layers. I didn't see that."

Elise shook her head. "I think she just put you into a nice little box so she didn't get hurt, then made you stay there, even if she was the one lashing out. But hell, that was weird."

"I don't know," I said, blushing, hating myself just a little. "You know, people can fall in love when they're twenty, but they don't know what they want with the rest of their lives. Still, they found their person. For me? I feel like you need to fall in love with yourself first. Figure out who you are before you can find who you connect with."

She blinked at me, and I wasn't even aware I had said the words aloud. "That's very deep. And I agree with you."

I shrugged. "Or maybe she and I just weren't right for each other. I don't know. I'm still learning about this whole school thing. This whole relationship thing." I winced, looking down at her. "Sorry. Like I said, I'm not good at this."

"I'm not either. But I think we're both better at it than anything she just threw at us."

That made me laugh. "I sure hope so. Because, hell, I didn't realize I was a launching pad for the rest of her life. I swear I'm not a douche. I don't sleep around. I didn't before her, and I'm not going to start now."

"I get it," Elise whispered.

I was exhausted and a little annoyed. I hadn't realized that Mandy had seen me in that way, and I was irritated with myself for not even standing up for myself or Elise. Elise seemed to understand since Mandy had spoken so quickly and had dashed away before we even had a chance to respond. But it still felt weird.

The rest of the party died down early, but it only made sense. We were in the middle of the semester, and most people had papers or exams coming up.

In the end, only my roommates, Elise, Mackenzie, and I had stayed. Even Elise's roommates had left, saying they needed to work on papers and other things. I didn't know if that was true, but seeing Pacey so forlorn and awkward about it was odd. I ignored it. It was what I was good at—at least for now. I needed to focus on Elise. Not Mandy, not my roommates' drama, not anything else. Elise.

And that wasn't even right. I had told myself that I needed to focus on work and school, and now Elise came first. Or maybe it was all just blending together.

Jesus, I needed a drink, or to go to sleep and stop wallowing. I wasn't a wallower, yet here I was, muddled in my thoughts.

"Is everything okay?" Mackenzie asked, then sighed as I looked up at her. She had a large trash bag and was cleaning up. "Sorry that I'm just stepping in and cleaning. I figured I could help. I'm staying the night," she said, blushing. "And I'm not good with messes. Is this okay?"

I laughed and held up my empty trash bag. "I need to start cleaning up, as well, so you're not alone. Thank you, though."

"It's no problem. But really, are you okay?"

I shrugged. "Yeah, just a long night."

"I can see that. I saw Mandy here." She winced. "Sorry. I try not to judge people, but sometimes she can be catty when she's trying to pretend that she's okay."

Elise walked up then and started to help me stuff garbage into the bags. "What do you mean?" she asked.

"Yeah. You think she's hurting? Did I do something?" I asked, afraid that that was the case.

"No," Mackenzie said. "I don't think she and Jeff are doing as well as she'd like us to think," she said. "And now it sounds like I'm gossiping, and I'm not a gossiper. I just happen to know things."

"Is it gossip when you're just trying to explain why she was so rude to us?" Elise asked, and I nodded.

"Yes, what she said."

Mackenzie sighed. "I guess you're right. Anyway, I don't think their relationship is going too great. And because of that, she's trying to prove to herself that she ended the relationship with you for a reason other than her just being cruel and thinking that she needed to."

"I don't know her as well as I used to since we aren't in the same circles anymore." Mackenzie looked at me. "She wasn't thrilled that I've stayed with Sanders as long as I have. I mean, I'm happy. I don't need to keep bouncing around from guy to guy to find that happiness. She's welcome to, but sometimes she hurts people along the way."

"Yeah, she does," I said dryly. "And it's starting to make me feel like I'm a pushover, and that's not what I am."

"Of course, you're not," Elise said, frowning. "You knew what you wanted, and that's fine. She's just trying to rewrite history, and that's not the way things work."

"I don't know. But I'm kind of done letting her take up real estate in my head. You know?"

"Exactly," Mackenzie said.

"What are you all talking about in here?" Sanders asked, strutting in. He had a beer in his hand and handed another to me. I accepted it, even if I hadn't been sure I wanted one.

"I wasn't sure what you wanted, Elise, I'm sorry," Sanders said.

"I'm fine for the night," Elise said. "But thank you."

He kissed Mackenzie on the top of her head, and she smiled up at him warmly, pure bliss on her face. The two of them seemed great. They got one another and were happy. It was odd to me to think that you could find happiness so young and make it work. But then again, maybe you could. They had.

I did my best not to look at Elise just then, not with where my thoughts were headed. It would be a little too weird if I did. Not when I was trying to formulate my thoughts.

Mackenzie perked up. "Oh, by the way, if you guys happen to hear of a house looking for roommates, let me know. I'm trying to find an apartment or at least something to live in for the next year. My roommates are all seniors and are graduating. I should've been fine, but now they're changing up the lease where I'm currently living and doubling the rent. It's a little ridiculous."

I winced. "That sucks." I looked up at Sanders, but Mackenzie gave me a slight shake of her head.

I wasn't going to ask, and I didn't even know if we were ready to have a woman live with us, but if her living with Sanders wasn't a good idea, I wasn't going to step in the middle of that. Plus, it wasn't even my place.

"If I hear of something, I'll let you know," Elise said. "It's too bad that we only have a four-bedroom," she said.

"I know. I get along with all of you so well, but I think having five of us in your house might be a little too much."

Elise laughed. "Sadly, yes. Because then you'd have to have a bunk bed with one of us, and that's not exactly what we want."

"So, what are we talking about?" Pacey asked, Tanner and Miles behind him.

"Just living situations and life," Sanders said. "Anyway, good party tonight."

I shrugged. "It was okay."

Sanders sighed. "School's tough, and everyone's stressed

out. They're either lashing out or hooking up. Pretty much the norm."

Elise snorted, and I wrapped my arm around her shoulders. "Pretty much."

She and Mackenzie started talking, as did the guys. I just looked around and figured that maybe I had found part of my place. Part of what I needed.

I hadn't expected them or this, and I still wasn't sure what I was doing, but I would find my way. I had to.

I didn't want to become the person that Mandy thought I was.

And that meant I couldn't hurt Elise. I couldn't hurt my friends.

Somehow, I had to find a way to keep that promise.

Chapter 12

Elise

ME: *I'M SO NOT IN THE MOOD TO GO TONIGHT.*

Dillon: *Just don't let your parents see these texts.*

I cringed.

Me: *Dear God. I would never hear the end of it. But no, I will not let my parents see these texts. They will never know.*

Dillon: *That's good. But I hope it's not that bad. It's just dinner, right?*

I wasn't exactly sure how to explain a lifetime of failing to live up to my parents' expectations in a text. Dillon had gone through hell, literally in some cases, and had come out stronger. My petty grievances with how my family treated me weren't even in the same realm. I didn't know how to complain about my family without sounding like a petulant child. And maybe that was an answer in itself. That it was just hard to stand up to people who didn't see me as an adult and who had never truly understood my choices.

Dillon: *I'm sorry. I didn't mean to trivialize anything you're going through.*

I let out a soft smile and shook my head even though he couldn't see me. I didn't understand how he came to understand me so quickly, how he understood *everything* so quickly. It wasn't as if we'd been together long. It had only been a couple of months at this point, yet he knew how to calm me down when things got a little weird or complicated. And I wasn't sure how I felt about that. I hadn't expected Dillon Connolly. Therefore, I had no idea what to expect next.

Me: *My parents, hopefully, will be satisfied with merely dinner.*

I sidetracked, but I knew he'd let me be. I wasn't sure what I was supposed to feel anyway. Not when it came to school, or Dillon, or going home to people who still saw me as the perfect thirteen-year-old they could mold into their ambitions.

Or maybe I was just thinking a little too hard about all of it and layering where nothing existed at all.

Dillon: *Have fun. Text me when you're done. You're sitting in their driveway, aren't you?*

I cringed.

Me: *Yes, but with the way the driveway is, you can't see. They don't know I'm creeping here.*

Dillon: *They probably know.*

Me: *Thanks. I'll see you soon.*

Dillon: *I hope so.*

I blushed, but did my best to push thoughts of Dillion from my mind. I needed to focus on my parents and this dinner. I loved them; I really did. They just expected so much from me and sometimes I had to wonder about the reasons behind their visions for my life and why their intensity had increased over time. They hadn't always been like this.

I put my phone on silent, tucked it into my bag, and checked my reflection in my rearview mirror. I added a bit more concealer under my eyes since I hadn't been sleeping much. Between exams, papers, and Dillon, I wasn't getting as much rest as I should. My parents would notice at a glance. They were doctors, and they could always tell, but I could at least try to hide the worst of it.

I added some lip balm since it wouldn't add a shine or color to my lips. My mother had strict guidelines for what she liked to see on her daughter. And, sometimes, I didn't care. Other times, I just wanted to get through dinner without too many arguments, and that meant falling in line. As it was, I was going to disappoint them because I wasn't switching majors as they wanted.

I might as well not stoke the fires while I was at it.

I put my bag over my elbow, got out of my car, and made my way down the long path towards my parents' home. I had grown up privileged. I knew that. I was blessed and was well aware that I didn't have to fight for many of the things others still did. My goal was to work in a field where I could help others and not just people who came from the same background as I had.

I wasn't sure my parents would understand that, but I couldn't change their minds in an instant, even though I'd been trying for years.

I rang the doorbell and waited for my mother to answer. Mother always answered the door, even though she was as much an established and prestigious doctor as my father. But there were certain norms in the household. Mother opened the door if there was no staff on hand, and Father would greet me by the mantel. It was what they had always done. It never made any sense to me, but I let it go.

My mother opened the door and smiled politely, the pearls around her neck glistening. She studied my face, her gaze moving down to my perfectly lovely cardigan I had paired with my dress, as well as my sensible heels. She gave me an approving nod after glancing at my eyes, and I was grateful that I had bothered to put on these clothes rather than something I was a little more comfortable in. She took a step back and gestured for me to walk into the house.

"Elise, I'm glad you're on time." No *hello*, no *I love you*, no *how are you*—just a quip about promptness. I had arrived early because I was afraid that traffic might delay me, and I'd stayed in the car and texted Dillon until it was time for me to go into the house. Being early was too inconvenient. Being late was never allowed. Being on time was somehow perfect. I usually liked to be early, so I ended up waiting around for my parents most days until the exact, promised time.

"Hello, Mother," I said and kissed her cheek as she leaned down. She was three inches taller than me, and since she wore more elevated heels—at least for the day—it made for a more noticeable height difference. I knew she'd done it on purpose, for the same reasons I wore sensible heels around her. Or that I didn't wear flats because my mother thought flats were for girls in ballet. I happened to like them, but I wasn't going to get into that fight with her tonight.

"Your father's near the mantel as always. Go say hello to him. I'll get your club soda ready."

I hated club soda and would rather have regular soda,

juice, water, or God forbid something alcoholic, but I still wasn't of legal age, and there was no drinking in our household. At least not for me.

My parents drank their normal martinis and whiskeys, but I wasn't even allowed to acknowledge its existence for another three months.

I swore my parents were the WASPs of old living in Colorado, and I didn't quite understand how they'd ended up here.

"Hello, Father," I said and kissed his cheek as he leaned down.

"Elise. You're looking well." He narrowed his eyes partially.

"I noticed the bags, as well. Elise, darling, are you using the night creams I sent? When you own your practice, you're going to need to make sure that you have the face to match. People won't want to come to you for specialties if you look old and haggard."

I was twenty years old. And yes, I wore night cream. But not the same one my mother slathered on every evening. She was welcome to do whatever she wanted to her face. It was hers. However, my body was mine. But I wasn't going to fight tonight. The big argument was coming, so I didn't want to chum the waters. At least, not yet. I was sure that my thread was about to snap. I guessed we'd see how long this lasted.

"She's not going to be in a practice. She's going to be at a major hospital or university. That's how you get into the best programs. She can't just be a resident in some old practice." My mother's eyes tightened, ever so slightly. "We've already discussed this."

"How about I go get that club soda?" I said, turning on my heel.

"Yes, yes, you know where it is," my mother said, continuing her argument with my father.

I was exhausted already. I didn't want to deal with any of this.

By the time I got my drink, we were ready to sit at the dinner table. Mother had had the meal catered as they both worked long hours. I was surprised that we'd even made dinner happen, but I wasn't going to look a gift horse in the mouth. I loved my family. They gave me the opportunities to do what I wanted. To have choices. I just needed to be allowed to finish making them. And that was the crux of it.

Dillon's childhood and life had been so much harder than mine. I had to make sure that my family understood that I needed to be my own person, one who made autonomous decisions.

Knowing that didn't make this evening any easier.

We sat down for roasted chicken with rosemary, and three types of vegetables. There were no potatoes or rice pilaf or anything of the sort on the table. We had long since given up most carbs, though I knew my dad snuck in a roll or two at work.

I wasn't going to rat him out tonight. Or ever.

"How are your classes going?" my mother asked.

"They're great."

"All As, I assume?" my father asked, his attention on his plate.

I nodded. "Yes, it's been a tough and challenging semester, but I've enjoyed it."

"Of course, you're getting all As. We would expect nothing less."

In other words, if I got anything but As, they would be disappointed in me, and I'd have to hear another lecture. It didn't matter that I was paying for my semesters through scholarships and loans. That's still what they wanted.

I was also taking at least three extra credit hours more than most people, which was why I couldn't get a job as I wanted. I'd taken the loan to focus on those three to six extra credit hours a semester. That way, I could work on my double major. Only I wasn't sure my parents truly understood why I was doing it. They never expected me to get a job. They had wanted to pay for school so I was always under their thumbs. When I politely declined, they assumed that I had just meant I was good enough to get a scholarship; therefore, I had to be the best. Yet they were still putting me under their thumbs.

I needed to get out of this situation. Tonight would be the big talk. I pushed my food around my plate, my stomach growing heavy. I wasn't sure I could eat anything but the few bites I had already taken. My mother noticed, her eyes narrowing again.

"Have you set your schedule for the next semester yet? We've looked through the pamphlets and tried to call your counselor, but once again, they wouldn't speak to us."

I ground my molars. "Because I'm nearly twenty-one. You don't have the authority to discuss my grades or anything else with the school."

"We want what's best for you," Father added.

My mother waved it away, even as my father ground his teeth. "That doesn't make any sense. We're your parents. We tried so hard for you, darling. We want to make sure that you have everything you could ever need or want."

I held back a sigh, not sure exactly what she meant by

that. *They'd tried so hard for me?* "My grades are good, and I've been working on my schedule. It's a little more complicated as I'm nearing my final year. That means I have to be careful about what classes overlap for the last two semesters. But I'm going to be taking a couple of summer classes, as well. They're online so I can work on an internship, but it's getting done."

Both of my parents stopped eating and looked at me. My mom tilted her head.

"Internship?" she asked. She looked over at Dad. "Did you discuss this with her? I thought we were waiting until after her fourth year to work on internships. And I was going to get her first."

They began arguing again, talking about their plans from before I was even born and what their child needed to accomplish. Honestly, with all their ideas of children and futures, I was always surprised that I was an only child. The amount of success they imagined for mc always seemed like something for far more than only one child.

They always had plans and worked hard to achieve them. In another life I'd even appreciate them. I'd had everything I'd ever wanted, including their love and attention even with their busy jobs, but they were also demanding. So much so that it was hard not to be bitter about it. I let out a low growl. I hadn't meant to let the sound escape, and they both looked at me.

"Excuse me?" my father said, his voice low.

I might as well begin here. "I got the internship on my own. It's going to earn me credits, and though I won't get paid, I'll still be saving money when it comes to school since my summer classes don't count towards the scholarship."

"You know we'll pay for it," my mother said, and I shook my head.

"No, I'm sorry. I don't need that. I have it handled."

"Where exactly is this internship?" my mother asked, her voice steely.

I set down my fork and knife and raised my chin. "As I said, I'm going to be a physical therapist. I'll be working at a clinic, behind the scenes, and taking in as much as I can. I still have a lot of school and classes to come after I get my two bachelor's degrees. So, yes, I got my internship. It was highly contested, but I did it."

Dillon had been so proud of me. He and the boys, as well as my roommates, had thrown me a party. Just us and Mackenzie, where we had sheet cake from a grocery store and cheese and other random appetizers. It had been fun, sweet, and I had felt so proud of myself.

And all of that turned to dust at the look on my parents' faces.

"No," my mother said. "That was not our plan."

I hated this, but I was determined to stand up for myself. "That wasn't your plan or Dad's. Though the two of you have separate plans from each other. And neither of them is mine."

"After everything we've done for you, you're going to do this?" my mother asked.

"Yes, I guess so. But I'm not doing it to you. I want to be a physical therapist."

"You want to be common. You want to be in debt for the rest of your life. You're not going to be a real doctor. What kind of hack do you think you are? The next thing we know, you'll want to be a chiropractor."

Mom and Dad began yelling at me and each other, and I shook my head, putting my hand on the edge of the table.

"I knew it was going to be like this, and I can't do it. I've already made my decision. You don't pay for anything for me. I'm here because I love you guys, but you need to stop."

"You don't get to talk to me like that," my mother said.

"And you don't get to talk to *me* like you are. I am your daughter, but I'm not a little girl. Nor am I a minor any longer. I've made my decision. I've been doing so for a while. You need to let me."

"No, you've made your mistakes and are going to live with them." My mother searched my face and snarled. "It's a boy, isn't it? It always comes back to a boy." She glared at my father. "I swear, this is your fault. It's always your fault."

My dad threw up his hands, pushed back from the table, and stomped out of the room without another word —his usual modus operandi. My mother's gaze turned to me again. Her eyes narrowed into slits. "Well, who is he?"

My heart thudded, and I swallowed hard. "I have no idea what you're talking about."

"You were never a good liar. Is he the one putting these thoughts into your head? That he can be the one who makes all the money and takes care of you? Well, he's wrong. Now, you listen to me. No matter how much money he makes, you have to do better. Because you are a woman. Everything you do will be twice as hard. He gets everything he wants just by existing, and he probably gets between your legs, as well."

I blinked. "Excuse me?"

"Oh, don't act all pure to me. We've never been a family

who's discussed purity as something important. We know sex is biological and needed for those who desire it. However, if you are going to waste your life for some boy, don't come back here. You said your semester was hard? I bet it was because your attention was divided. First, you live in that house with those girls with no ambition. With little Corinne and her happy, lucky life where she's never had to work a day for anything. And now you're with some boy? What does he want from you? What are his ambitions? Where does he come from? Nobody. He's probably nobody. If he was somebody, you would have introduced him to us or said something."

I just shook my head. "I haven't even told you if I'm dating someone. And from the way you're speaking, I wouldn't. It's none of your business anyway." I stood up and grabbed my purse. "I'm going. Goodbye, Mother."

"No. You listen to me."

"I don't have to. Not tonight."

"Fine, if that's your parting shot, I'm going to take mine. Boys are nice, and they get the job done every once in a while, but know this... All of these plans you have for your life? It's going to be hard. You think your little junior year is hard now? It's a whole lot harder out of school, honey. We are just trying to help you here. But you're throwing it back in our faces. You're spending all your time with this boy. And your roommates. No wonder school is so hard for you. It shouldn't be. This is your easy year. Next year will be just as hard. And you think you're going to be able to do well on this scholarship and take classes? No, not with your attention divided like this. So, you think long and hard about what you want from your life. Because if you keep throwing back what we do to help you in our faces, we're not going to be here when you fail. And you will fail. Spectacularly."

This time, Mother took her martini and walked from the room, leaving me alone, with her having the last word.

I shook my head, my entire body quaking. Somehow, I made my way to my car.

I hadn't even realized I was crying until I was halfway down the highway.

I saw that Dillon had texted again, just saying *"good luck"* and asking me to call him when I was done with dinner, but I didn't say anything. I couldn't.

Because no matter how pushy my mother could be, she was right. This semester had been harder than it should have been because I spent more time with Dillon than I had planned.

As I'd said before, I hadn't planned on Dillon Connolly.

And now I was afraid that with me spending so much time with him, maybe I was standing in my way. I could push my parents away. I could make my own decisions, but what would happen if those decisions were wrong?

What happened if I stood up for myself? And if Dillon was by my side when I did so?

Chapter 13

Dillon

I LOOKED DOWN AT MY PHONE AND FROWNED. ELISE STILL hadn't texted me back to tell me how her dinner had gone with her parents, and I was getting a little worried. I knew she was busy and had classes and friends and a life outside of me, but, somehow, I'd turned into a stage-four clinger.

Or maybe that wasn't right. I just wanted to know how she was. I knew it would be a big dinner, one where she made sure her parents understood what she wanted for her future. I hated that I couldn't be there for her, but neither of us was ready for that part of our relationship, and me being there would only be a hindrance. That wasn't what tonight was about. I wasn't the center of attention. And I was fine with that.

I just wanted to know how she was doing.

And I wasn't about to text her for the third time just to ask.

I would only be invading her space and annoying the fuck out of her. Of course, if she didn't text me back by the end of my shift, I would either have to text one of her roommates or stop at her house on my way home. I needed to make sure she was safe. She didn't need to talk to me, but I had to make sure she was okay.

And, unbeknownst to me, I was in a full-on relationship.

"That is the fifth time you've looked at your phone. Girl troubles?"

I looked over at Aiden and shrugged. "I don't think so."

My brother winced. "That's never a good sign if you have to qualify it."

"I'm pretty sure I said that phrase to you at some point."

My happily married brother just smiled a little evilly. "It's the truth. You helped me out of a sticky situation when it came to Sierra. I guess it's my turn."

I gave Aiden a look. "I don't know if I want your advice. Sometimes, you're a little scary."

"You're lucky I like you, kid, and we're in public, or I'd slap the crap out of you."

"You're so nice," I said, and Aiden just snorted.

"I'm not trying to be nice. I never try to be nice."

"Well, that's the truth," I said dryly.

"You're such a dick sometimes. It's like you're my brother or something."

That warmed me, and I couldn't help but give him a sloppy smile. Aiden rolled his eyes but smiled right back. We had been doing good at this whole brother thing for a while now, even though we weren't that new at it. Every once in a while, though, I was reminded of the fact that I hadn't been raised with them. I didn't share in their stories from their time growing up, nor did I have the connections and memories the others did. But they were so good at making sure I was part of everything now. I didn't feel the lack. Even though I could've easily let myself do so. My brothers were good men and took care of me.

Aiden's eyes narrowed, and he tilted his head as he studied me. "Is there a reason you're looking at me like that? Do I have something on my face?"

I tried to grin to lighten the mood a bit. I didn't want to get too emotional since we were working, and I was already worried about Elise.

"I think there's some processed wing sauce on your chin. Tasting the wares, were you?"

My brother's eyes narrowed even further, and his cheeks reddened. "How dare you utter such foolishness. Number one, if anyone ever heard you, I would have to kill you—and possibly them, as well. Number two, I would never dare grace these lips or these walls with processed wing sauce. We make it from scratch, you asshole."

"But you're still making wings," I teased.

Aiden flipped me off this time. "You're an ass. And, of course, I'm making wings. It's a bar. They just don't realize they're eating fancy wings."

"Is that what you call them now?"

Aiden groaned. "I'm going to end up with wings at the new restaurant."

"Just to annoy the highbrow people that come in and eat at your restaurant?"

"We're not going hoity-toity highbrow."

"And what's wrong with that?" I asked honestly.

"Nothing at all. I'm finding my groove. Now stop changing the subject. Why do you keep looking at your phone?" Aiden asked, and I shook my head.

"Elise isn't texting me back. I want to know how her dinner went with her parents."

My brother gave me a knowing look and then went back to plating an order. We were slow tonight, mostly because it was late on a weeknight, and we'd already hit our two rushes. But we still had a few orders to fill.

I was working in the kitchen tonight, though I had been up front for most of the evening. Now, Aiden was alone because his other cook was out thanks to a sprained wrist and a long day, and I had filled in. I didn't mind, and my brothers made sure they compensated me for my lack of tips. Plus, I got to hang out with Aiden. I had once thought that this was what I wanted to do for the rest of my life, but maybe I'd help again in the kitchen with Aiden more often. I just wasn't sure. I needed some time to figure out what I wanted. And I was blessed as fuck to have a family who understood that.

"Do you know if she's avoiding you? Maybe she just had a long night. Or her phone's off."

I sighed. "My mind's already gone through a thousand different scenarios. I'm just overreacting. She's fine. Everything's okay. I'm just tired, I guess. Or maybe I'm not used to this."

"For a guy who was so good at helping all of us settle into our relationships, you've never had a serious one of your own."

I shrugged. "No. I haven't. I guess that makes me kind of an asshole for forcing you guys to listen to me before."

Aiden shrugged. "No. You're not an asshole for that.

We didn't have to listen to you. We could've ignored you, acted like you were just some kid. But we didn't. We wanted to know what was up. We listened to you. Still do. We like you. And you're smart. You evidently knew what you were talking about, so I guess now you should listen to your own advice."

"And what advice was that? It's been a couple of years."

Aiden laughed. "Yeah, it has. You guys are young. You have time to figure things out. I know you've got a thousand things on your mind, though. And you texted her, I take it?"

I winced. "Twice. Once to see how it was going, another to ask how it went. I don't want to be *that guy* and text a third time, acting like a possessive jerk."

"You're right. You don't want to be that guy."

"It would be easy to become him, especially since I just want her to be all right, and I don't know how to make that happen."

"You can't hold the world in your hands. You can't make her feel like she can do everything either. But you can stand by her side and help."

"Is that what you say to Sierra?"

Aiden snorted. "I have never once been able to tell my wife what to do. I can guide her down the path, but then she shouts at me, pushes me off the path, and finds her own. And that's why I love her. Because she takes no shit, no prisoners, and knows I will do the same."

"I do love your wife."

"Watch it."

"Not like that, come on."

Aiden just gave me a look. "So, what kind of dinner was this with her parents?"

"One where she was supposed to explain to them that

she's going to stick with the major she is paying for, to be a physical therapist, and that she wants nothing to do with being a doctor like they are."

Aiden winced. "Oh, that's going to go well."

"Elise got scholarships and is pretty much paying her own way. Even if they were paying for her school, I don't know if it's okay for them to direct her in that way."

"I think if you go into a partnership with your family where they pay for your school, there needs to be an understanding of what that means. In terms of actually passing classes and graduating, but not directing them down a path to a major they want nothing to do with." Aiden gave me a pointed look.

"I know you guys would pay for my classes, but if I keep doing as well as I am, then I'll get the full-ride for the rest of my years at this school."

"And that would be fucking great," Aiden said, finishing up another order. "But if, by chance, you don't get that full scholarship and only keep with the partial, don't get a loan. Not these days where interest rates are insane. Let us help."

"You guys have kids to worry about."

"And everything that Brendon touches turns to gold. Let him use his fancy money. Hell, let us help you. We may not be billionaires, but we're not in debt either. We can help you. You're not in an Ivy League school getting a degree in underwater basket weaving. You're working towards something important. *To help with the family.* So, let the family help you."

I winced. "I haven't been good about seeing it that way."

"No, you haven't. But I figured I'd start here, and then let Violet and the girls get to you later."

"They're going to gang up on me, aren't they?"

"You know it. The only reason we even let you work like you are is because it's with and for the family. If we didn't have a place of business where you could work with us, you wouldn't be."

"I need to make my own way, Aiden. Earn it."

"And you do. You have." There was a lot in that statement, and I stiffened.

"I know. Thanks."

"Anyway, we like you, kid."

"Thanks," I said dryly.

"What? Now, work on this last order and then check on Brendon and Cameron. Brendon's upstairs working on the books since it's nearly tax time. And Cameron is behind the bar. If they're good for the night, head home."

I shook my head. "But it's not the end of my shift."

"Well, go check on your girl, then."

"And that's not being too possessive?"

Aiden shook his head. "It's just checking on her. You told me she was having an emotional evening. Just make sure she's okay. Or see if she'll text you back. If you show up there with her favorite treat or drink, hand it off, say you were thinking of her, and then walk away. That's not being too much. That's just showing you care. Hell, we're allowed to do that, you know? Guys don't have to be gruff and in the corner hiding their feelings and shit all the time."

I looked at Aiden, blinked a few times, and then threw my head back and laughed. "I can't believe you of all people said that."

Aiden flipped me off again. "Oh, fuck you, too. I am in touch with my feelings."

"You are not. You're a growly asshole who doesn't know

the meaning of showing emotion to anyone but your wife. And even that's like pulling hairs."

Aiden raised a brow. "Got a problem with it? At least, I'm married."

"Are you saying you want me married at this age?" I asked, my heart doing that twisty thing in my chest, thinking about Elise. We were not even close to that, but hell, the thought of being with her for longer than a minute? I liked it. I liked it a lot.

What the hell was wrong with me?

My brother rolled his eyes. "Go take this order out, and don't come back until you talk to your girl."

"And not in a stalkery way."

"Yes, don't stalk her, asshole. You're a romantic, one who reads all those books about what women want. You should know more than me."

"When I was giving advice, I was just talking out of my ass because I had no idea what I was doing."

Aiden just shook his head. "You know more than you think you do. Go talk to your girl. After you serve that table, of course."

I nodded and picked up the plates. I headed out to the front of the brewery, where a couple of tables were still filled. One group was already eating. I had the food for the other. It looked as if it would be a smooth close for the evening, and for that, I was grateful. Sometimes, we were crowded right up to the time we needed to close the door, and I was exhausted on those days, even if my tips were excellent.

"Okay, guys, I have wings, two wraps, and the sampler."

"That's us," one of the guys said. "Your bartender there? Cameron? He already got us some extra plates. You can just toss it all in the middle, and we'll fight over what we want."

"That sounds like the easiest plan ever for me." I did as they asked, nodded, made sure they had everything they needed, then headed over to Cameron.

"I heard Aiden say you were on your way out the door," Cameron said.

"Yeah, I have homework and stuff."

"And Elise?" Cameron asked, and then Brendon was there, as well, standing behind the bar.

"Were you all listening to that conversation?" I asked, a little unnerved.

"No, Aiden just mentioned that we were supposed to make sure you went home and checked on your girlfriend. We don't know what it's all about, but we're sure he'll fill us in."

"Y'all are worse than the girls."

"Don't let Harmony hear you say that," Brendon said, then paused. "Or any of them. Including your girl."

"You're right," I said, cringing.

"Anyway..." Cameron didn't get a chance to finish what he was saying because his eyes narrowed, and the hairs on the back of my neck stood on end.

"There you are, boy. Kind of annoyed I had to find you here."

I felt the blood drain from my face, and Aiden came out from the back. All three of my brothers glared over my shoulder. I swallowed hard and turned to see Dave. My father. The man I never wanted to see again.

"Jesus, you work in a bar? Well, I guess it's a good thing for me. Yo, barkeep, could use a beer. Whatever you got on tap here but not any of that pussy shit." He slurred his words, then started to rub his arm as if in pain...or needing another fix.

"I do believe you walked into the wrong place, sir," Cameron said, and I knew he recognized the man.

After all, he had my eyes.

And I had a feeling that all three brothers knew what Dave looked like. They had hired a private investigator to find him at one point, and I had wanted nothing to do with it. I had been trying to find my way, learn who I was as a Connolly, and they had been gracious enough not to tell me what they'd found. But they knew that this was my dad.

Hell.

"You should go," I said.

Dear old Dave's eyes narrowed. "You should stop talking back to me." His breathing quickened, and he rubbed his arm again, fisting his hand as if waiting for something.

The two tables with customers all turned to us, a total of five guys with narrowed eyes who didn't look as if they were interested in joining in on the fray or watching the party while eating popcorn. Instead, they looked ready to push the guy out of the bar and help us.

It was an odd sense to have, but one you figured out after working at a place like this for a while. These guys would help with Dave, but I didn't want anything to do with that. I wanted them to enjoy their evening without drama. I didn't want the embarrassment of my sperm donor standing in front of me, acting like an asshole.

"I've already told you once..." I began and heard Cameron curse under his breath. I hadn't mentioned that Dave had stopped by the house. "I told you already that I don't want you here or in my life. You need to go."

"You owe me. It's best we get it done now so I don't have to make a scene." He looked around the place and held out his arms. "And, you know, it'd be nice to make a scene in this pretty place."

"You guys keep eating," Brendon said casually from behind the bar. "Bill's on us. We're going to go take care of this. You need anything, Aiden here will be able to help you."

"You're making me stay here?" Aiden mumbled.

"You're closest to them. It's the first name that popped into my mind."

I shook my head, putting up my hands so my brothers would stop speaking. "I've got this," I said and then moved forward. "You should go. I'm done with this."

"You owe me."

"Like I said before, I will call the cops if I have to." I pulled my phone out of my apron. The guy who I hadn't known for my entire life spat on the floor before leaving.

I put my shaking hands down and slid my phone back into my apron pocket. "If it's all the same to you, I'm going to head home."

Cameron put his hand on my shoulder, and I flinched.

He cursed under his breath, and I didn't bother looking up at his face. I was afraid of what I might see there.

"He came to the house, then?" he asked.

"Yes," I whispered. "But it's fine. He just wants money or something."

"And you didn't tell us?"

"No. I didn't."

"Because you think you can handle it," Brendon whispered.

"I did, didn't I? He's just blowing off steam. He'll get

bored, and then he'll leave for good." Even I didn't believe the words coming out of my mouth.

"And what if he comes to the house again? Or one of our homes. What if he figures out where we live and comes when the girls are there alone? What then?"

Ice filled my veins, and my mouth went dry. "Shit. I didn't think." I hadn't wanted to. I'd wanted to push away the problem so no one would have to deal with Dave. But Dave wasn't going away. Not easily. Damn it.

"No, you didn't. Because you're a Connolly, and you have your head up your ass trying to protect your family by ignoring the situation and thinking you can handle everything yourself. Well, now that we know, we'll handle it. *With* you. But don't think you have to do it all on your own."

"It's fine. He's not your dad. You don't have to deal with him."

"I had to deal with a dad who wasn't the greatest either," Brendon said slowly. "Remember?"

My mouth filled with sawdust, and I nodded. "I remember."

"You don't get to do this alone."

"I'm fine. I just need to go. Check on Elise." My hands shook, and I honestly didn't know what to do.

"You do that. But maybe we need to sit down as a family and talk about who this man is. And exactly where he's been."

"I don't want to," I said quickly. "I have shit to do. Work and school and Elise and just…everything. I don't want to deal with him."

"It doesn't seem like he's going away, Dillon," Cameron said softly.

I knew that, but I was in denial right then. How could

the man tweaking out on *something* be the man who'd fathered me? "Yeah? He just walked out. He's good at that. He's nothing to you guys. And, yes, I guess we'll all talk it out later because that's what we do, but just give me a minute, okay? Let me think."

Brendon opened his mouth to say something, but Cameron shook his head. "Go. Go home, hang out with your roommates, check on Elise, do whatever you need to do to remember that that guy doesn't matter. But in the morning, we're going to talk. Because you're our family. Our brother, Dillon. You don't get to do this alone."

I fisted my hands at my sides. "There's nothing about this that's anything. It's nothing," I lied.

The pity in their gazes was something I didn't want to deal with. They'd all had shitty parents and had led more challenging lives than I had ever dealt with. Yet all I wanted to do was run away and not think about any of it.

I couldn't, though, because it was always there in the background, reminding me that I had come from worthless-ness. That I had been nothing. That I had only made it as far as I had by the grace and power of my brothers.

And I still hadn't earned it.

No, I remained the son of a gutter trash whore and whatever John she felt like having that night. That's what the kids in school had called me once, and that name would never leave my mind.

I grabbed my things and headed out.

I looked down at my phone, but Elise still hadn't texted. Maybe that was good.

She could deal with her things, and I knew she was strong enough to do so.

I didn't want to taint her with mine.

Chapter 14

Elise

"Do you know where I put my psychology book?" I asked as Corinne leaned against the doorway.

"The last time I saw it, it was on your desk where you were working, but that was last night. Did it fall under the bed or something?"

I scowled, dropped to my knees, and looked at the perfectly lovely book under my bed. "How do things move around my room like this? Like, how did this even get there?"

"Because when you're stressed, you start randomly moving into different positions trying to study. I don't know how you make it work. Sometimes you end up curled in a ball upside down while reading, and I always find that very uncomfortable."

I sighed, reached for the book, and pulled it towards

me. I hugged it to my chest and sighed. "I'm having a nervous breakdown."

"You're not, but you are stressed out. Do you want to come out with us? We're all going to get some coffee and maybe lunch."

I shook my head. "No, I need to focus."

"That's all you've been doing since your dinner with your parents. You haven't even seen Dillon since then."

I held back a cringe at that. "I've seen Dillon."

"In passing at the coffee shop as he went to class. It was awkward as hell. He kissed your forehead, you both looked at each other like you wanted to say something, and then he went away."

"Well, I'm sorry that I'm not having the perfect relationship for you," I said, none too kindly.

"Stop being a jerk," Corinne stated. "Tell me what your parents said. We know how much they love me."

"They don't dislike you," I corrected.

"But they sure as hell don't like me. I'm the bad influence." She rolled her eyes and then laughed.

"Little do they know that I'm probably the worst influence."

"Exactly, but it's fine. I will be the poor little bad influence in this family just for you. However, I wish you would tell me what they said."

I shook my head. "Just more of the same. I think I'm pretty much on the way to being disowned." I did my best to ignore the twinge I felt at that.

Corinne's eyes widened. "Seriously?"

"Seriously. They each have ideas for who I should be, and then went on a tirade about how I'm not working hard enough, studying hard enough, or being good enough to be their precious daughter."

"Did they actually say that?" Corinne asked, her voice low, angry.

"Not in so many words. But after Dad stormed off when I said I wasn't going to work on whatever internship he decided I should be in, or what my major should be, Mom grilled me on why I'd had such a tough semester."

"You are not having a tough semester. Yes, you have more to do than you did last semester, but you're not flailing around or coming unhinged. You're working your ass off just like before."

I sighed and pressed the book closer to my chest. "I'm focusing too much on outside things when I know I need to study."

"You're always studying. More so than usual. Don't let your parents taint what your goals were—or are."

"I'm not. My parents may be wrong about a lot of things, but they were right about the fact that I need to focus to meet my goals." I didn't get into all the untrue and rude things my mom had said about Dillon, a boy they had never met.

"I don't see the problem. You're getting good grades. You're sleeping, you're hydrating, you're taking care of yourself. And school isn't just about getting good grades and working yourself to the bone. You're allowed to have a life."

"I have you guys."

She tilted her head, giving me a pointed look. "And not Dillon?"

Tears pricked the backs of my eyes, and I shook my head. "I have Dillon, too. I just need to remember that I'm young, and we're not talking about marriage or anything. I need to not lose my head over a boy when things can change so quickly. Things got a little too serious too quickly already. We were only supposed to be a one-night stand, remember?"

I knew I was floundering, scaring myself into changing things, and that was a problem. I was glad Corinne was here to help me figure it out, but that didn't make my heart any less heavy.

"How serious has it gotten with Dillon?" Corinne asked softly.

"We're sleeping together," I whispered.

"We both know that's not the only thing that means you're serious," she said dryly.

"So says the virgin." She flipped me off, and I let out a sigh. "It just seems like a lot. And...I don't know how. I think about him too much. Like he's always the person I want to talk to in the morning, even before you."

"I'm not going to pretend that doesn't hurt a bit, but it sounds like a good thing. Dillon hasn't done anything to upset you, has he?"

I shook my head. "If anything, he should be upset with *me* since I've been pushing him away."

"Then don't do that anymore."

"I don't know what I want, and that's a problem."

"Do you just not want to get hurt, or do you want to focus on school and think Dillon is distracting you from that?"

"I don't know."

Corinne stared at me and then shook her head. "I hope you figure it out soon. I love you, you know."

For some reason, tears started falling down my cheeks

then, and I cursed. Corinne was on her knees in a second, sitting down next to me and holding me close. "I love you, too, you idiot."

"You're always the sweetest to me." I sniffed. "I'm sorry."

"Don't be sorry. I think you need to apologize to yourself. You always let your parents twist you up inside."

"Only it's not just them this time," I said softly.

"Maybe. So, think about what you want, and don't let yourself or Dillon get in the way of that." She kissed the top of my head. "I need to meet Mackenzie and Natalie at the coffee shop, but I'll talk to you soon."

"What about Nessa?"

"She and Pacey are out studying." She waggled her brows.

I raised mine. "Really?

"I think it's just studying, but damn she has a crush on that man."

"And you don't?" I teased.

Corinne blushed, something I loved seeing. It was hard to tease her because she had such a thick skin and could tease harder right back.

"I think he's dreamy, but he's more of a friend than anything. I like having friends." My best friend shrugged. "And you're one of them. But I think Dillon could become one, and not just as the guy you're sleeping with. Make a decision so I don't end up getting close and then get hurt. Because it is all about me."

That made me laugh, and my tears dried up. "Okay, I will think about what I want in life so I can make you happy."

"That's all I ask."

Corinne kissed the top of my head and then headed out.

"Make good choices!" she called out, and I shook my head before standing up and putting my book on the table.

The doorbell rang soon after she left, and I frowned, wondering who it could be. I went to the door, looked through the peephole, and steeled myself.

It seemed I would have to figure out what I wanted sooner rather than later.

I opened the door, and Dillon stood there, his backpack slung over one shoulder, and his hands in his pockets. "Hey," he said. "Sorry for not calling ahead. I left the library and was passing your house. Thought I'd say hi."

"Hi," I said softly and stood awkwardly in front of him. After a moment, I took a step back, realizing that I was just letting him stand on the porch. He walked in.

"Hi," he said again before he leaned down and brushed a kiss against my lips.

I nearly cried again and figured I must be hormonal or something. I didn't always cry at the drop of a hat, and I wasn't a fan of doing so right now.

"Studying?" he asked.

"Yes. Or trying. I lost my book."

"Was it under your bed?" he asked dryly.

Something twisted inside. I wondered what it could be. How did he know me so well? Maybe we were spending too much time together. Was I taking him away from his future plans? Between his family, work, and studies, I knew he was having trouble catching up in some respects. Not all of his courses had transferred, and he had to work double-time on some things. Was I standing in his way? Or was I just telling myself that so it wouldn't be so hard when I thought of him standing in *my* way?

Once again that voice in my head sounded like my mother's. Not mine. And I hated it.

"Do you mind if I study with you?" he asked, searching my face. "I can leave if you need space, but I figured since we've both been so busy recently, we haven't seen each other that much."

I winced. "I'm sorry. I have been busy."

"I get it. You're working, we have papers, and it's a little intense. But we haven't talked or seen each other beyond a passing glance since your dinner with your parents. How did it go?"

I knew he would ask that, so I sighed and gestured for him to come into the living room. I already had a few notebooks out since that's where I had been studying when I realized I'd lost my book. "It went fine. I guess."

"What do you mean?"

"They're forceful in what they want me to be. And I get it. They saw me becoming one person and steered me that way, and I'm not exactly doing what they want."

"You're in college, getting a degree, and you have a career plan. I'm not quite sure how that isn't what they want."

"But I don't want to become a heart surgeon, or a family practice doctor, or an oncologist, or anything that my parents set aside for me."

"And while those are all admirable and tough disciplines, they aren't the only things that exist."

"I know that. Yet it doesn't make things easier when it comes to what my parents see for my future."

"You can talk to me..."

There was something in his gaze that I couldn't quite read. And I didn't understand why I was having such trouble with it.

I would like to tell him...everything. And maybe that was the problem. Perhaps I liked him so much that I was ignoring everything else around me. I wasn't ready for a long-term relationship or anything that would lead to marriage and babies and a life I didn't even know I wanted. And it wasn't that I couldn't want that. It was more that I didn't know who I would be next semester, let alone after. And if things got too serious, I didn't care if I got hurt in the process. That'd be my fault.

But I refuse to hurt Dillon. And everything just hurt too much.

Or maybe I was burying myself in my drama and ignoring the fact that we hadn't talked about where we were or how serious my feelings were toward him. I was having that meltdown I had so studiously ignored, and I needed to focus.

"You okay?" Dillon asked again.

I smiled brightly. "I'm just fine."

He tilted his head. Stared at me. "You're lying. I mean, if you're not okay, you can tell me that. If I need to go, you can tell me that. I just wish you would talk to me."

"Dillon..." I began.

He shook his head. "I know we didn't go into this thinking we would be anything but a fun night together, but that changed a while ago, and we both know it." He paused. "Maybe it changed a bit too fast."

My heart raced, and I looked up at him. "What?" I asked, wondering how he could read my thoughts and why it hurt so much.

"I just... I need you to talk to me. I like the sound of your voice. I like listening to you. But you don't talk."

"Maybe I don't want to," I said, defending myself even though I knew this was my fault.

"And why don't you?" he asked, his voice icy.

"Because I don't know what I'm doing. I need to think, okay? I just need to write things down and think about it, and then I'll be okay. But I can't do that if you're here because you always scramble my thoughts, and it's hard for me to focus."

He nodded tightly, his eyes going blank. "Fine. Breathe. I understand. When you're ready, I'll be here. You need to be ready, I guess." And then he turned on his heel and left, surprising me.

I hadn't meant to say what I did because I'd needed to understand what I felt about him first. And honestly, I'd needed to know what he felt about me. And yet, he had left so quickly. He was hurting. Hurting so much more than I had thought possible. And I didn't know why.

But because I was selfish and self-indulgent, I didn't ask. I was so worried about my problems that I didn't even think about his.

He'd left the door open after he walked out, and I wondered why until I looked up and saw Mackenzie in the doorway. "I think I interrupted something," she said, her eyes wide.

"I just...I think I fucked up," I said and promptly burst into tears.

Mackenzie ran in, slamming the door behind her, and held me close as I sank to the floor. "It's nothing you can't fix. We're one step away from being teenagers. We're supposed to be moody. Our brain chemistry is still figuring itself out. It's okay, just breathe. We'll find a way to fix this."

I sniffed and wiped my face. "I don't know. I'm such a jerk. I can't focus, and I know it's not Dillon's fault. It's mine. It's my parents'. But mostly mine. And I'm taking it out on him."

"Because you trust him and know he can take it."

"But that's not fair to him. I screwed up."

Mackenzie reached for the tissues, and I took the box, wiping my face with one as I pulled a few more out. "I'm such an idiot."

"You're right, you are, but we all are sometimes."

"Really?" I asked, laughing.

"Of course. I'm an idiot all the time when it comes to Sanders. And we've known each other since forever. But we talk it out, and we figure things out. Sometimes, it takes a little bit longer than I would like, but we do. You and Dillon just need to talk. And even though they say it's so easy to have open communication and talk to one another, it's not. Finding that balance where you can open yourself up and know that you might be hurt but trust the other person not to hurt you? That is the bravest thing you can do. I know school is hard, and I know that you've been dealing with your parents, and even though I'm not your roommate, and we're new to being friends, I understand. You just need to figure things out, and that's fine. But maybe you should figure things out with Dillon. He's a good guy. If you don't know what you want, if you think it's all too much, then tell him. But make sure that he knows that he's important, too."

"I screwed up," I said, shaking my head.

"Maybe. But he left quite quickly, don't you think?" she asked.

I narrowed my eyes. "How long were you standing outside the door?

"I realized I was supposed to meet the girls at the coffee shop and not here. As I was pulling out my phone, I kind of heard you guys through the open window. I'm sorry."

I glared at the window and let out a breath. "I'm sorry for embarrassing you."

"Oh, you didn't. But I also didn't want to leave in case one of you needed me. I know, I mettle. It's what I do."

"Sometimes we need that. I like you, Mackenzie."

She smiled softly. "I like you, too, Elise. Now, go find Dillon. Figure it out and talk with him. I know people say that all the time like it's easy, and I know it's not, but you can do it. And, Elise? You're allowed to have a life. You don't need to focus on just classes, on only your major. Because you already are, and you're doing it brilliantly. But you need time to decompress. And between Dillon and us, we can make that happen."

I let out a breath and nodded. "I should go see him."

"He's probably on his way to the boys' house now. Go."

She helped me up and wiped my face. "And maybe add a little concealer."

That made me laugh, and I held her close, wondering how I could rely on so many of my friends so quickly. Maybe I was overwhelmed, but it wasn't their fault.

I needed to apologize to Dillon and ask why he'd had such pain in his eyes. I had a feeling it had nothing to do with me.

Chapter 15

Dillon

I FLUNG THE BACK DOOR OPEN AS I STOMPED INTO THE house, my hands shaking. Why was I so fucking angry? Elise was allowed to want her space. It wasn't like I needed to be next to her at all times. But hell, why did I feel like she had punched me in the gut instead of just talking to me?

Pacey stood in the kitchen and frowned as I walked by. "What's wrong, Connolly?"

"I do not understand women." I practically snarled the words and did my best to calm down. I didn't like being on edge, and yet I couldn't seem to pull myself back from it.

Pacey blinked and took a moment to respond. "I was under the impression, at least according to your brothers, that you understood the complexity that is women. You're the one who helped them in their relationships. It's your *thing*."

I was tired of that being thrown in my face. How young and naive I'd been when I thought I could help my brothers with the seemingly obvious. "I was wrong. Or maybe I just understand *their* women. I don't get anyone that I'm supposed to be with. Not that I know I'm supposed to be with Elise because, according to her, that's not the case."

Pacey set down his coffee. "What happened with you two?" He paused. "Wait. When did this occur? I thought you were at the library. Did you stop at her house? Or call her?"

"Why do I feel like you know where all of us are at all times?" I asked, a little concerned.

Pacey waved a hand in the air. "I see all, and I know all. At least that's what I want you to think."

Sadly, not even Pacey's humor could bring me back from the brink of insanity at the moment, so I answered his other question. "I left the library and figured I should stop by since I was close. We haven't talked much, and…fuck it. I just wanted to see her face. But, apparently, that was too much."

"What happened?"

I ran my hands over my hair. "I don't know. One minute I was asking if she wanted to study or sit and talk, and the next, she said everything was too much, and she couldn't deal with it. That she needed to focus on school and anything but me. I don't know what the fuck I did wrong."

"You didn't do anything wrong," Pacey said, sighing. "At least, I don't think you did."

"That's very comforting. Thank you," I said dryly.

"I do my best. Now, do you know what this could be

about? Because we both know Elise isn't the type of person to end things with you in such a way as to hurt you."

That Pacey knew that about her as well as I did, comforted me at the same time it cut because Elise *had* pushed me away. "I don't know. School? Her family? I don't fucking know. Because she's not *talking* to me."

Pacey's gaze didn't leave mine. "And did you tell her about what's going on with you?"

I froze, unnerved. "I haven't had the chance."

"If you would've had the chance today, if she hadn't been going through her own shit and hadn't decided that she needed time or whatever the hell happened, would you be speaking to her right now about it?"

I swallowed hard. "I don't know," I whispered, and the idea that I wasn't sure shamed me.

"It seems that she isn't the only one who needs to talk about her issues. *If* she has issues to begin with."

I scowled. "You're not very helpful."

"I'm immensely helpful. You just don't want to hear what I'm saying. Because it's difficult."

"I hate you sometimes." I set my bag down on the table behind me and sighed. "Not really. Shit. I don't know what I'm doing, Pace."

"Well, as I usually don't know what I'm doing yet am excellent at faking it, come sit next to me and tell me all."

"There's nothing to tell. She needs space, and I'm going to give it to her. It doesn't mean I have to like it."

"And why does she need space?"

"I don't know," I grumbled. "I guess everything's too much? I have no idea. She's not talking to me."

"Okay, she's not doing that, and you asking her isn't

getting it done. Give her the space she requested. The peace she needs. She'll come to you when she's ready."

I shook my head, hope spurting and dwindling at the same time. "Will she?"

"You have to hope so. And while you're waiting, you need to figure out what you want."

"I guess that's easier said than done," I grumbled and leaned my head against the wall. "I wasn't expecting her, Pace."

"No one ever expects the good ones," he mumbled. I frowned at him. "Have you ever been in love?" I asked and winced. "I'm sorry. I didn't mean to say that aloud. I mean, you're welcome to tell me, but I'm not going to force you."

"I should ask the same of you, then," Pacey said, neatly dodging my question. I let him, however. I didn't need to pry.

"No, I haven't. I've dated, as you well know, but I haven't been in love."

"And why do you think that is?"

I snorted. "Are you my psychologist today?"

"If I have to be."

"As I told Elise before, we're twenty years old. Not everyone is going to find their soulmate or fall deeply and passionately in love when they're our age."

"You're right. They aren't. But they could. My parents did."

That was the first real gem of information I had ever gotten from him. For all Pacey liked to speak about being open and communicative, he never told us anything profound about himself, other than the fact that he'd been raised in Europe and had lived in the US for a few years.

"I know this is hard," Pacey began. "But give her a

moment to breathe and think and then talk it out. If neither of you is ready for something serious, be open about it."

Why did the thought of walking away twist something inside of me? We weren't supposed to want more than we had, and yet that wasn't entirely true. Since the beginning, we'd lied to ourselves regarding what we wanted and kept creeping forward. Now, I wasn't sure if I wanted to go back to a time when I wasn't near Elise. When she wasn't part of my daily life and thoughts.

"Hell, I'm not good at this."

"Most people aren't. That's why it takes communication, as I said."

I pinched the bridge of my nose. "And I guess that means I need to tell her about what's going on with Dave."

Pacey nodded. "You do. I thought you would have before this, honestly."

I sighed. "I haven't been able to. Elise hasn't been talking to me. I was going to bring it up with her today, but it didn't exactly work out."

The other man studied my face before giving me a quick nod. "Then tell the girls, or I can tell Nessa."

"You and Nessa?" I asked, raising a brow, intrigued.

"No, we're just friends." His gaze shot off into the distance for a moment, and I had to wonder if what he said was accurate.

Pacey pulled out his phone, checked the doorbell camera, and grinned. "I think it's time for you to answer the door."

I stiffened. "I hope to hell that grin means it's not Dave."

Pacey's face sobered. "I would not be grinning or answering the door if it was him. We'd be calling the cops."

"Is it Elise?" I asked, afraid yet desperate that it was.

"Of course. Now, go get her. The house is empty because I'm heading out. That will give you guys some privacy."

"You're sitting in here, barefoot, drinking coffee. You don't need to leave on my account," I said as I headed towards the front door.

"Oh, don't worry, I can drink my coffee outside. Or anywhere. I just need to find my trainers. Good luck, and don't fuck up."

I rolled my eyes at that but oddly felt better. At least, I hoped so. I didn't know what I felt about Elise, but it was enough that I wanted to know more. I was just afraid that she would get hurt in the bargain. And I didn't know what to do about that.

I opened the door and met her gaze. She looked at me, her lower lip wobbling for a minute. I reached out for her, and she sank into my hold. Her body molded to mine as her arms tightened around my waist. It felt as if she were home, that *I* was home. And I couldn't stop the emotion from pouring out.

"I'm so sorry," we both said at the same time, and I let out a rough chuckle.

"Elise," I whispered.

"No, let me," she mumbled against my chest before pulling away. "I'm having a rough week, and I've been a jerk. I'm sorry for pushing you away. I'm not exactly sure what I'm going to do about anything, but I shouldn't have treated you like I did."

I shook my head and then kissed her brow. "I shouldn't have walked away so quickly."

"We're not good at this, are we?" she asked softly.

I wanted to hold her forever, but I knew we should take a breath and at least get out of the doorway. "Probably not. Come inside. We can talk."

"I thought that was my line," she said.

"Maybe, or perhaps we should both *actually* talk."

I pulled her inside, then closed and locked the door behind her. Once we were safely in the house, I kissed her softly on the mouth. She sank into me, wrapping her arms around my waist once again. I felt as if this was what I'd been waiting for all week. The moment she touched me, I felt fulfilled.

"I'm sorry for leaving. There are a few things I need to talk to you about, and I think they got all tangled up and I looked for an excuse to walk out."

"What is it?" she asked. "What's wrong, Dillon?"

I shook my head. "You first. Because I have a feeling that I'm going to need a drink after I talk about mine."

"We're a pair, aren't we?" She bit her lip, and I wanted to lower my head and lick away the sting. I restrained myself. Barely.

"Maybe," I whispered.

"Can we go to your room?" she asked and blushed. "Not for that," she said, laughing. "Only because I want privacy."

"We can. We have the whole house to ourselves, though. Pacey made sure of that."

"But you have four roommates with keys. And I think Mackenzie has one, too."

"She does, and since she helps with our grocery shopping because Sanders sucks at it, I don't mind."

"And you're okay that I'm not ready for a key yet?" she asked carefully.

I snorted, and she narrowed her eyes. "I'm not laughing at the idea of you with a key. I find it humorous that you and I both keep falling into a trap where we compare ourselves to Sanders and Mackenzie, who have been dating since they were in diapers. We don't need to compare ourselves to them or anyone."

"I guess that means it's a no on the key. And for that, I'm grateful. And no, you're not getting a key to the girls' house."

"That is just fine with me."

As we walked up to my bedroom, I held her hand, remembering the first time we had done this and how nervous yet excited I had been. The nerves that I held this time were far different, and I wondered what would happen once we finished talking to one another.

"Talk to me," I said as I pulled her onto the bed with me. We tumbled into one another, moving to sit against the headboard. She snuggled against me, and I was grateful. We could see each other's faces if we turned a bit, but for now, we could speak while just listening to each other's breathing. And maybe that was good. I didn't know if I could tell her everything if I had to see her face.

"Dinner with my parents went off like I expected. With a bit of a twist."

I stiffened, forcing myself to relax my hold so I wouldn't hurt her. "How?"

"They went on and on about my major and how I wasn't good enough, how I wasn't making the right decisions...and it got progressively worse as the night went on."

"I'm sorry. You didn't need to deal with that."

"No, I didn't. And it got me all twisted up, and then Mom started talking about you."

I blinked and pulled away slightly so I could look at her. "What?"

"I didn't tell her I was dating anyone, mostly because it's none of their business and I didn't want them to overreact when I already had enough to deal with. But Mom could find no other reason for me to be distracted, so she made up this guy I was dating. The fact that you're real wasn't lost on me. She went on and on about how I needed to look out for myself and not let a man lead me or change my ambitions. She was mean about it, and it somehow got twisted up in my head that the reason this semester has been hard and that I'm doing too much or can't keep up is because I'm with you."

I swallowed hard, my stomach twisting. "Oh?" I wasn't sure what I was supposed to say to that, so I leaned back and listened.

She shook her head, tears falling again. "I hate fucking crying," she grumbled, and I leaned down and kissed the tears from her cheeks. "It's fine. You're allowed to cry."

"It's just because I'm angry. At her. At myself. But not at you. I may be overextending myself and trying to do everything, but that's not your fault. We have time with each other and with others, and I hope I'm not taking up all of your spare time either. But you've never pushed me into anything that I didn't want. Yet, somehow, I let my mother make me think differently for a second. Maybe it's because I wanted to because I was scared. I don't know, and that's something I need to figure out. But I didn't need to lash out at you today in the process. Nor did I need to make you feel like anything but who you are—and that's someone I care about. That I enjoy spending time with."

"I see," I said, relaxing and yet tense all at the same time. Mostly because I had no idea what I wanted, and ultimately, I couldn't help but like what I had right here, especially in my arms.

"I don't know what's going to happen in the future, Elise, but I enjoy spending time with you. And I'm not going to stifle your ambitions or stand in the way of what you want. You only need to tell me what you want so I can make sure I'm not stepping on your toes."

"You're wonderful, Dillon. I was all twisted up inside for reasons that had nothing to do with you, and yet your face was the one that ended up getting twisted up in all those thoughts. I'm sorry."

"You've apologized, and there's nothing else to apologize for. Other than on my account."

She frowned. "What do you mean?"

I explained to her about Dave and about what'd happened at the bar. She paled, staring at me. "Are you okay?"

"I am. Well, as okay as I can be when I'm dealing with the dumbass that is my father."

"You don't have to call him that. You can call him by his name or any number of horrible nicknames. You don't have to call him your dad or your father."

I frowned, studying her face. "Why?"

"Because the corners of your eyes tense, and your whole body stiffens whenever you say that. And I can usually tell when you're thinking of him in that fashion. It's hurting you. You don't need to call him by a title he's never earned."

And right then, I knew I was falling in love with Elise. And that was going to be a fucking problem.

"I don't even know what to call him. It's just easier to use that so people understand the twisted connection rather than just using a man's name. I use Dave around my brothers and roommates now. I get it. I just don't know what to do."

"I get that."

"So, there's something that we've all been worried about, and I need you to be safe."

She nodded as I explained to her about how my brothers were worried that my dad might show up anywhere that I had been.

"Do you think he's following you to find out where I am?"

"I honestly don't know. We're not posting pictures on social media, so it's not like he can follow us around. But he could be taking that beat-up truck to follow me to you. I just want you to be aware. Okay?"

"Do you think he could hurt you? Us?" she asked, her voice filled with fear and worry.

"No. I don't know. I don't know him. And that's why we're all worried. My brothers and sisters-in-law are all taking steps to ensure that they're safe, and I just want you guys to make sure you keep the security system on, and your doors locked."

"We always do. We're a group of women living near a college campus."

"Now you have one more thing to worry about," I grumbled. "I'm sorry about that."

She reached up and brushed her fingers along my jaw. "Don't take this on. It's not on you."

"Sure as hell feels like it."

"Between the two of us, we're excellent about putting our parents' worries and damnations into our decisions. And we should stop doing that."

"Easier said than done," I whispered.

"Tell me about it. But if we make a conscious effort, maybe we can pull through this in the end."

I kissed her softly again, but I didn't let it go any further. Instead, I held her close, and we lay there, talking about our weeks and just breathing, living.

She sank into me, and I felt the tension release from her. I wondered what the hell we were going to do when we realized that we were no longer just being casual.

Though perhaps, in the end, there had never been anything casual about us.

As I had thought before, I was falling in love with Elise Hoover. And I had no idea what would come of it.

Or what would happen when she realized what I felt.

Would she run? Or would she stay, possibly frightening us both.

Chapter 16

Elise

"TO FINISHING THE HARDEST EXAM OF THE SEMESTER," Dillon said and clinked his glass to mine. I took a sip and sighed at the sweet taste. We were at the Connolly Brewery and each drinking root beer. It wasn't exactly a fancy date consisting of champagne and chocolate-covered strawberries, but it was what we needed. The two of us sitting in a corner at a place that felt like home to Dillon and was quickly becoming one of my favorite spots. We still each had a couple of months until we hit twenty-one, so there was no drinking the true wares for us yet, but we didn't need alcohol to have a good time. Aiden was in the kitchen, making us a special meal that wasn't on the menu in celebration of us finishing our exams. I was grateful for what was on its way because I was starving, and I knew that anything Aiden made would be extraordinary.

"I think your stomach just growled. Thinking about Aiden's meal?"

"Your brother makes amazing food. I can't help it." I said, blushing.

"Well, thank you," the chef himself said as he walked towards us, plates in hand.

"You're eating what I give you, and you're going to like it," he grumbled to Dillon, though the light in his eyes danced.

"Thanks," Dillon said dryly.

"You're welcome. Behold, your dinner."

He explained each of the meals in such detail that I wondered if he was also a writer in his spare time. My mouth watered with each additional item mentioned, and then my eyes widened as Cameron brought even more.

"How are we supposed to finish all this?" I asked.

"Oh, I'm pretty sure we're going to be sneaking bites when you're not looking," Cameron said, joking.

Brendan showed up with yet another set of plates, and I shook my head. "There's enough here to feed an army."

"The Connollys are their own type of army," Dillon said dryly.

"And you know, your guy here could probably make food nearly as good as I made." He raised a brow at Dillon. "I said *nearly*," Aiden growled out as Dillon's eyes brightened.

"That's nice of you," Dillon said. "I feel all warm inside."

"Well, you're about to feel full. So eat, be merry, and happy exam day."

I shook my head as the brothers walked away and then looked at the smorgasbord in front of us. "I feel like the rat on *Charlotte's Web* when he's singing and dancing among all his food."

"Please do not use that comparison out loud when Aiden's around. He may kick you out of the brewery forever—and me along with you."

I blushed. "Yeah, as soon as I said it, I realized it was wrong, but I couldn't help it. It all looks amazing. I don't know where to start."

"Let's just dig in. My mouth is suddenly watering to the point that I'm going to drool on the table, and if I do, Aiden will kick us out for another reason."

I snorted, and the two of us dug in. The Connollys did indeed stop by the table, taking a small plate away with them. I knew that Aiden probably had more food in the back, but they had wanted to join in. The bearded bartender I had met at one point was also there, coming over with his wife just to say hello.

I knew the other customers probably wondered who we were and why we were afforded such treatment, though most seemed to know who Dillon was and waved and said hello. They congratulated us on passing our exams, and it felt like we were one big family.

Much better than my actual family, who I hadn't talked to since our disastrous dinner. Not that I wanted to, but it would have been nice to text them and let them know that I had passed, and things were looking up.

Only I wasn't sure they would allow that to happen.

By the time we were done, I was beyond full and leaning on Dillon's shoulder, happily sated and sleepy.

"We should get you home," he mumbled. "I know you don't have class in the morning because it's your off day, but there's still more papers to finish. Sadly, the semester must continue on for a little bit longer."

"Don't dampen my mood," I whispered.

"I'm sorry." He kissed the top of my head, and we slid out of the booth. Dillon's brothers had already cleared away everything, but when I reached for my wallet, Aiden was there in a flash, growling.

"If you think you're paying for any of this, I'm going to have to slap my brother for you. I would never hit you, but Dillon's fair game."

My eyes widened, and Dillon rolled his eyes. "Be nice. You're going to make her think that we're a weird family."

"That ship sailed long ago," Aiden added dryly. "Have fun tonight. Don't do anything I wouldn't do. And if you do, do it twice."

I laughed and couldn't help but hug Dillon hard at the blush on his cheeks.

"I swear they're doing their best to embarrass me as much as possible now since they missed out on most of my teenage years."

"At least they're consistent," I said, laughing. "Come on, let's head home."

"Your place or mine?" Dillon asked.

"As my bag is already in your truck, yours."

"I didn't want to assume," Dillon said quickly. "You're okay with spending the night?"

I blushed. "Of course. We've done it before, after all."

"That was sort of an accidental falling asleep thing. This is planned."

"You have a bigger shower than I do. Another reason we're picking your place."

"I see. It's not about me and wanting to spend the night and having way too much fun. It's all about my shower."

"I'm so glad you finally learned the truth. Yes, I'm having an affair with your shower."

"It's the removable head, isn't it?" he asked, his voice low.

I stumbled and fell into him. "Dillon!"

"What? You're the one who started it."

"But I didn't think you'd end it with an orgasm in the shower joke."

Safely in the truck, I knew my cheeks were bright red.

"As I've given you an orgasm in my shower before, I don't see the problem here."

"Oh my God," I mumbled, shaking my head. "You know, I'm getting better about freely talking about sex, but sometimes I can't help but giggle like a schoolgirl."

"It'll only get worse once I start giggling like a school-girl," he said dryly, and I laughed.

"Only two more weeks of exams, and then we're finally free."

"Until the next semester."

"And the next," I said, sighing. "So, what are you doing for the holidays?" I asked as we made our way south from downtown Denver to the university.

"Staying here as usual. I'll be working most of the time, but we're closed on Christmas Eve and Christmas Day. We want to make sure the family and staff have a chance to spend time with their families."

"That's great. I love that some places are open because not everybody has somewhere to go, but since yours is family-owned and operated, it makes sense that you guys want to spend time together."

"Brendan's pretty sure we lose money in the deal, but even he has to agree that sometimes family is more important than profit." He paused as he turned into his driveway. "Just don't let him know I said that aloud."

I laughed and got out of the truck as he turned it off. "I promise I won't say that. However, you know he thinks it, too."

"Of course, he does. But it's a lot more fun to picture him as this money-hungry, egocentric dude."

"I'm sure it is," I said dryly. Dillon picked up my bag, and we made our way inside.

Mackenzie and Sanders were already in the kitchen, Sanders working behind Mackenzie as they cleaned up their meal dishes.

"Hey, you two, how was dinner?" Mackenzie asked.

"Amazing," I said, leaning over to hug my new friend around the shoulders as her hands were filled with soapy water.

"Next time, you're going to have to bring us," Sanders said. "I've heard good things about your brother's food, and I'm a little jealous."

Dillon smiled. "He was saying that he wanted to do another meal tasting for the restaurant. Maybe I'll get him to agree to add my roommates."

He looked over at Mackenzie. "And their girls."

"Thank you," Mackenzie said dryly. "I would hate to miss out on *the* Aiden Connolly's food."

Dillon blinked, and I laughed at the expression on his face. "I wouldn't say *the* Aiden Connolly in front of Aiden, though, Dillon may freak out."

"I'm just saying. We don't need his ego any bigger than it already is."

"What? My parents took me to the restaurant where he was the chef before everything changed, and it was so good. It doesn't live up to what it used to be, though, at least according to my parents. They were back last week and said the food has gone downhill."

I leaned into Dillon as he nodded. "We've heard that, too. And I think Aiden is a little conflicted about it."

I frowned and looked up at him. "Why?"

"Because he didn't leave the restaurant on the best terms because of the way that they treated him. But it was his other home for years. He doesn't want to see it go downhill, but I think he also likes the fact that it's obvious he was so needed."

"That makes sense."

"Anyway, we're headed up for the night. We're completely full and could use the time to just digest," Dillon said, and I knew I blushed.

From the way Mackenzie and Sanders looked at us, they knew what we were about to do.

"Everybody's already in their rooms for the night. Pacey still has an exam in the morning, and I think Tanner and Miles have that huge paper due for their joint class in economics."

"Oh, I have to take that class next semester," I said, shuddering. "Is it going to be hard?"

"From the way Miles and Tanner were both going on, it sounds like the end of the world," Sanders said dryly.

"Yay, something to look forward to."

We said our goodbyes, and I slid my hand into Dillon's as we made our way upstairs.

Feeling like I was at home, even in a place that wasn't mine, was so comforting.

We were still doing our best not to talk about exactly who we were to each other and where we were going in our relationship, but we were also more comfortable with one another. As if we were finding new levels to who we were together, without letting ourselves get too caught up in titles and labels.

Neither of us had mentioned spending the holidays together, but we lived in the same town and would see each other. Still, I would be forced to go to my parents' for Christmas, and I didn't want Dillon subjected to that. And I hadn't been invited to his place, other than casual remarks of them seeing me around.

We weren't ready for that kind of step, and I was fine with that.

I didn't want to think about it too hard, though, or I would stress myself out again and complicate things.

Dillon set my bag on the loveseat in the corner and rolled his shoulders back. "Did you have fun tonight?" he asked, and I smiled.

"I had a great time. And not only because Aiden is one of the best chefs I've ever met. It's a privilege to eat his food."

"As I said, don't tell him that, or he's going to get a big ego."

"I thought you said he already did." Dillon shrugged and came forward, slowly brushing my hair away from my face.

"He does, but I guess he's a Connolly. It's inherent."

"And yet, I don't think you do."

"That's not what my brothers or roommates would say."

"Maybe, but you also seem to have some sense of

240

humility. And you mentioned once that you'd thought about becoming a chef, but I didn't know you were good enough for Aiden to even talk about."

Dillon shrugged and blushed again.

"Well, I don't have anywhere near his talent, but I was learning."

He kept brushing my hair back from my face, slowly leading me towards the bed as he did. I didn't mind. It was what I wanted. And this felt normal, like coming home.

I was happy.

For the first time in a long time, I felt happy.

"If you ever want to cook for me, I'd love to taste-test."

"Anything you want, Elise. Anything."

And then he kissed me.

I returned the kiss, slowly running my hands up and down his back.

When he gently placed me on the bed, lifting my legs so I didn't have to make an effort to get onto the mattress, I sank into him, wanting more. He tasted of dinner and all Dillon. I loved his flavor, and I knew if I weren't careful, I could love everything about him.

So, I didn't think about that. I just let myself live in the moment.

That was something I needed to remind myself over and over again. That I needed to live in the moment.

We slowly kissed each other, letting our hands do the talking.

And when I sank into him more, *needing* more, he slowly stripped me out of my clothes, and I did the same to him.

He licked my breasts, paying particular attention to the nipples, and when he knelt between my thighs, lapping at my clit and spreading me for his gaze, I blushed but pressed myself against him, needing more. He sucked and he blew cool air on me, and when he latched on, eating me out until I nearly bucked off the bed, I came, clenching my thighs around his face. Blushing, I let my knees fall to the sides, and then he was over me, sliding a condom over his rigid length before moving between my legs again. I brought my legs around his waist, tugging him closer. When he slid into me, I groaned, stretching. This felt like something we had been doing for eons. It felt like peace, perfection. But I pushed those thoughts from my mind once again and just lived in the moment. He kissed me, paid special attention to my neck, my breasts, and then he began to move. We met thrust for thrust, both of us arching. And when he rolled onto his back, and I lifted my hips to ride him, he played with my breasts, and I slid my hands over his, tangling my fingers with his as he cupped me. I met his gaze, his eyes dark. The look I saw there—one of so much emotion, the kind that neither of us would dare speak of—was too much. I came, my body shaking with the orgasm as I fell into the abyss.

It was perfection. It was everything.

And it was utterly overwhelming.

He came with me, shouting my name as I screamed again, slamming into me one last time. I fell onto him, and he collapsed, both of us sweat-slick and holding each other. I could barely breathe, could hardly keep up, but I didn't care. All that mattered was Dillon and me. And this, just for the night.

He kissed me, and we cleaned ourselves up before we crawled back into bed, both of us still naked and pressed against one another. I fell asleep with my head on his shoulder and his body wrapped around mine. And I felt like I was home.

THE NEXT MORNING came far too quickly, but I still had an afternoon class, and Dillon had a mid-morning one. We showered together, and I got my morning shower orgasm. Laughing, we got ready for the day. Once we were decent, we stumbled downstairs, him carrying my bag, and me wishing I had coffee in my veins.

Everybody in the house was already up, and they looked at us as we came into the kitchen. I knew I was blushing from head to toe. From the looks on their faces, they were well aware of what we had done.

Miles cleared his throat. "Hey, guys," he said.

I looked between all of them and ducked my head. "Hi," I said.

I could feel Dillon scowling. "What's up?"

"Oh, nothing. We just..." Mackenzie began and then blushed, hiding behind Sanders.

Sanders rolled his eyes. "We just realized how thin our walls actually are when we're not playing music."

He said it quickly, and everyone scowled at him.

In sheer mortification, I swallowed hard, blinking.

"Oh my God."

"Sanders," Dillon growled.

"What?"

"We don't talk about it," Mackenzie snapped, standing up for us. "I'm sure they can hear us, too."

"Oh, we can," Tanner mumbled.

This time, Mackenzie blushed. "See? We just pretend it

isn't happening because all of us will have to deal with it at one point. Sorry."

I shook my head, knowing that I shouldn't be embarrassed. I might be bright red at the moment, but I still raised my chin.

"You know what, if I'm old enough to have sex, I'm old enough to deal with the fact that others might be able to hear me enjoying it. Sorry."

"No worries, sounded like you had fun," Sanders said and ducked Tanner's fist though he wasn't fast enough to avoid Mackenzie's elbow.

I cringed but mumbled my thanks as Pacey handed Dillon and me two travel mugs.

"Here's your coffee. We've got you. And we won't discuss this again," Pacey said softly.

"Thank you," I whispered.

"We might be discussing this again," Dillon grumbled to Sanders but led me out the back door anyway.

"Sorry about that," Dillon said.

I shook my head and got into the truck with him. "I should have realized, but I didn't factor in how loud I would be. Louder than usual."

This time, Dillon's smug look made me roll my eyes. "Glad I could make you forget."

"Jerk," I mumbled.

"You're a jerk," he said, and I leaned back into the seat and smiled.

"Yes, my jerk."

I was happy. I was trying to find my balance. Maybe I was floundering in some ways, but I was making it work.

I had my friends, I had Dillon, his friends, and maybe I'd be able to work things out with my family. I had to hope so. We just needed some time to breathe, and we'd make it work.

Things were finally starting to work for me, and I would let them.

"Let me walk you in," Dillon said.

"Dillon, I'm fine."

"But I want to kiss you on your doorstep. Let me."

I blushed. "Okay, I'll let you."

I smiled again and then opened the front door, only to have the world shatter around me.

"Corinne?" I asked. There was no response.

My best friend lay on the floor, her white pajama top strewn about her as the cup next to her lay shattered, coffee spilled around her.

Her eyes were open, vacant, and I screamed.

Chapter 17

Dillon

I USUALLY HAD WORDS FOR ANY OCCASION. I WAS THE GUY others could lean on if things were heavy or too much. I'd learned to be that way when I moved to Denver and my family had gone through hell. I'd thought I could handle anything. Watching Elise break down, albeit silently, told me I'd been wrong.

So wrong.

I barely remembered my mother's funeral—not that we'd had one for her. It had only been Cameron and me, as none of her so-called friends had shown. We hadn't had a graveside service, just a small moment in time when we gathered around the coroner and identified the body. I wasn't sure if that counted as a funeral or just a goodbye that never made sense. But it was what we had done.

And now I was here at a time of true mourning, a funeral with shattered hopes and dreams and one that was breaking my family and friends.

When we had walked into the girls' house, everything had changed. Elise had started screaming, and then it finally hit me what we were seeing.

Corinne had only been twenty years old. Healthy, vivacious, and full of life.

And a brain aneurysm that nobody had noticed had taken her life. A brain aneurysm that doctors might not have even been able to see even if they had run scans out of the blue for no reason whatsoever.

Corinne Prince was dead. At twenty years old. And I still couldn't quite believe it.

I knew Elise didn't believe it at all. She wasn't allowing herself to grieve or even think about what had happened.

I wasn't sure if she could.

As soon as we had seen Corinne, I had tossed my phone to Elise and told her to call 911. Corinne had been home alone, as the rest of the girls had already been out at their classes. No one had been there with her when she died.

I had taken CPR training and had tried to see if there was anything I could do, but she'd had no pulse, no breath escaping her lungs.

But I still tried. If I hadn't, I wasn't sure that Elise could have forgiven me. It'd been futile, though. Confirmed when the paramedics said that there was nothing they or anyone could do.

And then they had taken her away. Pronounced her DOA.

Dead on arrival.

She was gone, and it was the most heartbreaking thing I'd ever witnessed. I would never forget the sound of Elise's scream.

Everything moved at a different pace after. As if waiting for death passed in a blink of an eye when it was proven that life could be shattered in those precious moments. But the paperwork and notifications and process of death took its sweet time.

I wasn't sure if everybody agreed with me on that, nor should they. After all, nobody had signed up for this, yet here we were, at the funeral of a young girl I was getting to know. One that Elise had loved and had had in her life since they were five years old.

Corinne's parents stood off to the side, watching the workers lower their baby girl into the ground. I stood with Elise, the rest of my roommates and hers around us as we wondered what we were supposed to do now. You weren't supposed to die when you were our age. You were supposed to have a life and a future and wonder what choices to make for your next path. You weren't supposed to watch someone your age die. You weren't supposed to get there too late to stop it.

But we had. The doctors had all explained that there was nothing we could have done, even if we had been at Corinne's side. According to the authorities and those in the know, she had died quickly and without pain. I wasn't sure if they had said that to alleviate her parents' fears or if it was the truth. My sisters-in-law had all explained that what the doctors had said was true. It had been swift and sudden. She might've felt a slight headache before everything changed. But then again, we weren't sure what to believe. Not when the girl I loved was in so much pain.

And it wasn't like I could tell her what I felt or what I wished I could do to make her feel better. This wasn't the time, and I was honestly afraid there wouldn't be a good time. But this wasn't about me. It wasn't about any of my friends. It was about a friend we had both lost, and the girl I loved, watching her best friend be laid to rest.

"How does something like this happen?" Miles asked from behind me. It wasn't the first time he had said something like that. The others were all in their Sunday best, saying goodbye to a girl they might not have known well but had known enough. Pacey was dressed in all black. Even his shirt and tie were dark. He wasn't speaking to anyone, wasn't saying anything. He just stood there looking lost while Nessa leaned into him, tears pouring down her face. I had known that Corinne and Pacey were close, but I never knew what the relationship was. It wasn't that of a boyfriend and girlfriend, Corinne had explained that to us. But it had been something. And now, the girl was gone, and there was nothing we could do. My family and all their significant others stood behind me, even though they had only met Corinne once when she came to the bar.

But they were there for me, Elise, and for the girl who had died far too young. Because that's who my family was. They were good people who cared about those in their care, even if we were all too late to do anything about it.

Natalie stood between Tanner and Miles, tears sliding down her face as both men tried to console her. Mackenzie and Sanders were off to the side. Mackenzie wasn't crying at all, but her eyes were wide, her face pale. I hadn't heard her utter a word, not even when Sanders asked her how she was doing. She was just as lost as the rest of us, and nobody knew how to deal with grief. We had dealt with our fair share of heartache, at least in my family, and I knew sorrow must've touched everybody here, at least in some respects. Nobody lived in this day and age without understanding at least some semblance of it. But this was different. This made no sense. There were no answers, and damn it, it wasn't fair. But as my brothers had said before when they lost their friend when I first moved to town, life wasn't fair, and it ended far too soon for too many of us.

Elise wasn't speaking at all, and she sure as hell wasn't talking to me. I didn't know what to do about that. She wasn't doing anything. We stood there, watching the proceedings take place. Her parents had come for the start of the funeral but had left soon after. They hadn't even spoken to her. I had only known who they were because Corinne's parents had mentioned their names.

What were you supposed to do with something like that? With people who didn't even acknowledge their daughter but still had time to say goodbye to her childhood friend? Maybe they had done it because they knew the drama of seeing her would be too much for a funeral. If that was the case, I understood that. They'd still come to pay their respects but hadn't wanted to intrude. I really wanted to think that was the case.

When the final words were spoken, and Elise leaned into me for a second before stiffening, I squeezed her hand. She let me go almost immediately and walked away towards Corinne's parents. I stood there, not knowing if I should follow her or not. Pacey didn't move. Neither did Miles or Natalie. Nessa still leaned on Pacey; Mackenzie, and Sanders did the same with each other. But it was Tanner who moved forward and reached out to squeeze my shoulder.

"Come on. We have to settle dirt on top of the casket, or the rose in your hand, and then we'll head to Corinne's family home for the wake."

He said it, and we all nodded like we understood.

"Thank you," I whispered. "I don't know what I'm doing."

"We've got you," Violet said from behind me, and I sighed as my sister-in-law spoke. They had all been through this before when they lost their best friend. It had been heartbreaking for them, and I hadn't even known the woman they'd buried. But they had gone through it, too, and yet somehow found a way to heal.

Maybe we would be able to do the same.

I didn't know what I was supposed to do for Elise.

"Come on, she's going to need you, even if she doesn't say so," Violet said, and then we moved. I laid the rose on top of the casket while others gently tossed in dirt and muttered blessings and memories. I had never done this before. I didn't know what I was supposed to do, but I followed along and copied what others did. I looked at Elise, but she looked right through me as she stood by Corinne's parents. Corinne's mother held Elise's hand in a tight grip, and I knew that Elise needed space to help her friends' parents. I would be there when she was ready.

I would do what I could to make things better. I just didn't know what she'd *let* me do.

I sat in the back of Cameron's SUV as he drove most of my roommates and me towards the place where the wake was being held. My brothers had come to carpool for us so we didn't have to drive. They seemed to know that we were all a little lost and not sure what to do. I would be forever grateful that I had them. Miles' parents had shown up for the funeral, as well, for a girl they hadn't known. Still, they had wanted to be there to support their son. There were so many connections, so many people trying to help their kids who might not be minors in the eyes of the law any longer. We'd always be children to them, though. All of us were a little lost, and I didn't know how we'd ever be found again.

"She's going to need you," Violet said from the front seat. Her hand rested on the baby bump that got larger by the day. "She may push you away, may act as if she needs space and can't focus, that you're too much. But she'll need you."

I swallowed hard. "I'll do what I can, but I don't want to push her. I already almost pushed too much before, and it ended with our first fight. I don't want to do it again."

"You'll find a way. Just do what she needs, make sure she's hydrated and fed, even if she doesn't want to eat."

"How are they supposed to go back to that house?" Miles asked, his voice low.

"We'll see what happens when they're ready. Until then, we'll let the girls sleep at ours," Pacey said, and I was grateful that Nessa and the girls weren't in the car with us. They were going with Corinne's family, leaving mine to help us get to the next phase of saying goodbye. "We'll make room for them," Pacey added, and Tanner cleared his throat. "Yeah, we will. I don't know what they're going to do after...well, after. But we'll find a way to make it work."

"You guys are good people," Violet said as she turned to us, her eyes full of tears. "I'm so sorry, but you'll be there for each other. You have each other. Never forget that."

I nodded, and we each got out of the car, making our way inside. People were somber. A light so young shouldn't be extinguished like this, with no one to blame but God himself. At least that's what someone had muttered under their breath when we walked in. Really, there was no one to blame. It hadn't been a prolonged illness that we could come to terms with. It hadn't been an accident where we could blame a stop sign or a drunk driver. It had been a moment in time, something that had taken her so quickly that nobody even had time to breathe.

I tried to find Elise, but I couldn't. I didn't know where she was or what I was supposed to do. But I would give her the space she needed. I wouldn't forget that she might need the space, but she needed someone, as well.

Finding that balance nearly broke me, but I had no idea what to do. I barely knew Corinne, but I had liked her. She had been the one to dare Elise, to set us on this path, and now she was gone. I couldn't change that. I couldn't bring her back.

"What are we supposed to say?" Miles asked softly.

"Nothing," Pacey said, his voice low. "There's nothing you can say. But from the way it looks, people will soon want to tell stories and remember her. So you'll tell a happy story about the girl who's no longer here."

He cleared his throat. "And you'll make sure that people remember her happy and alive, not only the feelings they have now. You have to do everything you can to make sure others remember her."

I looked at the other man, trying to understand what I had missed. Maybe I hadn't missed anything. Perhaps they had just been friends, and this was how Pacey dealt with things. I wasn't sure, but I wished there was something more I could do. All of my friends were in so much pain, and there was nothing I could do about it.

I let out a breath, and we moved around the room. My

family was wonderful, and Aiden had brought food. It was what we did, we found a hole for what was needed, and we filled it.

Corinne's parents were in the corner, speaking with Aiden as I walked up.

"Dillon," Corinne's mother said softly. "Thank you again for offering your brother's services," she said, her eyes shiny but her tears not falling yet. "We truly appreciate it. We had some of it covered but having Corinne's friends take care of the details has been wonderful. I wish we had been able to get to know you before this," she said, holding out her hand.

I swallowed hard and nodded. "Corinne was great. She was nice and made me laugh and introduced me to Elise. I'm just so sorry."

This time, her mother let her tears fall, and her father squeezed her around the shoulders.

"She was always doing that, setting people up so they got with the people they needed to. We love Elise like our own daughter." There was something there, but I knew I wasn't going to get into it now. "We love her. So, you be there for her. This will be just as hard on her as it is for us. She's so good about closing people off. So, make sure she doesn't do that."

Corinne's parents knew Elise pretty damn well for them to say that. And the fact that they were worried about their daughter's best friend when they were so mired in their own emotions meant the world to me. I nodded, said my condolences once more, and walked away to look for Elise. I saw people I knew from campus and others I didn't that must have been from Corinne's life before she moved here. I wasn't sure what I was supposed to do, but in the end, I found Elise at the back of the house, sitting on the back porch all alone, holding a glass of water and staring out into the distance. I knew she needed space, that it was likely why she had come out here, but now that I was here, I didn't know what to do with my hands. I sat next to her without saying anything and let out a breath.

She didn't lean into me, didn't move towards me, just sat there, blinking.

"I'm so sorry," I whispered after ten minutes of silence where nobody came out to talk to us.

Elise still didn't say anything.

"Can I get you something to eat? Anything? What do you need, Elise? I'm here for you."

Still no words.

"Do you need me to go? Do you need some space?"

I quit speaking, letting her mourn in a way that I didn't fully understand. I was not a part of this for her, and I knew I didn't have to be. These were her emotions, but I needed her to know that I would be here for her when she was ready.

She turned towards me, her eyes hollow. "I think I need some space."

I nodded, my chest aching. "I'll make sure someone knows you're out here, but I'll leave, let you breathe."

She shook her head. "No, just...the semester's over, and I just... I don't know what to do. I already told you that this was a lot, and I didn't think I could do it. And now with Corinne..." Her voice broke, and I knew she couldn't finish the statement. "I need you to go. I need to be alone."

I felt a pain in my heart, and it was as if a cavern had erupted within my soul, breaking me into a thousand pieces. But I didn't say anything about my feelings. I swallowed hard and nodded. "You don't need to do this alone. So many people care about you, Elise. We'll be here for you."

She looked at me and then blinked, not a single tear falling from her eyes. "Where was I when Corinne was in pain? When she was dying? I wasn't there. My best friend in the world, and I wasn't there. I need you to go. I need to think. And I can't do that when you're around. I can't do anything."

"It wasn't your fault," I said softly, trying to hold on. But I wasn't sure there was anything I could hold onto.

"Maybe. But I wasn't there. My best friend died alone with broken shards of porcelain around her, and coffee splashed into her hair and across her face. She died, and I wasn't there. So, yes, I need you to go. I need to just *be*. Because I can't *be* with you around. I'm sorry."

And then she turned away but still didn't cry.

My mouth went dry, and I swallowed hard one more time, trying to breathe. I knew she was doing this because she was scared, and me pushing her right now would be the worst possible thing.

Instead, I stood on shaky legs and turned to see Nessa and Natalie and Mackenzie standing there. They had all linked hands and gave me pitying looks. But I knew they were just as upset. So, I nodded tightly and knew that they would comfort Elise where I couldn't. I was too much for her right now, and I understood that.

But I would be there when she was able to think clearly again. And I wouldn't be pushed away so easily. Still, for now, I would let her be. And I wouldn't make a scene.

I walked away from the girl I loved into a house full of

mourning and pain and knew that nothing I did would change things or make them better.

This was the beginning of the end. And I had to do the one thing I hated.

I had to walk away from the girl I loved.

And hope to hell she would let me walk back in again.

Chapter 18

Elise

"ELISE, DARLING, YOU NEED TO EAT."

I looked at my mother and shook my head. "I had an omelet this morning. I'm not hungry for lunch." I hadn't been hungry for breakfast either, but I had forced it down, mostly because I knew my mom wouldn't stop hounding me. Something twisted deep inside. The fact that my mom cared enough to be here for me, that she was alive in order to do it at all, broke something within me, and I didn't know what to think. Everything hurt. How could Corinne be gone?

It didn't make any sense. My best friend should be walking through that door at any moment, telling me it was all a joke that had gone too far. I would hate her forever for it, but I would still love her until the end of time. How could she be gone? My best friend since we were five years old, could not be gone.

"I know you did, honey, but will you please eat lunch with us? We're so worried about you, and we don't know what else to do."

I looked at my mother and sucked in a breath. Tears ran down her cheeks, and I didn't understand. My mother *never* cried. She got emotional, yes, but she always held herself in check. I remembered my grandmother once saying that she had done it as a child and hadn't stopped. And I had never been comfortable enough to ask her why. But here she was, crying in front of me. My dad stood in the doorway in his sweater, the one he wore when he was stressed out with work. There were holes in the sleeves, and it was coming undone at the ends. My mother had knitted it for him when she was pregnant with me because she had promised herself that she would learn how to knit. She had made me booties and other cute things that I had worn for as long as I could fit into them. She had knitted a blanket that I still had somewhere. And she had knitted Dad that sweater. She hadn't made anything else after that. I hadn't been sure if she'd quit because she hadn't wanted to fit into a certain box when it came to being a doctor's wife in their circles, or if she'd chosen to quit on her own.

I had never asked.

Because I was so busy trying to find out who *I* was, and I hadn't taken a step back to realize that I didn't know who my parents were as adults either.

Maybe I wasn't supposed to know those things. Perhaps children never did. But Corinne's parents would never be able to see how their daughter grew up. And Corinne wouldn't be able to question why her parents had made the choices they had—both good and bad.

I hated that.

I swallowed hard, tears falling freely now. My mother sat next to me on the couch, looking through the window at the trees.

"I'm not hungry, but I'll eat dinner. I promise. I'll take care of myself. But I don't think I can stomach anything right now."

My mother nodded and squeezed my hand. I squeezed back, afraid of what I'd do if she let go.

"We don't know what to do for you, honey. We want to help, but we don't know what to do."

My dad cleared his throat and moved to stand next to the edge of the bay window so he was in our line of vision but not too close. There wasn't room for him on the couch, but he was still there. My throat tightened, and I held back more tears.

"We want to talk to you about what happened," my dad said, and I stiffened. "If you can't talk to us, talk to your friends. To Dillon. Anyone."

"Dillon and I are over," I said, wondering why that was the first thing that came out of my mouth.

My dad's mouth tightened into a thin line, and he nodded. "I'm sorry to hear that. We only know his name because of your roommate. Nessa mentioned him in passing. I didn't mean to pry, even though that's what we do so often. I'm sorry."

I didn't understand these people in front of me. They weren't acting like my parents at all. But then again, I wasn't acting like myself. And yet I couldn't find the energy to act like anyone other than who I was in that moment.

Corinne wasn't here. If she was, everything would make more sense. I would be able to breathe again. Things would go back to normal. I'd be able to stress out over my major and what my parents thought I needed to do with my accomplishments. I'd be able to freak out over a boy and wonder if I loved him or not. But instead, I was sitting with my parents, wearing black and wondering why my best friend had to die.

She was only twenty years old. You weren't supposed to die when you were twenty. You were supposed to live forever. She hadn't even had her first legal drink. She'd never had sex. My best friend had died a virgin. She'd never been in love and had died alone. I hadn't been there.

"Please, talk to us," my mother whispered. "Please, Elise. We don't know what to do."

"I don't know what to do either. She's gone, mom. Corinne is gone."

My mother swallowed hard and squeezed my hand again. "We know, honey. I'm so sorry. She was such a sweet girl."

I gasped. "You hated her."

My mother sat back, her eyes wide, the look on her face one of shock. "No, we didn't."

"You always said that I needed to make new friends. That she wasn't making the right choices."

My mother shook her head. "No, the two of you were joined at the hip for so long that you pushed others away when you were younger. And maybe we were meddling, but we loved Corinne. We may not have understood her because she was so vivacious and loud in her choices. But that was because, well...your dad and I are shy."

I snorted. "What?

Dad sighed. "We're not shy with you, but with others? It's taken a while to make the people you see today. We were raised not to speak out, not to do anything but stay in our lane and not make waves. We made waves in our careers, but not in anything else. You were always brighter than the sun when you were with Corinne, and she was your focal point, the star in the sky that shone against everyone. We may not have known Corinne as well as we should have, and that's on us, but I will forever be glad that she was in your life."

I swallowed hard, not understanding. "What are you guys talking about?"

My mother sighed. "It took so long to get pregnant with you," my mother said.

I frowned. "What?

"It took us so long. So many treatments. We lost three babies before you. You were our rainbow baby, as they call it. And yet the three before you? We didn't get to name them. We didn't get to hold them in our hands and in our arms and say goodbye. You were it for us. And somehow along the way, we wanted to make sure that you had everything, and we twisted that. And now, Corinne's parents will never be able to watch their child grow up. Never watch her fall in love or get married or find her happiness. Their memories of their daughter will be frozen in time only to fade away if they're not careful. But I know them, darling. They will keep her memory bright, but I don't know how they'll move on. We never moved on after losing our first three children, and I would break if I lost you," my mother said, her voice shaking.

"And I'd be broken right alongside her," my dad added. This time, the tears flowed freely down my face.

I choked, my body shaking. "All of this was because you love me?"

"Yes. And we were wrong. We're not going to push you like we have been. We're going to do whatever we can to make up for the choices we made when it came to you. We will always trust the choices you make, even if we question them because…we do have some experience with some things."

"I don't understand," I said again. "You guys were so mean."

"And we were idiots," my mom said, throwing up her hands. "Stupid idiots who thought we knew best. Maybe we do in some things, but not everything. I'll listen now. I promise I will. But don't push me away. Don't push us away. Let us be part of your life. Corinne's parents will never get to hold their daughter again, and I don't know what I would do if I never got to hold you. If you walked away forever and we didn't have you in our lives. I'm sorry that we lost so much time. That we were such horrible people. But I love you, Elise."

"I love you, too. So fucking much," my dad said, and I blinked at the vulgarity. Dad never cursed in front of me. I hadn't been sure he knew how.

"Maybe we should get to know you as an adult, rather than the little girl in our heads."

I looked at my mother, so confused, and it felt like my heart kept breaking over and over again. Shattered into a thousand pieces where I knew it could never be glued together with any type of emotion or connection.

"I just want you to be happy, and I don't know how we can make that happen. But we'll always be here. Even if we make mistakes again, we'll atone for them. We'll do something."

I shook my head. "I don't know if I can think about any of that right now. But I don't want you to atone for anything. Corinne doesn't have any more time, and I don't want to lose time wondering what if and what we lost. I just want things to go back to normal. Or a new normal where you guys are proud of me, and Corinne is still here, making me laugh and giving me dares and telling me truths."

"Dares and truths?" my mom asked.

I shook my head. "It's a long story."

Mom squeezed my hand, and Dad came closer.

He cleared his throat. "I'd love to hear it, if you think we have time."

I looked at my parents. I knew that Corinne was never coming back. As much as I wanted her to be here, she *couldn't* come back. Rationally, I knew that I couldn't have saved her, that no matter how fast I was, I would never be fast enough to stop an aneurysm.

But I couldn't get over it in a blink. I didn't know if that would ever happen.

Somehow, I would have to find a way to breathe again.

I just didn't know how to do that.

And so I sat between my parents, and I told them about the dares and the jokes.

We ate lunch, even though I didn't think I'd be able to, and I cried hard, and they held me close. When we got to Corinne's final dare, I skated over the truth, but the knowing look in my mother's eyes said that I hadn't done it well enough.

"So I take it this dare was Dillon?" Mom asked.

"Are you going to tell us what happened with you and

that boy?" my dad asked, sounding very fatherly and not so judge-y.

"It didn't work out," I said, shrugging. Nothing about what I felt for Dillon or the thoughts filtering through my mind were casual, but I wasn't sure I could voice them. Not even to myself.

"When did you break up with him?" my mother asked.

"Why do you think I'm the one who broke up with him?" I was deflecting, and we all knew it.

"When?" Mom asked softly.

"At the wake, because I'm a horrible person."

My mother shook her head. "We all make terrible decisions in grief. We make big ones, small ones, and a lot of them are terrible. Were you thinking about breaking up with him for a while?"

I shook my head. "Honestly, the only time I thought about it at all before was after our conversation here."

My mother had the grace to blush, and my dad sighed.

"We're not used to this whole adult you. And that's on us."

"I'm not used to this whole adult me either. But I don't think I can fix what I broke. I was mean. I said I couldn't take it anymore, that it was all too much. I told him to go."

My mother shook her head. "It's been three days. Has he texted? Because to me, that says you need space, not that it's over."

I pressed my lips together and nodded. "He's texted. Every day, just to check in on me and tell me that I don't need to respond. But he also said he wanted to hear my voice because he likes the sound of it."

My mom's eyes filled with warmth, even as my dad gave

me a skeptical look. "Either that boy is in love with you, or he's using the best lines."

That made me laugh, and I honestly didn't think I'd ever be able to laugh again. "Dad."

My dad shrugged. "What? I was a twenty-something-year-old-boy before. He is twenty-something, right? And not some forty-year-old going back to school?"

I snorted. "He's a month older than me."

"Good. We're going to want to meet him."

My heart twisted again. "But we're not together, Dad."

Mom leaned forward. "I don't know if that's quite true. I think you should talk to him."

"Do you think this is a time for me to make big decisions?" I asked my mother, tossing her words back in her face.

She put a finger in the air, marking it as a little invisible point. "Or you're just fixing the decision that you made before. Your teachers have given you the rest of the semester off so you don't have to worry about school, but you already finished your coursework, so that's no problem. You have time before the winter break. Before he goes home."

"He lives in that house, Mom. His family is from Denver. They own the brewery, remember?"

My mom nodded. "I was just making sure that he was still going to be here for the break. Because I want to meet him."

"Mom," I said, laughing again, surprising myself. I was still crying off and on, but this was a conversation I had always wanted to have. Maybe not about Dillon per se, but feeling so open.

I only hated that it had taken losing my best friend for

us to do this. Maybe we would have been able to do this without that, but I wasn't sure. I could still hate the process that had brought us to the outcome.

"You should go see him."

"Right now?" my dad asked. "Shouldn't we run a background check first?"

I narrowed my eyes. "You wouldn't."

"I know people."

"Are you in the mob now?" I asked.

"As I said, I know people." He snorted and shook his head. "Do you know if he's at home?

I looked down at my phone, checked the time. "He should be. If not, I don't know. But you're right. I need to fix this, figure out what I want."

"You can always text him."

I shook my head at my mom's words. "As I said, he likes the sound of my voice, so he deserves to hear it when I grovel and apologize for being so mean to him at the wake."

"If he's any sort of man, he's not going to blame you for hurting at your best friend's funeral," my dad growled.

"Just because I was hurting doesn't mean I'm allowed to hurt others."

"Maybe," my mother added. "But perhaps you two should just talk." She looked over at Dad. "Look at us, honey, we're being so adult about this whole thing. Our daughter's dating. In a serious relationship, it sounds like. We're growing."

"Growth has its advantages."

I didn't know if this bubble of peace in tragedy would stick, but I leaned into it. The relief that slid through me at the fact that I felt like I could come to my parents again was worth its weight in gold.

I missed Corinne so damn much.

I sat with my family for another hour as we talked about nothing because we could. Because Corinne didn't have that option.

Suddenly, I found myself in my car, headed towards the guys' house.

I missed them all so much. They'd all come to the funeral—even their families. They were there for us, and I knew from Nessa that the girls were staying at the house on college row. Mostly because we weren't sure if we could go back to living in the home where we had lost someone we loved. Nessa and Natalie had mentioned something about our landlord, and I felt like if we ended up roommates again, we would likely be living elsewhere. I wasn't sure I'd be able to stay in the place we had lived with Corinne. Maybe not wanting to be there made me a horrible person. I would never be able to walk into that living room again without seeing Corinne there, death in her eyes and a small ghost of a smile on her face. The last one she'd ever have.

I sniffed, annoyed with myself for crying. I was here to see Dillon and apologize. I didn't need to be a puffy mess. I pulled into the back of the home since street parking was hard to come by, then rolled my shoulders back.

I didn't see his truck, but he could still be here. Sometimes, he parked on the street when they were saving a spot thanks to the snow.

I slid out of the car and zipped up my coat as a cold breeze hit. I knew a storm was coming. If I weren't careful, I'd be snowed in here.

That might be comforting, but it could also be another achingly horrible thing to add to the day.

I took a few steps, heard a crunch behind me, and turned.

I saw a shadow, and then something hit me upside the head.

I fell.

And then there was nothing.

Chapter 19

Dillon

"All done, then?"

I looked up as Pacey walked towards me, his bag slung over his shoulder.

"Yeah. The semester's over. Let the holiday season commence."

I knew I sounded exhausted, and not just from school, but Pacey didn't say anything about it.

"You mind giving me a ride back?"

I frowned. "You didn't drive yourself here?" I asked, looking around the parking lot on campus as if expecting to see his car amongst the dozen or so there.

"I rode in with Miles. I didn't feel like remembering what side of the road I should be on."

I snorted. "Yes, because after so many years of driving in America, you're suddenly going to drive on the wrong side of the road."

"Excuse me. You treasonists are driving on the wrong side of the road."

"You're half treasonist if you're going by that logic."

"Fine," Pacey grumbled, his lips crooking into a smile. "I suppose you have me there."

I smiled, feeling lighter than I had in days, though I knew it wouldn't last long. "Of course, I do. And come on, my truck's over here."

"Are you ever going to buy a new one?" Pacey asked, looking at my older-model truck that had probably seen better days. It reminded me of Dave's pickup for some reason, and I held back a shudder. That guy's vehicle had been older, hadn't been taken care of, and was full of rust. Mine was just older. Not antique or classic, but one that had a lot of miles on it and would probably need to be put to pasture soon if I didn't overhaul the engine.

"Maybe, but I'm going to have to wait on a few more tables before I get there. She's doing me all right for now." I tapped on the hood and looked up at the dark sky. "That storm's coming in a bit early."

"That's what my app said," Pacey said as we both piled into the truck. "It's going to be a fun one tonight. We may be able to use the fireplace."

"Do you know how to use a fireplace, or are you going to end up smoking us out?"

Pacey just raised a brow. "Of course, I know how. Why don't you?"

"Because I've never had a fireplace before."

"Really? That surprises me since we live in Colorado."

"Didn't need them much out in California. At least, where I was in California. And none of my brothers have one in their homes. I think Brendan wants one, and they'll probably end up getting one in the next house they buy, but as of now, I don't know how."

"Well then, we'll have to teach you. Look at you, growing up."

"Jerk," I said.

Pacey smiled. "I try."

"How did your exams go?"

Pacey shrugged as I turned down the street. "Fine, as always. It's amazing what happens when you take the time to study. Sometimes, you know the material."

"Only sometimes?"

"Well, other times things don't work out the way you want. However, this semester I seem to have gotten lucky."

He was quiet for a moment, and I kept my eyes on the road, the snow coming down a little bit harder now.

"I hope the rest of the guys can get home through this. I don't like the look of this stuff on the roads."

"Spoken like someone who didn't learn how to drive in the snow."

"I didn't. I didn't feel like I ever needed to learn."

"That fills me with so much confidence. Maybe I should have been the one who drove."

"And we'd end up on the wrong side of the road, as you said." I snorted.

"Are we going to talk about the elephant in the room?"

My hands tightened on the steering wheel. "What elephant?" I asked, trying to act casually.

"I don't know, the broken look you've been sporting, like you lost a part of yourself."

I shook my head as I pulled around to the side of the house. With the snow coming and the plows working in the morning, it was best to park on this side and save the spots in the garage for the rest of our roommates. I didn't mind my truck being here, and it wouldn't be easy for them to find spots later in this storm.

"Have you talked to her?"

I sighed, my hands clenching. "No. I texted Elise to check on her, but she hasn't replied. Although Nessa said that she's talked with her, so I know she's okay. Not today, however. I'm going to try again and hope she at least gets back with Nessa."

"I can't believe Corinne's gone," Pacey said, his voice hollow.

I let out a breath. "I can't either. I know she was your friend."

Pacey looked away, his voice low when he spoke. "She was. And she wasn't supposed to die. It wasn't supposed to be like this."

"I'm sorry."

"Yeah. Me, too. I hope you and Elise figure it out."

"Hell, me too."

We got out of the truck, each zipping up our jackets. The temperature had dropped in the ten minutes it had taken me to drive home, and I wasn't looking forward to how cold it would get this evening.

"Are the girls staying tonight?"

"As far as I know. It'll be a full house."

"Yeah..."

"Do you know how you're going to fix this?" Pacey asked, his voice low. "I mean with Elise."

"I don't know if there is any fixing it. She's just so broken, at least according to her, and I can't simply step in and make things better. Plus, I don't want to be the guy who hovers and forces her to listen to me and then bullies my way into helping."

"Maybe you can be the guy who's sort of in the middle of that. One who helps even if she pretends that she doesn't need you to."

"Yeah, I'm going to have to find a way. Because I love her, Pacey."

"I know," Pacey said softly. "We all know."

"Well," I said with a dry laugh. "I just figured it out, and I'm pretty sure that Elise doesn't know."

"Somewhere deep down, she does. And maybe that's part of why she's scared."

"That doesn't help me feel any better."

"Maybe not. But if you love her enough—and I know you do—you'll wait for her."

"Of course, I fucking will. It's not over. I'm just giving her the space she needs."

"Good," Pacey said as we walked up to the front doors, stomping our feet to get the snow off.

"That's damn good."

We took off our shoes, and I visibly shivered as Pacey went directly to the fireplace. Nobody else seemed to be home, and I hoped they arrived soon. The roads weren't getting any better—not even for a native Coloradan.

"You want to start some coffee?" Pacey asked.

"I can do that. Though I thought you'd want something stronger."

"Oh, we can do that, too."

My phone buzzed, and I looked down at it, frowning.

Nessa: *Have you gotten ahold of Elise?*

I frowned, typing quickly.

Me: *No. Why? Is everything okay?*

Nessa: *Her parents said that she was on her way to talk to you, but I can't get ahold of her. I wanted to make sure she was there. With the roads so bad, I'm worried.*

My heart thudded, and I looked around. I called Nessa instead of texting back. "She's not here. The house is empty."

"Damn it. Will you check to see if her car is there or something? Maybe she fell asleep like Goldilocks in your bed while waiting for you."

"Jesus, I hope so. Okay, I'm going to check. I'll let you know." I hung up, my hands shaking. I padded in my socks towards the back door and frowned when I saw her car.

"Pacey!" I called out.

"What? Talk to me."

"Nessa said that Elise came here. Her car is here, but I don't see her."

"Shit, I'll go check the rest of the house. But it's quiet, Dillon. And she doesn't have a key."

"I know," I said slowly, pushing down my fear. I ran down the back-deck stairs in the snow, wearing only my socks, and headed towards her car. It was empty, the engine cold, and I looked around, my heart thudding. "Pacey! Did she get in?"

Pacey was on the deck, shaking his head. "No. I'm going to call the girls. Maybe she went to them when she couldn't get in. But how, given her car is here? And why would Nessa be looking for her, then? Fuck. It doesn't make sense."

"I'm going to check the grounds. I don't know. I just have a feeling." And it wasn't a good one. It was too damn cold out here, and Elise was hurting. I *needed* to find her. Now.

"There's an old shed out back behind those trees. Maybe she's in there getting warm."

I met his gaze, and then I ran, heedless of the fact that I still wasn't wearing shoes. I could barely breathe, bile filling my throat. She had to be fine. She had to be. She was just staying warm.

And then I saw the spots of blood on the snow, and I ran faster.

"You're going to tell me where he is. I need money. I didn't mean to hurt you, but Jesus Christ, you scared me."

"Please, just let me go. I promise I won't tell anyone. Please."

I nearly tripped because I recognized those voices.

Elise and...Dave.

Why the fuck was my father talking to Elise? If he hurt her—

Holy fuck.

I kept running, knowing I should call out to Pacey but not wanting to startle them. I got to the shed, nearly sliding in the snow over the pine needles. My socks were drenched, sticking to the bottoms of my feet, but I didn't care. The door was open, and I could barely see what was going on. Elise sat there, blood caked to the side of her face as she held her knees to her chest, her whole body shaking. Dave stood in front of her, pacing, his whole body vibrating as if he were tweaking. He had a fucking knife in his hand, one of those hunter's knives that I only saw on TV.

I didn't know what to do, and yet, I knew I had to do something. Dave was obviously on something, and he wasn't thinking clearly. And Elise was hurt.

I didn't think. I just hoped to hell I wasn't making a mistake.

"Dad?" I asked. I couldn't say, "*Dave.*" Not when I wanted him to focus on me. Calling him by his first name would piss him off. Right? What the hell was he doing? What the hell was *I* doing?

Dave whirled, his eyes going dark. "You should have been here. Why weren't you here?" And then Dave lunged. I ducked out of the way, ignoring the hot sting in my skin as the knife slid through. It was only a graze, but still, I shouted. And then Elise was there, pushing at Dave.

"Dillon!"

"Get to Pacey. Get out of here."

"Not without you."

I met her gaze over the other man's head. Dave was on something that made him far stronger than he should be. I didn't know what it was, but he was definitely tweaking.

He shoved at us. Thankfully, however, not with the knife.

I tackled him, my adrenaline surging, and the blade skittered across the ground. Elise jumped on it, holding it in her hand as her arm shook.

"Get Pacey. Call the cops." I knelt on my dad, my knee on his back as I pinned him down. "Stop it. What the hell were you thinking?"

"I just needed a few bucks. She was there. I didn't mean to hurt her."

"Dillon?"

"Get Pacey."

"She doesn't have to. I'm here. Let me help, Dillon. The cops are on their way."

Pacey rushed in, Tanner, Sanders, and Miles with him, and they all held Dave down. I ran to Elise. I didn't care that she probably still wanted space. I saw the blood on her, and I couldn't breathe.

"Elise?"

"I'm fine. He surprised me. I'm fine." Her teeth chattered, and I could see each of our exhales. It was so fucking cold out, but she was okay. She had to be.

She leaped into my arms, and I held her close, dropping to my knees. We fell, holding each other, and I felt the hot warmth of her tears on my neck. I was crying, as well, not able to hold back any longer.

"You're fine, you're fine."

"I was so scared, but you're here."

I kissed the top of her head and held her as my new friends and roommates pinned my dad to the ground, and Miles ran out to direct the cops.

I had no idea what the fuck had happened or how we had ended up here. But Elise would be fine, damn it.

Somehow.

I just hoped to hell she forgave me for what Dave had done.

Chapter 20

Elise

"ARE YOU SURE WE SHOULD LEAVE?" MOM ASKED, AND I looked up at her and smiled. "I asked you to drop me off, and you did. I'm grateful, but I could use some time with them, okay?"

My parents stood in front of the couch, looking down at me, worried expressions on their faces. It had been a day since the attack, and unlike my home, I didn't want to lose the ability to ever walk into Dillon's again. Even if he didn't forgive me and we ended up never being together, I didn't want to lose that.

So, my parents had dropped me off at Dillon's with the rest of my friends and their families and were now about to head out.

"I want to stay for a bit. Is that okay?" I asked, even though that had been the agreement when they drove me over here. I had a slight headache but didn't have a concussion and would be fine. And I'd only needed two stitches. Apparently, wounds on your head bled easily and copiously, and that's why I had been in the shape I was in while in the back shed.

"That's okay," Dad said, holding my mom's hand. "We wanted to see the place. It seems like a nice home," my dad added, looking around.

"It is," Dillon said from behind the couch, clearing his throat. I looked over at him, and he put his hand on my shoulder, squeezing it slightly. "You guys don't have to go," he said. "You're welcome to stay."

My parents looked at each other and then at Dillon, shaking their heads. "No, we'll give you two some time. I know your brothers and their wives just left, as well as a couple of the other parents, but we wanted to make sure Elise was okay."

"I am," I said, self-conscious now.

"Well, just let us know if you want us to pick you up, or if someone else will. We're here if you need us."

I knew my parents were worried, but I had to do this. I needed to stop being scared of my shadow. Everything had happened so quickly, and I hadn't realized what had been going on.

Dillon's dad had been strung out on meth and had needed money to pay his debts. Somehow, in his drug-addled mind, he had convinced himself that Dillon would have it for him. And vowed he would get it no matter the cost.

I had just been in the way. He had seemed remorseful after, as if he hadn't wanted to hurt me. At least at first. But then Dillon had shown up, and everything had changed.

Dillon's dad would be in jail for a little bit and would hopefully get the help he needed, but he was out of Dillon's life forever. Once again. And I couldn't be more grateful for that.

My parents leaned down and hugged me, and I sighed.

"We love you," Mom whispered.

"Yes, we do," Dad said, and then they left, Miles leading them out.

"We'll give you two some privacy," Pacey said, and Tanner, Sanders, Mackenzie, Nessa, and Natalie all nodded before dispersing, headed towards the kitchen and study areas. I was pretty sure they could probably hear us unless we were in Dillon's room, but they were trying to give us some semblance of privacy. And that's how I found myself alone with Dillon for the first time in days.

He sat in front of me on the coffee table, his forearms resting along his thighs. "Hey," he whispered.

I swallowed hard. "Hey."

"I'm so fucking sorry," he said. "I'm so sorry he hurt you. I hope you can forgive me, but I'll understand if you can't. It must have been so scary. I don't know what would have happened if I hadn't gone out to that shed, gotten there in time."

I shook my head. "But you did. You were there. And this is not your fault." I leaned forward, putting my hand on his. "It's not your fault, Dillon. In all honesty, I came over here in the first place to apologize to you."

He frowned. "Why would you need to apologize to me?"

"Because I pushed you away because I was scared. Because I couldn't deal with my feelings. And, honestly, I'm not there yet."

He pulled back, his face going blank. "Not where?"

I winced. "I'm not dealing with all of my feelings. But I need to. I already talked to Mom and Dad, and we're going to start with me seeing a therapist. Because I need to talk about Corinne. It's tough for me to do so, but I shouldn't have pushed you away. I didn't need to make things worse. I need... I don't know what I need, but I didn't need to do what I did to you."

"I understood why you did it, though."

"Well, I don't. So that's something I need to deal with." I sighed. "I'm so sorry."

"How about this? How about we stop apologizing to each other? Clean slate, or at least as clean as it can be."

He moved so he sat next to me on the couch and then brushed my hair away from my face. He was careful of my wound, and I saw the way his jaw tensed. "I almost lost you. I don't know what I would have done if you had been hurt any more than you were."

"He could have hurt you." I looked down at his arm. "You got stitches, too."

"You're right, I did. But I'm going to be fine. And so are you. I still blame myself for what happened."

"Don't. I'm fine. And you're fine. We're going to be okay." I swallowed hard. "I don't know how to feel about losing Corinne, and that's something that will take me a while. I'm broken inside, Dillon, but I want you to be by my side when I figure things out. Can you do that? Can you be here?"

He sighed, leaned down, and gently pressed a kiss to my lips. I nearly cried, but I held myself back, afraid that if I started crying, I wouldn't be able to stop or speak.

"I love you, Elise."

I blinked, then looked up at him. "What?"

A small smile played on his lips. "How could you not know that? How could you not see it whenever I look at you?"

I swallowed harder, traced my fingers along his jaw. "I hoped. But I thought maybe I just saw what I wanted to see." I let out a breath. "I love you, too, Dillon. I don't know what's going to happen next. I don't know what I'll feel in terms of everything else in my life once I let myself think, but I do know that I love you."

His smile was bright this time, and he kissed me again. "Then we will have to do this together. Whatever comes next is you and me. Our path won't be easy, Elise. We know that. But we can do it together. You and me. Us, against the rest of the world. Just don't leave me again. Don't push me away."

"And don't blame yourself for what others do to us," I whispered.

"That, I can promise you," he said and then kissed me again. I heard cheers from the other side of the house. Dillon groaned, and I started to laugh, ignoring my oncoming headache.

"It's about time," Sanders called.

Mackenzie punched him in the shoulder as they walked in. "Stop it. We were supposed to pretend that we weren't listening."

"And yet you were the one who cheered the loudest," Pacey drawled.

I laughed, leaned into Dillon's side as our group sat down around us, and began making plans to destroy the shed and build something new. Most of us would be dispersing for the holidays to spend time with family, but somehow, we would come back together.

Plans needed to be made, and I didn't want to lose this connection. I'd already lost so much. I didn't want to lose anything more. But as long as I had Dillon at my side, I knew I could do anything. We still had the rest of our futures to plan, but I knew that I wanted Dillon to be my forever. He was no longer my one night, no longer a dare. He was mine.

And I would thank my best friend to the end of time for gifting him to me.

Bittersweet promises and all.

Chapter 21

Dillon

I LEANED ELISE AGAINST THE WALL AND KISSED HER HARD on the mouth. "Hi," I whispered.

She laughed. It reached her eyes this time, though maybe not as brightly as it had before. "Hello, there. I didn't know there was mistletoe above us."

I looked up and saw empty rafters. "I didn't realize I needed mistletoe to kiss you."

"Maybe not. However, it is a holiday party. I'm pretty sure mistletoe abounds." She sighed a bit, and I knew she was thinking of Corinne, of the first party she'd come here for. We'd almost canceled this one, but Elise had insisted we keep it going. Because Corinne needed to be remembered, and we needed brightness in this home. We all needed a point of light in the times when it felt as if there might not be one again.

I smiled then. "Secret mistletoe should make for some interesting pairings since it's mostly just our friends at this house party."

"That is true," she said, leaning into me.

"Let's go see the rest of our people."

It had been a week since the attack, over a week now since we had lost Corinne. Nobody was okay. Nobody was fully healed, but we were trying to make the most of it, even if it wasn't easy. And that meant having a holiday and goodbye party before the next semester started.

There were a few people from school that I didn't recognize, but this was a smaller gathering than the one we'd thrown when I first met Elise. Or the one where I'd first met Mandy, for that matter. Mandy and her boyfriend had not been invited, and that was fine with me. I usually didn't have a problem with my ex coming to these types of things because I tried to be nice to everybody, but she had been harsh to me the last time we spoke, same with Elise, and I didn't want her near the love of my life.

I couldn't help but let a small smile play over my face at that thought. The love of my life. Some people might think it was odd to find that love so young, but what did they know? If we were blessed, we would have a long life left to live, and I would have the one person I wanted above all others at my side as I did so. We would be able to change together, find out who we were as we traversed the rest of our school years and careers. And we would have each other to lean on.

Maybe it would be easier if we were single and weren't thinking about forevers and all of that, but we were doing exactly what we wanted, and that had to count for something. Or maybe it counted for everything.

Tonight, though, was about our group becoming a family, surrounded by others we didn't know as well, but they were still invited.

I kissed the top of Elise's head while we walked in, knowing that bittersweet feeling was back again. Corinne's picture was on the mantel, a small candle lit against the frame. She would forever be remembered in this home and in our hearts. I still didn't know how to reconcile the fact that she wouldn't be coming through the door again, daring Elise to kiss me, making a joke or having a laugh with us to remind us that we were supposed to be enjoying college and life, and not stressing out about the next paper.

It didn't seem fair that a girl so full of life and happiness wasn't here anymore, but it was my goal to live my life along with Elise in Corinne's memory. We'd find a way to make that work.

Once again, Miles was in the corner, this time with a girl I didn't recognize. They didn't seem to be arguing, just chatting peacefully. Tanner was on his phone, scowling down at it, alone this time, but Nessa and Natalie were near him, the two girls talking to each other. I knew they were searching for another house to live in, and my brothers were helping them. They would find a place for them to settle, along with Mackenzie if she ended up moving in with them as they'd talked about.

I wouldn't get in the middle of that other than to offer my brother's help with real estate. We'd find a way to make it work. For now, though, the house was a little busy with so many people coming in and out.

Pacey growled in the corner. I wasn't sure why, and I wasn't going to ask. For as open and helpful as Pacey was, the man had more secrets than I could count. And I wasn't going to pry them out of him, at least not during the holidays. These days weren't easy for most people, and I knew they wouldn't ever be easy for us. Pacey was in pain after losing Corinne—we all were. I just hoped he found someone to talk to about it soon. Yet only a blink of time had passed since the loss, and I didn't know what would happen next.

We all had memories and entanglements when it came to this time of the year, and finding joy in it was sometimes the only thing we could do.

Mackenzie walked in, a cheese board in her hand. "Hi there, have you seen Sanders?"

I looked at the small group of people who had come to celebrate a semester and a girl we all missed and shook my head. "No, he might be up in his room."

Mackenzie nodded, her smile a little forced. "Thank you again for hosting." Her eyes filled with tears, but she quickly blinked them away. "I just...thank you. It's nice to be included." She leaned in, kissed me on the cheek, and then did the same to Elise before setting the cheese board down. People attacked it with gusto, and Mackenzie smiled softly. She liked taking care of people, even if it was usually in her orderly way. I didn't mind, though, because I liked it when she cooked, and she was taking care of Elise, too. That was a plus for me.

Elise leaned into me again, and I looked down at her. "Hey," I whispered.

"Hey, there. I can't believe I kissed you in front of everybody in this room," she mumbled.

I raised a brow. "If I remember right, I'm the one who kissed you."

"But I asked."

"Maybe. Or perhaps we did what we should have."

"I still can't believe you're also the guy I saw across the coffee shop."

"When your mouth went slack, and you just couldn't help but fall in love with me?" I teased.

She rolled her eyes. "Yes, sure, that's exactly what happened."

I snorted and kissed her softly. "Merry Christmas, Elise."

"Merry Christmas, Dillon. I got you a gift, you know."

"I thought *you* were my gift."

"And what? Are you going to unwrap me later?" she asked, her voice low.

My dick went hard, and I swallowed. "Well, if you're going down that path…" I began and laughed. We'd been together the night before in quiet peace, but the teasing was slow to come. It would take time. We'd been through too much in the past month, and we were still finding our footing. But we would. Because we'd found each other. "I love you," I whispered.

"Hey, I love you, too. Now, let's get some cheese before the rest of the horde steals it."

"You always say the sweetest things."

I kissed her again before we went to join the others. I hadn't meant to fall in love at my age. Hadn't thought I ever would. I'd always been the one who helped my family when I could and watched my brothers fall in love one by one, each under harder circumstances than the last as the years went on. They had each come to me for and with advice. It had taken falling in love myself to realize the chance they had taken for that hope.

A chance I had freely fallen into.

One I would take again and again when it came to Elise.

She was more than my one night. She was my everything.

Mackenzie

After fifteen years, you would think I would be used to searching out and finding my boyfriend. However, it seemed to annoy me more and more these days. Mostly because finding Sanders sometimes took an act of God. My heart hurt too much at the moment to focus on others.

I knew he had to be in the house somewhere. After all, this was his holiday party his and his roommates'. I just needed to find him. Even though he was usually the life of the party, he sometimes liked to step away and give himself some space. It made sense. He was great at being the center of attention until it got to be too much, and he needed a break. Just to breathe. I was the same way, so I knew I would probably find him in his room as Dillon had said.

I waved at the others, though I didn't recognize a few. This wasn't my home, even though I had been staying here for the past week. I needed to find a new place to live, and through the worst set of unimaginable circumstances, I might've found some new roommates. But I didn't want to think about that right now. I didn't want to think about the fact that I would be a replacement. A placeholder for someone I truly adored and would rather have in my life with me living in a box on the street. I missed Corinne.

I shoved those thoughts from my mind and walked up the stairs. Sanders' room was in the center of the five bedrooms upstairs. Apparently, the guys had all drawn straws or something to find out which one of them would get the biggest room. I remember Sanders grumbling that he'd wanted the largest room, mostly because he had the most stuff, but he hadn't minded in the end. As long as he had had a place to sleep so we could go to class, he said he was fine. And that was good with me.

I heard rustling inside the room and figured he must be changing or something. I opened the door, a wide smile on my face.

And then the floor fell out from under me. I didn't know if I saw rage, anger, sadness, or an end of everything that I had thought purposeful.

Sanders sat on the edge of the bed, his pants down to his knees, his head thrown back in ecstasy. He'd tangled his fingers in the hair of some redheaded girl I had never seen before, and her lips were around my boyfriend's cock— around my future husband's cock.

Tonight was a *holiday* party. A party to say goodbye to a semester and a friend we all knew and loved and had lost too soon.

And my boyfriend was getting a blowjob from a girl who wasn't me.

She hummed, and Sanders let out a grown. I knew what was coming next. I'd given that man enough blowjobs in my life to know exactly what he looked like when he came.

He came hard, his whole body practically vibrating, and the girl lapped him up, the two of them not even realizing I was there.

Was I supposed to say something? Was I supposed to run out and yell and do something?

This wasn't happening. I had plans. Everything was in place. I was going to marry him, we were going to have careers and a family. Those were the plans we had discussed. It wasn't just me. We may joke that I was an anal-retentive bitch who liked things in order, but Sanders had been there right alongside me, making those promises, those plans.

We were supposed to get engaged next year. He'd told me so.

And now some girl was sucking him off.

I must have made a sound because the girl looked up, her eyes wide. She scrambled back immediately. Oh, this one knew what she had done. She wouldn't be so scared if she didn't know who I was. Even if I didn't know who the fuck *she* was.

Sanders looked at me then, tucked his now flaccid penis into his boxer briefs, and cringed. "Hey there, hon. I didn't know you were coming up here."

I just blinked. His words echoed in my head, and I tried to keep up. "Are you kidding me right now? You're getting a blowjob from a girl, and now you're blaming *me* for walking into the room that I have spent every night in this past week? Our friend *died* last week, Paul. We're still *mourning*, even if we pretend what's going on downstairs is a party."

Paul Sanders swallowed hard. "Hey, you know it's just for fun. It's only a blowjob. I mean, really, don't freak the fuck out. I'm just trying it out, babe. We're going to be together for the rest of our lives. I don't want to be with just you, though. I'm sure you've gotten off with some other guy or given a blowjob. I mean, it's what we do, right?"

My mouth filled with bile, and I felt like I surely couldn't be hearing what I thought I was. This was not happening. This couldn't be happening.

Instead of saying anything, instead of standing up for myself as I should, I nearly fell backward as I started to run. I ran right into Pacey's chest. Tanner was at his side, both of them glowering. Tanner fisted his hands at his sides as Pacey wrapped his hands around my arms, keeping me steady. Sanders finally stood up and zipped his fly.

"Hey, guys, can you give us some privacy? It's just that me and my girl have a few things to discuss."

"I...I need to go..." I whispered. I wasn't even sure I'd spoken aloud, but Pacey's hold tightened slightly.

"Oh, we're going to have this out right now," Tanner growled. "What the fuck do you think you're doing? I should kick your fucking ass for hurting her."

I looked up at Sanders then, not even recognizing him. But the boy I had loved with every inch of my soul sneered at Tanner. "Hey, this isn't any of your business."

I noticed that the girl who had been on her knees before now stood behind Sanders as if she were afraid I might hurt her.

How could I hurt her when I didn't even feel like I was inside my body at the moment? I felt like I was watching things from afar, wondering what the fuck I was supposed to do. And I should be doing something. I shouldn't just be standing here.

"Raise your chin," Pacey whispered in my ear, and I swallowed hard. "What?" I asked, barely breathing the word.

"Don't let him see you in pain. Don't let the world know. Don't let the others know. Don't break. Don't do this. Walk with me. Everything's going to be fine."

"No, it's not." My voice sounded hollow and tinny to my ears.

"Let the world see you're better than this. Don't let them see your pain. Don't let Sanders win."

And yet, Paul had won...hadn't he?

As Tanner began to growl at Sanders, and the two talked about whatever the hell they were talking about, Pacey put his arm around my waist and led me towards the stairs.

I didn't know what I was supposed to do, what I was supposed to say.

Because nothing was the same. Everything had changed.

My future lay behind me, the promises that I'd thought had been made broken and scattered in a heap of tattered remains.

If I wasn't Mackenzie, Paul Sanders' girlfriend and future...then who was I?

Who could I possibly be?

****

Next in the ON MY OWN series?

Mackenzie and Pacey pretend they don't need each other in My Rebound.

Want to read a special **BONUS EPILOGUE** featuring **DILLON & ELISE? CLICK HERE!**

A Note from Carrie Ann Ryan

Thank you so much for reading **MY ONE NIGHT!**

This book was about second chances, making mistakes, and finding your path. I hope you loved their story as much as I do.

Next up in the ON MY OWN series?

Mackenzie and Pacey pretend they don't need each other in My Rebound. Their romance starts off with heartbreak and ends with...well you'll just have to see. Pacey has secrets and Mackenzie has ambitions. And their love is explosive!

And if you're new to my books, you can start anywhere within the my interconnected series and catch up! Each book is a stand alone, so jump around!

Don't miss out on the Montgomery Ink World!

- Montgomery Ink (The Denver Montgomerys)
- Montgomery Ink: Colorado Springs (The Colorado Springs Montgomery Cousins)

- Montgomery Ink: Boulder (The Boulder Montgomery Cousins)
- Gallagher Brothers (Jake's Brothers from Ink Enduring)
- Whiskey and Lies (Tabby's Brothers from Ink Exposed)
- Fractured Connections (Mace's sisters from Fallen Ink)
- Less Than (Dimitri's siblings from Restless Ink)
- Promise Me (Arden's siblings from Wrapped in Ink)
- On My Own (Dillon from the Fractured Connections series.)

If you want to make sure you know what's coming next from me, you can sign up for my newsletter at www. CarrieAnnRyan.com; follow me on twitter at @CarrieAnnRyan, or like my Facebook page. I also have a Facebook Fan Club where we have trivia, chats, and other goodies. You guys are the reason I get to do what I do and I thank you.

Make sure you're signed up for my MAILING LIST so you can know when the next releases are available as well as find giveaways and FREE READS.

Happy Reading!

The On My Own Series:
Book 1: My One Night
Book 2: My Rebound
Book 3: My Next Play
Book 4: My Bad Decisions

WANT TO READ A SPECIAL BONUS EPILOGUE FEATURING DILLON & ELISE? CLICK HERE!

Want to keep up to date with the next Carrie Ann Ryan Release? Receive Text Alerts easily!
Text CARRIE to 210-741-8720

About the Author

Carrie Ann Ryan is the New York Times and USA Today bestselling author of contemporary, paranormal, and young adult romance. Her works include the Montgomery Ink, Redwood Pack, Fractured Connections, and Elements of Five series, which have sold over 3.0 million books world-wide. She started writing while in graduate school for her advanced degree in chemistry and hasn't stopped since. Carrie Ann has written over seventy-five novels and novellas with more in the works. When she's not losing herself in her emotional and action-packed worlds, she's reading as much as she can while wrangling her clowder of cats who have more followers than she does.

www.CarrieAnnRyan.com

Also from Carrie Ann Ryan

The Montgomery Ink: Fort Collins Series:
Book 1: Inked Persuasion
Book 2: Inked Obsession
Book 3: Inked Devotion
Book 4: Inked Craving

The On My Own Series:
Book 1: My One Night
Book 2: My Rebound
Book 3: My Next Play
Book 4: My Bad Decisions

The Tattered Royals Series:
Book 1: Royal Line
Book 2: Enemy Heir

The Ravenwood Coven Series:
Book 1: Dawn Unearthed
Book 2: Dusk Unveiled

Book 3: Evernight Unleashed

Montgomery Ink:
    Book 0.5: Ink Inspired
    Book 0.6: Ink Reunited
    Book 1: Delicate Ink
    Book 1.5: Forever Ink
    Book 2: Tempting Boundaries
    Book 3: Harder than Words
    Book 4: Written in Ink
    Book 4.5: Hidden Ink
    Book 5: Ink Enduring
    Book 6: Ink Exposed
    Book 6.5: Adoring Ink
    Book 6.6: Love, Honor, & Ink
    Book 7: Inked Expressions
    Book 7.3: Dropout
    Book 7.5: Executive Ink
    Book 8: Inked Memories
    Book 8.5: Inked Nights
    Book 8.7: Second Chance Ink

Montgomery Ink: Colorado Springs
    Book 1: Fallen Ink
    Book 2: Restless Ink
    Book 2.5: Ashes to Ink
    Book 3: Jagged Ink
    Book 3.5: Ink by Numbers

The Montgomery Ink: Boulder Series:
    Book 1: Wrapped in Ink
    Book 2: Sated in Ink

Book 3: Embraced in Ink
Book 4: Seduced in Ink
Book 4.5: Captured in Ink

The Gallagher Brothers Series:
Book 1: Love Restored
Book 2: Passion Restored
Book 3: Hope Restored

The Whiskey and Lies Series:
Book 1: Whiskey Secrets
Book 2: Whiskey Reveals
Book 3: Whiskey Undone

The Fractured Connections Series:
Book 1: Breaking Without You
Book 2: Shouldn't Have You
Book 3: Falling With You
Book 4: Taken With You

The Less Than Series:
Book 1: Breathless With Her
Book 2: Reckless With You
Book 3: Shameless With Him

The Promise Me Series:
Book 1: Forever Only Once
Book 2: From That Moment
Book 3: Far From Destined
Book 4: From Our First

Redwood Pack Series:

Also from Carrie Ann Ryan

Book 1: An Alpha's Path
Book 2: A Taste for a Mate
Book 3: Trinity Bound
Book 3.5: A Night Away
Book 4: Enforcer's Redemption
Book 4.5: Blurred Expectations
Book 4.7: Forgiveness
Book 5: Shattered Emotions
Book 6: Hidden Destiny
Book 6.5: A Beta's Haven
Book 7: Fighting Fate
Book 7.5: Loving the Omega
Book 7.7: The Hunted Heart
Book 8: Wicked Wolf

The Talon Pack:
Book 1: Tattered Loyalties
Book 2: An Alpha's Choice
Book 3: Mated in Mist
Book 4: Wolf Betrayed
Book 5: Fractured Silence
Book 6: Destiny Disgraced
Book 7: Eternal Mourning
Book 8: Strength Enduring
Book 9: Forever Broken

The Elements of Five Series:
Book 1: From Breath and Ruin
Book 2: From Flame and Ash
Book 3: From Spirit and Binding
Book 4: From Shadow and Silence

The Branded Pack Series:
(Written with Alexandra Ivy)
Book 1: Stolen and Forgiven
Book 2: Abandoned and Unseen
Book 3: Buried and Shadowed

Dante's Circle Series:
Book 1: Dust of My Wings
Book 2: Her Warriors' Three Wishes
Book 3: An Unlucky Moon
Book 3.5: His Choice
Book 4: Tangled Innocence
Book 5: Fierce Enchantment
Book 6: An Immortal's Song
Book 7: Prowled Darkness
Book 8: Dante's Circle Reborn

Holiday, Montana Series:
Book 1: Charmed Spirits
Book 2: Santa's Executive
Book 3: Finding Abigail
Book 4: Her Lucky Love
Book 5: Dreams of Ivory

The Happy Ever After Series:
Flame and Ink
Ink Ever After

Single Title:
Finally Found You

CPSIA information can be obtained
at www.ICGtesting.com
Printed in the USA
LVHW022100081221
705641LV00014B/1860